T0165284

Shogun Iemitsu

War and Romance in 17th Century Tokugawa Japan

Michael R Zomber

iUniverse, Inc.
New York Bloomington

Shogun Iemitsu
War and Romance in 17th Century Tokugawa Japan

iUniverse books may be ordered through booksellers or by contacting:

iUniverse
1663 Liberty Drive
Bloomington, IN 47403
www.iuniverse.com
1-800-Authors (1-800-288-4677)

ISBN: 978-1-4401-5563-5 (pbk)
ISBN: 978-1-4401-5564-2 (ebk)

Printed in the United States of America

iUniverse rev. date: 9/28/2009

Chapter 1

Oda Hideo

Oda Hideo, grandson of Dictator Nobunaga by one of his minor concubines, gently rubbed his eyes. He had slept poorly, tossing from left side to right and back again in a futile effort to recapture the sleep that eluded him.

It cannot be my tatami. It is the very best I could find, and it is nearly new, he thought. Even though he was rubbing them using the lightest pressure, his eyeballs felt like they were coated with an invisible layer of incredibly fine sand or dust. They felt raw and inflamed. Turning onto his back, Hideo smelled the sweet perfume of newly cut grass. His sleeping mat was *san sun* (three inches) thick, the cover beautifully and intricately woven, the sides rimmed with thick, black silk brocade. His sleepless eyes looked out the open door of the barracks, and he fancied the sky was almost imperceptibly lighter than it had been the last time he had looked—which was but a few moments before.

Time to get up, he thought. Then he stood in one fluid motion.

On the mat next to his lay a bundle of silk, or so it appeared in the semidarkness. The mat was well used, and fragments of straw lay near it on the hard-packed dirt floor, as though ejected by the weight of the bundle. From one end of the mound of silk came a soft but regular snore. Bending over the snoring end, Hideo poked one end of the bundle ever so lightly with the big toe of his right foot.

"Kobiyashi," he said in a low, husky, attractive whisper. The bundle gave no reply but only shifted shape away from the prodding.

Hideo smiled to himself, shaking his head, and stood erect once more. Slipping his bare feet into a pair of sandals, he tightened the sash around his outer kimono.

He automatically reached down to a beautifully lacquered sword stand within easy reach of his mat. His *daisho*, a matched pair of samurai swords, rested on it; the *wakizashi* sat above his *katana*. Only samurai could wear the katana, much less the daisho. The morning light was barely sufficient to reveal the raised, gold *mon,* or crest, of the Oda clan shining dully against the highly polished black lacquer *katanakake*. Hideo's swords were mounted in elegant black lacquer *saya* with russet iron fittings and *tsubas*. The black string-wrapped handles were of the highest quality, as were all of Hideo's sword mounts. A samurai's swords—good, bad, or indifferent—were his greatest earthly treasure, reflective of his character and ultimately symbolic of his life. Hideo's were excellent but also tasteful and restrained. They achieved the elusive Nipponese quality of *shibui,* or restrained elegance.

Choosing the *wakizashi,* Hideo thrust it expertly through his black silk sash and walked out the open passageway that served the barracks as a door. As his sandals crunched quietly on the pebble pathway, Hideo was very surprised to see that the tiny guardhouse was empty. His high, thoroughly noble forehead furrowed in perplexity.

"I know I heard Captain Yamashita tell Fujimori he was to have the dusk to dawn duty," Hideo shrugged his shoulders. There was no danger to Lord Arima or his domain. There was no credible threat to the shogunate. Since Shimabara, Nippon was almost too peaceful.

Now the sky was lightening perceptibly. The morning air felt heated despite the early hour.

Hideo wiped his brow, examining the sweat on the back of his powerful, fine-veined, brown hand. His nails were immaculately groomed, the whites almost perfect semicircles, and the cuticles supple and intact. Standing a full six *shaku* (feet) without his sandals, Hideo was statuesque. He continued to contemplate the unusual amount of sweat.

"So hot," he continued in an undertone, "already so hot."

Wiping his hand on his sash, he walked on, crunching small brownish pebbles as he went.

Stopping before a small temple with a pagoda-shaped roof, he paused for a moment. He looked over his right shoulder to make certain there was no one following him. Seeing and hearing nothing out of the ordinary, he slipped inside the structure. Once inside the entrance, he removed his sandals and placed them in a wooden niche designed specially to hold them.

Hideo's delicate nostrils flared, drinking in the heady scent of fragrant incense; yes, it was jasmine, his favorite. Hideo's finely formed nose was very different from the flattened features of so many of his comrades in the barracks. It bespoke his noble ancestry. Hideo loved fine incense. As the pungent vapors filled the air, he was transported by mental images of startling clarity.

He was eight years old when his mother died.

The Shimabara Rebellion had not yet been crushed by a coalition of Shogun Iemitsu's army and the Dutch navy. The current Shogun Iemitsu was enforcing Hidetada's 1622 Edict outlawing Kirishitanity to the fullest rigor of the law. On a hot August morning similar to this one, shogunate officials had crashed through the oiled paper walls of Hideo's modest, wood-frame house and overturned his mother's cherished tatami mats, searching furiously, probing, crushing, violating, and destroying with swords drawn.

Hideo's mother, Settsuko—well-known in the neighborhood for her long, raven black hair—stood mute and terrified at the sudden onslaught.

She had motioned him to her side and whispered in a soft melodious tone, "I'm so sorry, my son. We have been denounced. It is all my fault. Forgive me. I will always love you." Then she squeezed his small hand tightly, and Hideo suppressed a cry. She continued even more softly, inaudible to anyone but her son, "No matter what happens, say nothing about him," as she raised her beautiful, limpid black eyes to the sky.

He hugged her tightly by way of assent. Peeling his hands away, she placed a minute square of metal in his right one. Only a moment later, Settsuko was seized by two samurai in full armor as a third gripped Hideo's shoulder with an iron grasp. Hideo bit deeply into the flesh of the man's thumb, but the samurai never relaxed his grasp though the bite cut to the bone. His jaws nearly closed, and he could taste salty blood, unpleasant and metallic. He gave up fighting and wept silently as Settsuko was carried off. The samurai was as unconcerned by Hideo's bite as he would have been had the boy been a flea. He smiled at the youth's spirit. His face all but obscured by an enormous iron *menpo,* or face mask, he addressed Hideo in a soothing baritone. The iron mask was very fierce with hideout gilt teeth, a monstrous, detachable iron nose, and a devilish, bushy, white moustache.

"Son," he said, "Believe me, this is all for your own good. You'll be happy where you're going."

With a great effort of boyish will, Hideo choked off his weeping and stared with murderous intensity into frightening jet-black eyes, which were all but hidden behind the russet iron mask. In spite of himself, the heavily armored samurai started back a full pace.

"You have your grandfather's look. I never saw it myself; I am far too young. But I've heard others speak of it. Now I know they were telling the truth," he said in a voice filled with awe.

He never saw his mother again.

Hideo slowly returned to the present as he gazed upon the black *honoki* image of the Buddha of Compassion, lacquered and subtly gilded. It glowed softly in the warm light of guttering candles kept alight by wandering, saffron-robed monks and devout samurai in the service of Lord Arima. The lips of the image were thin and compressed; the eyes open only slightly between heavy lids; the hair rendered in tight coils covering the head. The face was nearly feminine in its features as the body sat serenely in the lotus posture on a huge blossom. All aspects of the statue beckoned the worshipper to kneel and be absolved, freed from the suffering and corruption of the world. The unknown sculptor had realized his vision, succeeding in inculcating an animate feeling of infinite mercy into the inanimate wood.

Commissioned by the previous Lord Arima, the bodhisattva was small compared to the Great Buddha of Kamakura near Kyoto. Hideo's first real *sensei* had taken him to see that Buddha in the hope that the enormous figure would overawe him and erase any lingering childhood *Kirishitan* thoughts by demonstrating the physical superiority and grandeur of the Lord of the Eightfold Path. Hideo was duly impressed at the time, but he remained steadfast in his mother's faith. Arima's man-size Buddha had the most marvelously sinuous hands, whose elongated fingers possessed a surpassing gracefulness that reminded him of Settsuko's own long, lovely hands.

She was the daughter of the last of Nobunaga's concubines, Hasui, and his last known child, born shortly after his death. Hasui was a lithe woman of considerable beauty and was unusually tall. The aging warrior was less attracted to her beauty—her almost perfect oval face and heart-shaped lips—than fascinated by her abnormal height.

Hideo's grandmother was an ardent *Keikyoto,* and Hasui's parents, followers of the Buddha who knew of Oda's hostility to their own religion, were only too happy to entrust their *Kirishitan* daughter to the protection of the most powerful man in Nippon. Nobunaga not only did not ask her to renounce her faith, he asked her to explain its teachings and doctrine. She was only too delighted to do so.

Prior to his taking her, Hasui was apprehensive, for she had never known a man, and Oda, though a Fujiwara by birth, had spent most of his life in battle. Strangely, she found him to be the most courteous lover imaginable. True, he was much older than she, but he was an absolute fanatic about personal hygiene, who devoted hours each day to the most elaborate and thorough ablutions comprising innumerable hot and cold baths with numberless oils, constant massage, mud treatments, and heated rubs more suited to an imperial courtier than a battle-scarred general.

Almost from his birth, Hideo had been regaled with detailed accounts of his grandmother, Hasui, and her life with Oda, the protector of *Kirishitans* and the ruler of Nippon. Settsuko was rightly proud of her mother, who perished in a fire of suspicious origin shortly before Hideo's birth.

Settsuko knew that Tokugawa Ieyasu, his son Hidetada, and now Hidetada's son, Shogun Iemitsu, kept a watchful eye on all descendents of the dictator, no matter how distantly or far removed. Even an unacknowledged connection, such as Hasui, was cause for concern to the Tokugawa. Iemitsu's prudence in all facets of politics was becoming legend, but his sensitivity to potential threats to the Tokugawa family dynasty was the most acute of all. Settsuko remained convinced that she—and not Hasui—was the intended victim of the fatal blaze, which conviction she kept secret from her son.

Iemitsu revered his father and grandfather and had paid close attention to every lesson in politics each offered in the months and years prior to their deaths. His father, Hidetada, was Ieyasu's third son, chosen for the shogunate due to his Buddha-like calm. Some said that Hidetada lacked Ieyasu's father's brilliance and that Ieyasu's genius had skipped ageneration to reach Iemitsu. Like Ieyasu, Iemitsu paid almost fanatical attention to the smallest details. One of the smallest was the eight-year-old grandson of Oda Nobunaga. Though Iemitsu was only slightly concerned about the remote possibility that the orphan child might be used by political factions for nefarious ends, Iemitsu nevertheless ordered that the boy be raised in a Zen Buddhist monastery.

The abbot, an old friend and correspondent of Shogun Iemitsu's, was charged on peril of his life to make certain that Hideo would grow up to be a devout follower of the Eightfold Path. Periodic reports on his progress were received by members of the Shogun's all-pervasive intelligence service, summarized, and sent on to the palace in Edo. The reports all spoke of Hideo's great piety. They were highly complimentary of and therefore pleasing to the Tokugawa government. As a young man, Hideo excelled in the martial arts as well as in the fine arts necessary to all followers of Bushido. His calligraphy was adequate, though his aptitude for tea ceremony was exceptional. His abbot often used him as an example of the well-rounded characteristics of all true samurai.

Hideo was, in many ways, his grandfather's heir as well as his father's. Both Oda and Shintaro, who died shortly after Hideo reached the age of five, were the essence of Bushido incarnate. For Hideo, the two men—the grandfather he never knew and the father he knew only a short while—blended together to form a shining ideal of the perfect samurai.

His violent separation from his mother caused Hideo to keep his own counsel at an early age. He would not speak of his grandfather; if another boy asked him about Nobunaga, Hideo simply said that his grandfatherhad died long before he was born. Hideo's reserve by no means meant that he was either taciturn or lonely. On the contrary, he was very popular with both masters and students at the monastery for he excelled at all the physical arts.

Upon reaching a certain age, he was sent to Lord Arima to serve in his personal army as a common soldier. His fine horsemanship and love of horses and his skill with the bow as well as the sword stood him in good stead not only with his companions in the barracks but with his liege lord as well.

Shortly after his arrival, an older, crude, and hardened samurai, Sato, made a rude remark about Hideo's ancestry. Sato jeered at him.

"See how the mighty have fallen. Imagine Oda's grandson—a flower of the mighty Fujiwara—a common soldier, forced to empty night soil jars." Sato laughed, hocked vigorously, and then spat a greenish glob of phlegm that landed on Hideo's right toe. Hideo stood motionless, fixing Sato with the same stare he had given Yoritomo after his mother had been taken. Undeterred and determined to see the grandson of Oda's concubine humbled, Sato hocked once again and spat, this time into Hideo's face.

"Take that, you little bastard," Sato snarled.

Very calmly, Hideo wiped his cheek and flung the sticky spittle to the ground, where it quickly coated itself with dust.

There were witnesses to the provocation, and one of the samurai—it happened to be Kobiyashi—rushed off, returning almost immediately with two wooden swords, or *boken*, that were used for practice. Sato seized the longer, heavier sword and took up a classic defensive posture. Hideo bowed elegantly, first to Kobiyashi and then to Sato, whose face—unattractive under the best of circumstances—took on a truly hideous expression.

"Fight, you bastard," he thundered.

Hideo calmly and deliberately assumed the seagull stance, his wooden sword outstretched with the edge facing his opponent, the blade parallel to his chest. The combatants advanced, and Hideo's sword was a white blur that stopped with the sickening crunch of hard wood on bone. Sato fell senselessly onto his back in the light brown dirt. Bright red blood gushed from a laceration above his right eye that was deep and wide enough to reveal the skull bone. The edges of the wound yawned open as if grimacing in pain. Hideo then he handed his *boken,* now having a long thin flap of skin and flesh clinging to the beveled edge, to Kobiyashi, who courteously returned his bow and whirled the sword 360 degrees to dislodge the bit of bloody flesh, which landed in the dust close to the small ball of Sato's dusty phlegm. Sato never spoke about the duel and, for the remainder of his long life, answered any inquiry by gesturing to the long, white, puffy scar on his forehead.

Hideo faced no more challenges from his fellow samurai.

While at the monastery, long before the duel with Sato, Hideo fully embraced Zen Buddhism as the most harmonious discipline for a would-be samurai. As rigorous as were the physical disciplines, some involving use of the staff, the intellectual and spiritual training was even more severe and demanding. He loved the gilded images of the Buddha and the aroma of jasmine as clouds of incense wafted to the eves of the central temple. He was enchanted by the voices of the saffron-robed monks as they prayed amid the bright flickering light of countless candles, some burning bright and others guttering as they died. Kneeling prostrate, arms stretched forward, with palms down, he would clear his mind of all worldly thought as Buddha asked. But as Hideo contemplated the void, and the physical world ceased to be, he did not pray to the gilded image before him, despite seeming to.

Standing in the temple near the barracks, in the first light of dawn on the August morning of 1646, Hideo gazed with great affection at the Buddha with exquisitely formed lips and smiled to himself.

No one ever guessed or ever will guess my secret. Do you hear me, Mother? No one will ever know, I promise you. He did not swear, for it was written that one should not, as no one could make a black hair white, and heaven was God's footstool. Hideo continued his internal dialog, *No, Mother, they will never know. If they did, they would have cause to fear another Shimabara, another Shiro. I am thankful to God I am content to remain as I am.*

As though the very thought itself was dangerous—which it was—Hideo turned and closely surveyed the interior of the temple. He looked through the doorway. Satisfied that he was alone and unobserved, he withdrew a small, rectangular object from deep within his sash. Contemplating it with a look of love, he placed it to his lips and kissed it with the greatest reverence. As tears glistened on his long lashes, he gazed upon the rectangle once again. Placing it back in his sash, Hideo once more prostrated himself before the Buddha and prayed in a voice that would have been inaudible from the temple doorway.

"Our father, which art in heaven, hallowed be thy name; thy kingdom come; thy will be done; on earth as it is in heaven…." He had just spoken the words, "For thine is the kingdom, the power, and the glory for ever and ever," when he heard the crunch of pebbles. He continued his prostration but left off the "Amen" as Kobiyashi knelt beside him and prayed that the Buddha would show him compassion and mercy in the day before him.

As Hideo raised himself, so did Kobiyashi. Fully two inches shorter than his friend, Kobiyashi was slightly bowlegged, with a thoroughly honest face, a shock of unruly black hair, and unusually bushy eyebrows that arched over deeply sunken, laughing brown eyes. His grandfather was little, if anything, more than a farmer when he had been conscripted into the dictator's army as an *ashigaru* and musket man just before the battle of Nagashino.

The farmer-samurai acquitted himself well as he and his comrades shot down the flower of the Yagyu cavalry, which consisted of hereditary nobility mounted on the finest horses in Nippon. Magnificent and costly, the Yagyu armor was proof against arrows but easily penetrated by lead bullets. Kobiyashi's grandfather was promoted to the rank of corporal, and although he returned to his village and his rice paddy, his son, Toshi, entered Lord Arima's service on the strength of his father's deeds at Nagashino. Toshi was assured that, despite his humble background, his unknown and unborn son would be a samurai in Lord Arima's guard.

Perhaps mindful of his humble beginnings, Kobiyashi tried the hardest to be a living embodiment of samurai ideals. He wished to act in the noblest tradition of Bushido. He became a student of samurai swords: their forging, their tempers, and their history. His knowledge of master swordsmiths was encyclopedic. He memorized all the Bizen smiths from the most illustrious, like Nagamitsu, to the most obscure one of the dozens who signed Sukesada. Kobiyashi could spend hours debating the merits of one school of swordmaking, exhausting the patience of those less enthusiastic than him. He detested the use of guns as ignoble and contrary to Bushido. In doing so, he ignored the fact that it was his grandfather's proficient use of the musket that made his father's samurai status a reality.

After the incident of Sato and the green phlegm, Hideo and Kobiyashi were all but inseparable, although there were times when Kobiyashi tried his friend's patience with his constant talk of swords.

Mopping his head with the end of his sash, Kobiyashi

complained, “Can you believe this heat? The sun isn’t even up yet.”

Hideo looked at him with a quizzical expression.

“Truly, the heat is suffocating. I think the festival will have to be postponed.”

Kobiyashi blanched.

“That’s impossible.” His voice sounded inappropriately loud and harsh in the temple. “Last night, I saw the carpenters putting the finishing touches on the pavilions and the reviewing stands.” He made a wry face as he realized Hideo was making fun of his enthusiasm. “You’re making fun of me. There’s no way the festival’s cancelled.”

Hideo tried hard to suppress the laughter that welled up in his chest. He thought of the sound a tree makes when it falls in the forest with no one to hear it, then the sound of one hand clapping. In desperation, he thought of the biblical passage in which the Christ speaks of taking the beam out of one’s own eye before regarding the dust mote in one’s neighbor’s. Nothing could stop the laughter. In a moment, Hideo was on his knees in a convulsion of laughter that left him weak.

“That look on your face,” he said, sputtering and choking. As he rolled onto his back, Kobiyashi put an oversized, sandaled foot squarely on Hideo’s solar plexus.

“Stop it! Stop it or I’ll stand on you with both my big feet.”

The reference to large feet only made Hideo laugh harder, because Kobiyashi’s feet were very big and often tripped him up in hilarious ways.

“Stop it! Stop it! You’re killing me!” Hideo gasped, still sputtering. Pausing for a moment to clear his lungs from the aspirated fluid, Hideo added, “You won’t need your enormous feet to kill me.”

Kobiyashi stood stone-faced for a moment, and then he too crumpled to the slate floor, laughing helplessly.

The two friends stepped through the temple doorway as

the sun was cresting the eastern horizon, hanging like some malevolent red eye, half open, in a cloudless, overheated, orange sky. Hideo squinted at the unusual sunrise.

"I don't know how this heat will affect the contest."

"Nothing will affect the festival, much less the contest," said Kobiyashi. "For months now, people have been talking of nothing else."

"No," said Hideo, "for months a certain samurai in the service of Lord Arima has been speaking of nothing else. A samurai known for his very big feet."

The witticism was not well received, for Kobiyasho was acutely conscious of his large feet. He therefore said nothing, but his round face lost most of its habitual animation and assumed a hurt expression.

Hideo softened his sarcastic tone and said good-naturedly, though with a touch of frustration, "Everything is Okisato this, Okisato that, Kunishige this, Kunishige that. There is more to life than swords, helmets, and bows."

In a sheepish voice accompanied by an equally ovine expression, Kobiyashi said, "I know, I know, I get carried away. It must be annoying after a while. I'm sorry, it's just . . ." He shook himself like a horse from mane to tail. "I can't help myself; I get so excited."

"You should save some of your enthusiasm for the right woman," Hideo said. "Women don't like talk of swords, armor, and matchlock guns."

Kobiyashi bridled.

"I don't like guns. Besides, women like me, and you damn well know it."

"Yes, it would seem Koetsu likes you, but then she is very young and doesn't know any better." Kobiyashi's love for Koetsu was pure, but he was by no means inexperienced.

"I admit my love for her is innocent, but you remember that time we were in Edo?"

"How could I ever forget so much sake and such women?

If only I could remember her name," Hideo said. Kobiyashi laughed heartily, dispelling the last vestige of ill will he felt from Hideo's remark about the festival contest.

"You were so drunk you vomited all over yourself, then you passed out."

"Yes, I admit it." Hideo took this with his habitual good nature. "The next morning my mouth felt like an *eta* had emptied a night soil jar in it. What was that girl's name?"

Kobiyashi laughed again. "Are you serious? I was drunk as well. I only remember Sasano's nipples. I have never seen such breasts. Aiyee! They were amazing. You know what they say?"

"No." Kobiyashi's question was rhetorical, so Hideo waited.

"Big feet, big man." By way of emphasis, Kobiyashi pointed to his groin.

"No," said Hideo, "I think the saying goes: Big feet to fill a big mouth."

Kobiyashi had completely recovered his equanimity because of the memory of his friend lying in a disreputable tavern, his kimono stained with his own vomit while girls of dubious reputation laughed at him.

"I do put my feet in my mouth from time to time," he admitted.

Hideo, delighted that his barb had fallen out of his friend's skin, said, "if your manhood were as big as your feet, you'd make a stallion die of jealousy."

Pleased that the conversation had moved far away from his relationship with Koetsu, which he cherished with exquisite care despite his womanizing, Kobiyashi slapped Hideo on the back.

"Any comparison with a stallion is fine with me." Kobiyashi raised his head, looking at the angry red disk of the sun, which was now cresting the horizon. "It's time to return to barracks."

"No need," said Hideo. "All troops except those with guard duty have leave to attend the festival until sunset."

"Do you think the Fragrant Blossom is open?"

Hideo snorted, "I doubt it. Hana was up late last night. Hana and Koetsu."

"How do you know?"

"I don't, but it seems they are always working late these days. At least, that's what Hana tells me." Kobiyashi was not happy to hear that his innocent Koetsu was working so hard. *If only I had the money to buy her contract,* he thought. The knowledge that this was an impossible dream tore at his heart and made his stomach churn. Koetsu was his first completely platonic love, and he felt very protective of her.

Hideo mopped his sweating brow and said, "Fragrant Blossom or no Fragrant Blossom, I want a bath."

"The river awaits," said Kobiyashi, half seriously.

"It's only three *shaku* deep," said Hideo.

"I suppose you have another idea," Kobiyashi said, disgusted. "I can't stand this heat. Let's go back in the temple."

"Wait," said Hideo, "the festival. They must have a bathhouse on the grounds somewhere. So many dignitaries from outside."

Kobiyashi shook his head.

"They will be guests of Lord Arima."

"Some, perhaps, but not all. Not everyone is pleased to be seen accepting Arima's hospitality."

Kobiyashi looked around and spoke in a barely audible whisper, "What are you saying? It is close to treason."

"I only say what everyone knows," Hideo said. "Everyone except for you."

"What? What do you know?" stammered Kobiyashi. All thoughts of a hot and cold bath vanished from Kobiyashi's mind. Hideo gestured to Kobiyashi, and the two men stepped several paces off the pebbled path.

"I know for a fact that Lord Arima is involved with something very odd," Hideo said.

"Hideo, you know you can trust me. I must know if there is anything going on. Unlike you, I have no illustrious ancestor." He pointed to the Arima crest on the collar of his kimono. "This," he tapped the crest embroidered in gold thread. "This is all I have in this world." Hideo looked at him and pointed at the Oda crest on the *saya* of his *katana*.

"No, you have this as well."

"But the Oda clan is no more."

Hideo shook his head in exasperation. "You have me, not my family. That is something."

"I still want to know what is going on in my lord's palace." Hideo looked startled.

"How did you know it was going on in the palace?"

Kobiyashi grabbed his right shoulder. "Now, Hideo. Give it up."

Hideo sighed. "I guess I would take an arrow for you." He continued, "Seriously, I would have told you, but the knowledge is extremely dangerous."

Kobiyashi squeezed Hideo's shoulder with a grip of steel. In pain, Hideo flicked up his right hand, the thumb tucked in so as to form a blade, and Kobiyashi's hand flew upright.

"Ow! That hurt," said Kobiyashi.

Hideo looked very seriously at his friend.

"All right, I will tell you, but remember I warned you." He drew a deep breath and began in a low tone, "I know that Lord Arima met with a barbarian very recently in Edo."

"A gaijin? Impossible!" Kobiyashi was incredulous.

"I knew you wouldn't believe me."

"Fine, let's go to the festival." Hideo turned and took a step when Kobiyashi abandoned his whispering and said loudly, "Wait!" Hideo turned to face him.

"Are you going to listen?"

"I'm sorry," said Kobiyashi, "the thought of a gaijin with

the lord—well, it is hard to imagine." Kobiyashi asked breathlessly, "What did the lord tell the foreigner?"

Hideo shook his head.

"I have said too much."

"Who told you this?"

"I was sworn to secrecy. I have broken my promise, because you are my friend. Don't ask me any more." Kobiyashi nodded.

"I understand, just tell me who told you."

Hideo paused for a moment in contemplation.

"I heard it from Shinbei. You must promise me you'll say nothing."

"I won't say a thing."

Hideo mopped his brow once more. "This heat is killing me. Let's go."

Walking back to the path, the two friends turned and began the five-mile trek to the festival grounds, their *tabi* crunching the gravel as they went. The heat was intense, despite the early hour, and within a short time, each man had sweated through his kimono, which stuck to his back. Sweat stained and darkened the white cloth, leaving the gold thread of the large Arima crest that decorated their apparel untarnished.

In less than five minutes, Kobiyashi stopped abruptly.

"This is ridiculous. I don't have my *jingasa*. You can die of heatstroke if you want. I'm going back to barracks." Hideo nodded wryly.

"I agree. No sense in being miserable. Let's get our hats."

As the sun rose higher, the air felt like the heat from a swordmaker's forge. Returning from the barracks, Hideo and Kobiyashi passed the first boundary stone on their way to the festival, their faces all but obscured by saucer-shaped, gleaming black lacquer hats emblazoned with the Arima *mon* in raised gold lacquer on the brim.

Touching the brim of his *jingasa*, Hideo said pleasantly, "You know, this was a good idea."

"I always have good ideas."

"Let's not get carried away."

"By the way, have you seen Shinbei?"

"Not for the past two days. Why?"

"I thought I heard Hankei say something about him to Yamashita."

At this, Hideo looked worried. "There was no guard on duty this morning. That never happens."

Kobiyashi looked at Hideo.

"I thought there was something very odd going on. When I left the barracks this morning to find you, Shinbei's *tatami* was empty and his swords were gone. Now that I think of it, even his *katanakake* was gone."

"That is very strange. His sword stand was gone? I left when it was still dark."

"Shinbei has been spending most of his time in the castle," Kobiyashi said. "Nothing good can come of a soldier spending all of his time with his liege lord. Differences in rank are hard to overcome. I hate to tell you this, but there has been some talk of Shinbei and the Lady Mariko."

Hideo suddenly felt sick to his stomach. Just when he thought his feelings were stable and calm regarding Mariko, the very idea that she would be even remotely linked with Shinbei made his heart faint and his belly boil. Kobiyashi could see the vein on Hideo's right temple fill with blood, and he was sorry he had brought up the subject. For a brief instant, Kobiyashi thought he could see Hideo's right hand move to his *wakizashi tsuka* and that his life might be forfeit. Hideo's mind went blank as it did when he meditated upon the void. The hand movement was involuntary, an unconscious reflex to protect itself from pain.

He knelt before Kobiyashi.

"Kobiyashi, you must forgive this stupid fool. You are my best friend. I have no right to be angry with you. My feelings for Mariko make me act like a horse's ass. I am *baca*."

Kobiyashi wiped his forehead with the free end of his sash.

"Blame it on this damnable heat. I meant no disrespect to the lady. It is I who must apologize for listening to rumors. She is my liege lord's daughter, and I would joyfully lay down my life in her service." Hideo rose and embraced his sweating friend.

"How fortunate I am to have a true friend," he said. "Kobiyashi, you are a great samurai. You honor Bushido. I am honored by your friendship. I salute you."

Somewhat embarrassed by such self-abasement from someone he esteemed—at first, for his grandfather, but in time, entirely for his own merits—Kobiyashi hurriedly changed the subject. "I can't understand what women see in Shinbei. He's a skinny runt of a man."

Hideo knew very well exactly what women could see in Shinbei. The runt, as Kobiyashi referred to him, possessed the ability to flatter a woman without her knowing it. He couldn't help feeling jealous that Shinbei would inevitably come into frequent contact with Mariko. He also seemed to have the confidence of Lord Arima, and his calligraphy was peerless. These thoughts irritated him like a cocklebur under the saddle blanket of his black mare, Amaterasu. Hideo had not been promoted to Arima's household cavalry, though he was permitted to stable his horse.

Using Buddhist breathing exercises, he proceeded to empty his mind of thoughts ofMariko. *Kobiyashi's right,* he thought. *Shinbei's a thin, bony runt. Mariko's no teahouse girl. She is beautiful, educated, and noble to the core of her being. Besides, she is samurai.*

Now the sun was fully risen, a fiery, incandescent, orange ball, and the oppressively hot night yielded to a day that promised to be the hottest of the year.

Chapter 2

Festival Morning

Hideo and Kobiyashi reached the festival grounds badly in need of a bath and refreshment. Despite the torrid temperature and even at this early hour, there was a frenzy of activity. The reviewing stands, built especially for visiting dignitaries, swarmed with carpenters who added small niceties. Others were completing the innumerable temporary structures that would house the food sellers offering tempting sweet bean cakes, sticky rice balls, grilled wood skewers of fresh mackerel, shrimp, and other ocean delicacies, all manner of radishes pickled in sweet rice vinegar, and whatever vegetables had resisted the ongoing drought. Normally there would have been a large tent or pavilion for the Kabuki theatre, but in deference to the heat, the theatre was a raised dais without walls or roof.

In the very center of the grounds stood an immaculate, raised platform of bamboo, *honoki*, and cedar—all covered with tatami of the finest quality. In each of the four corners were huge, outsize rice paper parasols that offered shade while allowing unobstructed views from almost any area of the grounds. Large silk banners, featuring the three hollyhock leaves that were emblematic of the Tokugawa shogunate hung from the sides of the stage.

Pointing excitedly at the banners, Kobiyashi said, "I can hardly wait for the contest to begin." He hugged himself in an effort to contain his enthusiasm.

With a powerful, sinewy right hand, calloused from strenuous sword practice, Hideo patted him on the back gently, like he would his horse, Amaterasu. He had not reckoned on the sweat that had rendered Kobiyashi's entire back wet and sodden. As he withdrew his hand, he turned it over, ruefully contemplating his soggy palm.

Brightening, he said, "Over there by the river. Do you see it? It's the bathhouse."

Feeling more like a wet dog than a samurai warrior, Kobiyashi's heart leapt. "Let's hurry."

Moments later, they lay naked, blissfully ensconced in a large wooden tub of comfortable dimension that was filled with clean, steaming water. Their kimonos were being washed, and their swords rested nearby on fine, unfinished red oak stands. Their *tabi* were already clean and free of dust, and large green bamboo vessels, brimming with cool, fresh water, stood within easy reach.

Genji, the bath attendant, was an older man worthy of the sumo contest. Rolls of fat cascaded down his hard, swollen belly. His great, full, sagging breasts had tiny dark nipples. His enormous bald head featured beady pig's eyes, which peered out over a flat, broad nose, which was ravaged by bright red pustules trimmed here and there with yellow pus. He gleamed with sweat. Kobiyashi was fascinated bythe twin rivers whose origin lay in his hairless armpits and ran down his fat, furrowed sides, finding their deltas in small pools near his huge, bulging, yellow feet. Despite his appearance, Genji smelled clean and was extremely deferential and most attentive.

"Would you masters like another dipper of hot water?" he asked in a thin, reedy voice that was startlingly at odds with his mountainous body.

"Yes, please," Hideo said politely.

Genji took a bamboo dipper large enough to fill a horse trough with two dips and plunged it into a massive, beaten-copper cauldron that rested in a wrought-iron stand over a bed of glowing charcoal.

Even in the superheated, subtropical air of the bathhouse, the dipper's contents smoked and steamed as Genji's oversized puffy white hand topped with stubby, fat fingers poured the almost boiling water down the side of the tub. Hideo was pleased to note that Genji's chubby fingers were clean, as were his short fingernails. The nails on both thumbs were scaly and rippled, so he looked at the cuticles, which were very short and irregular from excessive picking.

What does a man like Genji have to be anxious about? he wondered. *It lies in no man's heart to see into another.* Having concluded his philosophical musings about the attendant, Hideo sighed in utter contentment.

"Let's stay here all day." He sighed again. "We can go to the Fragrant Blossom for supper. I'm sure Koetsu would be happy."

Although Kobiyashi would have certainly liked to see Koetsu, his eyes grew wild and his round face distorted as he shouted in a booming voice, "Are you mad? We would miss the contest! Not to mention the food stalls, the famous people, and the shooting."

Hideo had no prejudice against firearms and knew that his grandfather owed his victory at Nagashino to *ashigaru* armed with guns. He even intended to purchase a good quality weapon, preferably a Kunitomo rifle with a large brass and silver dragon coiled down the underside of the fine, red oak stock.

From the very furthest tub, which was separated from the others by a fine *shoji* screen, came a deep bass voice. The screen disconnected the voice from its invisible source.

"That's the true samurai spirit. Those words are Bushido in action. I assure you that the contest will be magnificent."

Kobiyashi looked triumphantly at Hideo, who slid his long well-muscled body down the side of the tub to vanish beneath the hot water as penance for his lack of faith.

Speaking in a deferential voice, Kobiyashi boomed, "Who do I have the honor of addressing?"

Once more the deep bass spoke, "No one of importance. I will see you both at the contest."

The disembodied voice bespoke such a high degree of self-possession that he could only be one of the principal participants in the contest, perhaps the representative of Iemitsu himself. Kobiyashi's mind raced. It might be the shogun, for Iemitsu often went about in disguise as a high-ranking and wealthy samurai. The possibility that the speaker might be the shogun himself tantalized him. As Genji refilled the bamboo water vessels with fresh cold water, Kobiyashi gestured to him with his right index finger.

Rising from the fragrant, soothing water, Hideo allowed the liquid to stream down his face. His long hair trailed down his well-muscled neck in a satisfying weighty mass. Wiping his eyes and completely relaxed, Hideo looked first at the swords on the stand nearest him and then fell into a reverie. His earliest childhood memory was not of his beloved mother but of his father's swords.

The ritual was invariable. Before his father would kiss his mother, before his father would greet or dandle him, the man who had had the courage and audacity to marry the daughter of one of the Dictator Oda's concubines removed his sandals with great care and walked to the black lacquer, double sword stand and, employing ever greater care, first remove the long sword from his sash and then the shorter sword. Each was positioned with incredible accuracy so that the handle and guard were outside of the cradle formed by the arms of the stand. The long sword was always placed above the shorter one. Their graceful curves, shining black lacquer scabbards, and silk-wrapped grips fascinated Hideo. They were so intimately associated with his father—a kindly but serious man of few words.

Several times a month, his father would dismount the blades for a thorough cleaning, although Hideo never saw the slightest speck of dust or discoloration on either sword. First, his father would remove the bamboo peg of the long sword after drawing the blade, always with the razor sharp edge vertical. He would then replace the empty scabbard on the stand. Gripping the sword, he would rap the knuckle of his left wrist sharply with the palm of his right hand. This loosened the blade from the hilt, and Hideo's father never had to strike twice. The gold foil spacers and the gold inlaid, pierced iron guard would be laid out in a triangular pattern on a square of thin white silk in such a deliberate way as to ensure remounting in the same order.

Once, to demonstrate the inherent danger of the sword to Hideo, his father had touched the edge of the short sword ever so lightly with the ball of his strong thumb. As he raised it from the blade, he showed Hideo a finger with an almost invisible long line that proceeded to bleed for a few moments and seal itself, leaving only a few bright red droplets on the white silk. The demonstration only served to augment Hideo's interest in the mysterious weapons, which he saw as the source of his father's power, for he had seen farmers and merchants in the town treat his father with great deference and respect.

One time Hideo witnessed Shintaro's sword exercises, and Hideo cried out for fear that the blade would cleave the very earth and be damaged. The cry had broken his father's carefully and laboriously attained Zen state and nearly brought about the very thing Hideo feared most; his father stopped the downward motion of the sword barely a hand's breadth from one of the stone charcoal braziers on the edge of the minute vegetable garden. Sheathing the sword, his father walked the three paces to his son. Hideo could see the man he loved was angry.

"Hideo," he said with a stern, carefully controlled voice. "You must always remember two things." Although his father had never laid a hand on him, the man was capable of violence—his skill with the sword was evidence enough of that. Hideo shook like a maple leaf in an autumn gale. Seeing his son's terror, the father softened his fierce expression and his harsh tone. "My son, never forget that you are the grandson of the great Oda; his blood runs in your veins." He drew the great sword slowly. Hideo could see the clouds scudded in the steel. They seemed to move before his startled eyes. "Never forget," his father admonished him, "the sword is the soul of the samurai."

When Hideo saw Kobiyashi gesturing to Genji for some strange reason a tale Hideo's father, Shintaro, told him about the master swordsmith Masamune came unbidden to his mind.

Hideo could not have been more than five.

He had often heard stories of swordsmiths who used human blood to temper their swords while still red-hot from the fires of the forge. Shintaro dismissed these tales as absurd fictions.

"Human blood is very salty, and no artist would permit salt to come into contact with a blade," he told the wide-eyed boy. "Salt rusts polished steel as badly as acid or worse. After a battle, a samurai's first task is to clean blood from his sword, arrowhead—any iron or steel, even a *Kabuto*. Truly, human blood is a terrible corrosive." Hideo nodded his assent as his father continued, "Of course, the perfect water temperature is the swordmaker's most prized secret. You know that Masamune is the most famous of all artists in Nippon, even more so than Sanjo Munechika or Amakuni."

Shintaro sheathed the Yasumitsu and seated himself in the lotus posture. Taking five long meditative breaths, he began, "Masamune lived in Sagami Province almost five hundred years ago. He had an apprentice named Samonji. Samonji assisted his master with the hammering. He worked the bellows, swept, and cleaned the forge. Just outside the forge, under a thatched roof of its own, was the large oak cask holding the tempering water. When not in use, the barrel was very tightly covered with a close-fitting lid and handle made of cypress wood. The shed and its barrel were forbidden to all except the master.

"Many times Samonji would watch as his *sensei* plunged a newly forged, red-hot blade, which was carefully coated with gray clay, into the water barrel. At such times, the air filled with clouds of steam and a devilish hissing sound. Samonji was well aware of Masamune's renown, but he wrongly assumed that the greatness of his swords was a function of his having discovered the perfect water temperature.

"Samonji resolved to steal the *sensei*'s secret and forge his own swords. The apprentice normally rose with the dawn, sweeping and cleaning the forge long before Masamune awoke. One crisp morning in late autumn, Samonji left his warm tatami and went to the forge just as the dawn painted the wispy, low-hanging stratus clouds in the eastern sky crimson. The maple trees had recently shed their leaves, and their naked branches swayed gently in the morning breeze. There was a slight chill in the air, but Samonji's heart beat violently, sending surges of blood through his veins, and a cold sweat trickled from his armpits and beaded on his brow. He lifted the wooden lid offthe tempering water, setting it down as carefully as he was able to beside the barrel. As he slowly immersed his right hand in the water, he flared his fingers to record the exact temperature.

"He felt a shocking pain at the end of his arm. It was so wrenching that he urinated and defecated involuntarily. He drew breath with a sharp gasp and opened his streaming eyes to a horrifying sight. The tempering water turned red with blood, and his hand, with most of his wrist attached, floated on the surface like a starfish torn from its rock. He looked up and saw Masamune holding a gleaming blade with an expression at once fierce at the betrayal and sad that his judgment could have been so poor. Neither man spoke. Samonji turned and ran off as fast as he could, leaving Masamune to contemplate his water barrel, newly defiled with Samonji's blood and the severed hand that floated wrist down with the splayed fingers upright."

As he grew older, Hideo became less and less interested in weapons. Luxuriating in his bath and looking at his *daisho* where it rested on the bathhouse *katanakake,* he experienced a feeling of great fondness. This was succeeded by a sense of incredible good fortune, because he knew he was the owner of such a treasure.

Genji responded to Kobiyashi's raised finger by pouring another enormous dipper, full to the brim of nearly scalding liquid, which splashed on Kobiyashi's left shoulder, making him wince, but he said nothing although he thought to himself, *Baca, I didn't ask for water.*

"Who is the man behind the *shoji*?" he whispered to Genji. The attendant stiffened his huge ungainly body uneasily, and his pendulous breasts swayed as his swollen, naked feet with cracked, yellowing toenails rocked gently back and forth in agitation. He wished to offend no man, much less a samurai.

In a high, thin, reedy voice that jarred Kobiyashi's nerves, Genji said, "The man refused to give his name."

"You mistake me, bath man," Kobiyashi said. "I have no wish to pry. I simply want to know who answered me." The brief exchange was carried out in very soft voices, which were further deadened by the intensely humid atmosphere of the bathhouse.

Hideo spoke, nearly shouting, "If you want to know so badly, get out of your bath and ask."

Kobiyashi was both embarrassed and furious. He grabbed his bamboo drinking vessel and threw it at Hideo, who instantly ducked once more beneath the steaming waters. The container arced over Hideo's vanishing head, over the rim of the wooden tub, striking the stand with Hideo's swords, knocking it over. Horrified, Kobiyashi nearly screamed. He gasped and thrust himself vertically out of the bath and raced naked and streaming hot water to the swords, which lay like chopsticks, one atop of the other on the damp tatami.

Kobiyashi was morbidly sensitive about his treasured status as a samurai. Any affront to a sword affected him personally. His almost fanatic love for the sword began in early childhood.

There was a time in his life when this was not the case. In fact, Kobiyashi's father, a samurai of the lowest rank in the service of the Arima, had been concerned about his only son. At the age of two, Kobiyashi had not yet learned to walk, and his large motor functions were either awkward or impaired.

"What is wrong with your son?" Toshi asked his wife. Whenever Kobiyashi failed to measure up to Toshi's expectations, the well-loved little boy was Reiko's. She turned two mackerel on the small charcoal fire.

"There's nothing wrong," she said with considerable asperity, "he's taking his time. My son will be a patient man." Toshi snorted and bit back a sarcastic remark, temporarily distracted by the strong, enticing aroma of the oily fish as it cooked. He had only recently returned from extended guard duty with its diet of rice and pickled cabbage; the appetizing smell of fresh fish allayed his annoyance with his son's inexplicable behavior.

Only a few days earlier, Toshi had placed two objects before Kobiyashi. One was a brightly colored ball. The other was his *wakizashi*, which he drew from its *saya* and stabbed upright and quivering in the tatami. He looked his son in the eyes and spoke in an authoritative tone.

"Now, Kobiyashi, choose your destiny. You will follow the Eightfold Path or Bushido, the Way of the Samurai." To his chagrin and dismay, the toddler, who refused to toddle, crawled inexorably toward the bright ball, ignoring the shining sword blade. The boy hesitated at the very last moment, even as one chubby hand seemed destined to reach for the ball. Kobiyashi withdrew his hand and plunged it into his loincloth and, feeling around, grasped something that made the baby smile broadly. Exasperated, Toshi threw the ball, which knocked over the only ikebana arrangement in the sparsely furnished dwelling, picked up his *wakizashi*, and resheathed it in one fluid motion.

Sensing his father's displeasure, Kobiyashi stopped fondling himself and commenced crying piteously. Toshi raised his eyes to the bamboo ceiling and, calling on Amida Buddha to strengthen him, walked calmly from the single room as his son continued to wail. Kobiyashi had not failed his father's test; neither had he passed it as his father had wished. Ignorant and innocent, he had made a farce of things.

Unlike Hideo, whose love for samurai swords diminished as he grew to manhood, following his rather inauspicious beginning, Kobiyashi quickly developed an interest in swords that bordered on madness. Certainly, the sword could be said to be the soul of Kobiyashi.

Just a few days before his death from pneumonia, Toshi told his adolescent son, "Kobiyashi, there is more to the samurai code, more to Bushido, than the sword."

"Father, what is more valuable to the samurai than his swords?" he asked.

"Honor. Duty to one's liege lord, to Lord Arima."

"But what is honor and duty without the sword?" Kobiyashi asked.

Reiko, who dutifully attended her sick husband, smiled to herself, thinking, *Husband, you wished your son to love the sword, and you have gotten your heart's desire. Live with your wish.*

Toshi wiped his fever-withered hand across his forehead and ruefully contemplated the bands of perspiration on his palm. He rolled his bloodshot eyes to the ceiling and fell asleep, leaving his wife and his son to look at each other.

Kobiyashi spent nearly all of his free time, which, as a youth in the service of Lord Arima, was extremely scarce, listening to older samurai discuss and compare the virtues and defects of various swordmakers. There were a few books printed by the Honami family, who were sword appraisers to the imperial household and the Tokugawa shogunate, listing the cash values of some of the greater ancient artists as well as the characteristics that would enable the true aficionado to distinguish a genuine work from a student copy or a deliberate forgery. Often lesser-known swordsmiths carefully copied not only the style of a Masamune but the signature as well.

As the styles of fighting changed, many of the most precious blades by great thirteenth-century smiths, such as Nagamitsu, that were designed for use on horseback and were very long were cut down from the tang end, as the point and *mono uchi,* the most valuable striking edge, were tempered. This reworking was known as making a sword *suriage*, and often this removed the signature. There were several ways swordsmiths could retain the signature. One was to remove much of the tang but save some steel, folding the signature over to make it an *orikeshi mei*. Another was to inlay the old signature into the new tang. The signature in this case became known as a *gaku mei*. Other methods were to newly sign the blade using gold and silver, or red lacquer. Masamune often refused to sign his masterpieces, confident that anyone worthy to own one of his swords would recognize it by its sublime qualities alone.

Kobiyashi studied each and every sword, arrowhead, *naginata*, *yari*, *nagamaki*, and dagger in Lord Arima's arsenal, as well as any blade a samurai was willing to show him. After nearly two decades of obsessive study, to which he dedicated himself with fervor normally reserved to Buddhist fanatics, Kobiyashi regarded his sword knowledge as equal to an apprentice Honami.

The relative poverty of a samurai could be seen in the mountings of his swords, and Kobiyashi's father, Toshi, was far from being a wealthy man, scarcely a generation removed from the rice paddy. He had been issued his swords just prior to the decisive battle of Osaka Castle. They were *daisho* in the plainest but no less serviceable set of russet brown iron fittings, utterly devoid of finery such as gold inlaid dragonflies or hairy *minogame*—legendary winged turtles. The scabbards were of plain black lacquer; the blades were of original length but unsigned from Bizen province. Though essentially mass-produced and known as *kazu ichimono*, with none of the crab claw temper made famous by the school, Toshi's swords were well forged with straight workmanlike tempering and, in the proper natural light, even a trace of *utsuri*, the ghostlike recapitulation of the temper in the edge, in the body of the blade just below the ridge line.

Though the adolescent Kobiyashi loved his father's swords because they were the ultimate connection with his father, he passionately longed for a finer pair. He lamented the situation often and endlessly to Reiko. She was a dutiful wife and mother, genuinely thankful to her husband for marrying her and permitting her to leave an extremely unhappy home in which her father drank to excess and her mother beat her mercilessly in frustration for her own inability to thrash her father, still she did not really love Toshi. All her love, both maternal and otherwise, was reserved for Kobiyashi, and her husband knew it all too well. Toshi's wife was not overly grief-stricken when her husband fell asleep never to wake.

One afternoon, after returning from the barracks where he was attempting to master the arts of the samurai and failing miserably to please his calligraphy teacher, Yamagata, Kobiyashi was in a foul humor. He refused a proffered bowl of sweet rice and sat down dejectedly on a clean tatami. Reiko was deeply hurt, because she had made the rice especially for Kobiyashi, who usually ate her rice with a large appetite whetted by *kendo*.

"What is the matter, my son? Are you ill?"

"I'm sorry," Kobiyashi said, "it's just that when I see other boys' swords—boys no older than me—I feel ashamed."

Reiko smiled. *So it is only Toshi's stupid swords.* Then she had an idea. Without a further word, she walked to a *tansu* chest and started rummaging. Old sandals, *tabi*, kimono, and silks lay in an ever-increasing pile. Near the bottom, she found what she was seeking. It was a long bundle, wrapped in an old, stained, torn kimono. She handed it to her curious son.

Sitting in the lotus posture, Kobiyashi placed the bundle across his knees and began to unwrap the kimono. He loosed the red silk strings that tied it. He felt the heft and then the contents. His mother smiled.

"I only just remembered we had this. I know it is old." Kobiyashi's excitement increased, and he literally tore the kimono in his impatience. Within a very short time, Kobiyashi held a *naginata*, whose scabbard was adorned with the Yagu family *mon,* or crest. The pole was cut just below the parrying bar. He scissored himself upright and grabbed his *mekugi-nuki*, a tiny brass hammer. He pushed the bamboo peg that fastened the blade in its pole and smashed his left thumb knuckle with the flat of his right hand. The peg fell unnoticed to the mat.

Kobiyashi looked at the tang and almost fainted. His brown face paled and his hands began to sweat.

"Is it valuable?" asked his mother. He looked at the one-character signature, and then he sighted down the blade, studying the temper, which flashed down the edge like crumbled and broken clouds, thick and unbroken. The work in the blade matched everything he had ever heard of the artist. A tremor shook his entire body, and he knelt to avoid fainting.

"Son, are you ill?" his mother asked, anxious.

"Mother," he said in a breathless voice, "Mother, it's fantastic. Incredible. I can't believe it." With a lover's care, he set the blade on the old kimono and scooped the sweet rice with his middle and index fingers from the worn, brown lacquer bowl.

Reiko was undeterred.

"What is it, anyway? Your father never made a fuss over it. I thought it must be something of value or he wouldn't have kept it."

Kobiyashi set the bowl down and wiped his fingers with a small square of silk. Then he picked up the *naginata* blade, gazing with a look of a fond lover at the clouds floating in the bright steel. He paused for a long moment and then spoke in an awed tone.

"Mother, I am almost certain this sword is a masterpiece by the first generation Chikuzen Sa. He was famous for pole arms, both *naginata* and *nagamaki*." He looked with great care at the one-character signature on the long tang, which was sliced at an angle near the base, where Toshi's heavy blade had cut through the pole and the very end of the tang, severing both. A mosquito whined in Kobiyashi's left ear, and he deftly caught it with his left hand, crushing the life out of the pest.

"I am certain this signature is genuine, but my opinion is not official. I will have Tsunahiro take the sword to Kyoto for an official authentication."

"Are you sure it is worth so much trouble?"

"Mother, I've wanted to ask you for a long time, but I did not wish to give offense." Reiko walked to his side and took his face in her tiny, calloused, yellow hands. She was nearly a head shorter than her son, and Kobiyashi could see a lattice of crow's-feet around her limpid brown eyes. Reiko was aging before his eyes and he had hardly noticed. His extreme excitement yielded at once to a deep sense of sadness at the transience of life, then a few lines from a Buddhist monk played in his mind.

"Pursue not the outer entanglements, dwell not in the inner void, be serene in the oneness of things, and dualism vanishes by itself." His elders had often chastised him for excessive worldliness, a fanatical interest in swords, and his often-unchecked emotionalism. "Avoid the outer entanglements" was given to Kobiyashi as his own personal mantra.

Remembering this, Kobiyashi shed his melancholy almost instantly. He took his mother's hands in his own, entwining his long shapely fingers in her stubby ones, and gently kissed her graying black hair.

"My precious boy, you could not offend me if you tried. You are the best son I could ever have dreamt of. Kannon the Merciful smiled on me the day of your birth."

"So you won't be angry if I sell or trade father's swords?" he asked in a timorous tone, wholly uncharacteristic of his normal deep bass. Reiko wanted to reply sternly, but as she tried, a titter escaped, which grew in intensity until her small but wiry frame convulsed with laughter and tears flooded her crow's-feet and streamed down her cheeks. At first, Kobiyashi could not distinguish the nature of her tears, frightened that they might be tears of grief. Then, as she realized she was ready to wet her kimono, Reiko composed herself with great difficulty.

"Son," she said, literally gasping and wheezing for breath, "Son, your obsession with swords is simply crazy. Sword this, sword that. I still remember that day with the sword and ball, when your father was so disappointed that you couldn't choose. Then you become a sword madman. Sometimes I think you will marry a sword or a swordsmith rather than a woman."

Kobiyashi blushed as scarlet as his deeply tanned, healthy face permitted.

"Mother, I am not yet of age to marry."

"I know, I know," Reiko said. "It's simply that I worry about this sword mania. I am a woman. I know how women are. No woman will like being second to a sword."

"Can I trade father's swords, or will that dishonor his memory?"

Reiko looked up into her beloved son's eyes as she might have looked upon Amida Buddha.

"My son, your father was given his swords by the armorer of the Shogun Ieyasu. They were not his father's. Your grandfather carried a hoe, not a *katana*. My father carried a hay trusser's knife, also hardly a *katana*. You are second-generation samurai, a rank for which you must thank your father. He was a good husband." Here she raised her eyes to the ceiling as she lied without malicious intent. She went on, "My Toshi was a good man, loyal to the shogun and to Lord Arima. His swords are yours to do with as you will."

Kobiyashi loved his mother dearly. He had always unthinkingly taken her side in any family dispute or quarrel, a fact that mortally wounded his father and made Toshi's slipping out of this world that much more attractive to him and that much easier for him when the pneumonia called his soul back to the Buddha. Like a salmon that spends his life swimming upstream only to spawn and then die, Toshi had spent his life transcending being the son of a farmer and achieving samurai status for himself and his only son. He was content to pass on knowing that his family would be samurai by heritage for generations. This was a signal achievement in the hierarchical society of Nippon, and though the years between Nagashino in 1573 and Sekigahara provided opportunity for many sons of the paddy and soil to be ennobled, such chances for advancement all but vanished after Ieyasu assumed the shogunate.

Yielding to Kobiyashi's pleadings, Tsunahiro had attempted to trade Toshi's Bizen *daisho* for a finer set with little success. Kobiyashi grew more and more morose. He lost weight and his calligraphy deteriorated further. He was in grave danger of failing his examinations. Tsunahiro, a kindly, almost superannuated retainer in Lord Arima's personal bodyguard, had taken a liking to the spindly Kobiyashi.

Tsunahiro returned from Edo for the fourth time with Toshi's Bizen *daisho* without attracting any takers. Kobiyashi was crestfallen. The situation was extremely serious. If Kobiyashi's inability or unwillingness to master the art of calligraphy continued, not only would he forfeit any chance of future promotion, he would be in danger of losing his samurai status and becoming a *ronin*. He would make a very precarious way in a world where *ronin* were little more than bandits. Opportunities for young, failed samurai were virtually nonexistent. The only legitimate path open to such an unfortunate man was the Way of the Buddha at a monastery. Tsunahiro was only too aware of the potential for disaster in Kobiyashi's inattention to calligraphy. He had already discussed the sorry state of affairs with Shiro, the *sensei*.

Well advanced in years and highly esteemed by Lord Arima, Shiro was also a thoroughly competent samurai. Following the fourth abortive attempt to sell Kobiyashi's *daisho*, Tsunahiro approached Shiro.

"*Sensei*, I am concerned about Kobiyashi." Shiro grimaced slightly as if what he was about to say caused him pain.

"He is clearly a most earnest young man, but I fear there is something very amiss with him. He utterly fails to understand that the stroke of a *katana* and the stroke of the brush are one and the same. This is the true way of the warrior. This unity is the very essence of Bushido. Were I a younger man, there are times I could whip him, I become so frustrated." At this, Tsunahiro raised his right hand upright with palm facing out.

"That would have been proper years ago. Now it would only serve to make matters worse."

"I know," Shiro sighed. "I know it all too well. Kobiyashi is the most frustrating student I can remember." Tsunahiro's face crinkled as he smiled. Shiro scowled, "Why are you grinning?"

"My apologies, *sensei*. It's only that not so many months ago, I heard you shouting at the Lady Mariko. If I recall, it was something like 'You are the most difficult student I have ever had. Your characters are illegible—a disgrace to the name of Arima.'" At this, Shiro blanched and his wrinkles, especially the wattle around his neck, quivered.

His voice was shaky as he asked Tsunahiro, "You never told anyone?"

"Many are the stalwart samurai who would gladly shout at the Lady Mariko," Tsunahiro said with a twinkle in his eye. He paused and continued, "if they did not value their positions, if not their very lives."

"What about Kobiyashi?" Shiro asked, hurriedly moving away from a very dangerous subject.

"I will speak with him. I believe he will come around. Please show patience. He is a most worthy youth."

"I have been most patient," Shiro said. "Perhaps the young man would make a better priest than samurai."

"Buddha and Bushido are one," Tsunahiro said sharply. "They demand service, humility, and discipline; the one path no more and no less than the other."

"You forget yourself," Shiro said angrily. "I am master, not you."

"Aii, old man, I forget nothing, nothing at all. I promise you he will succeed." The samurai wheeled on his right heel and stormed from the room in a fury. Shiro walked to a raised dais on which lay a superb *suzuribako*, a magnificent lacquer box of polished black lacquer. Raising the close-fitting lid adorned with the Arima *mon* in intricately raised relief in pure

Chapter 3

The Hollander

Hendrik Visser sat on an immaculate hardwood floor sipping strong, fragrant tea from an ugly, fired clay cup that he knew was probably worth more than his home back in Hoevelaken. Here in Japan it was so very easy to be deceived by appearances, so easy to make an irrevocable fatal blunder. He turned the hot cup around 360 degrees, trying desperately to see the beauty and value of the artist's vision for the dark brown glaze that dripped here and there in an irregular and variable, seemingly random, pattern that he knew from previous encounters was anything but. He remembered the words of the Huguenot priest who had cautioned him to forget everything he believed about art when in Japan.

"There is very little in Japanese art and culture that is straightforward to a European," the priest told him. He continued. "Art that appears hideous and deformed and often grotesque to you is considered lovely, even beautiful. Images of deformed, leering dogs, their cavernous mouths filled with enormous teeth, decorate temples in the Chinese manner. They may resemble the gargoyles of Notre Dame, but they are neither for drainage nor for frightening devils and demons. On the contrary, they are regarded as attractive ornaments, while to us they are repugnant.

"The simple glazed cups they use in the *cha no yu*, which any European wouldn't give houseroom and which look like something only the poorest peasant would use as a last resort, are worth thousands of gold guilders. The key to success in Japan is to ignore everything you know and cast aside all preconceived notions and prejudices. Penetrate things, people, and concepts to their essential essences. Do not be misled by outward appearances."

At the time there in Rotterdam, Hendrik had thought that the man must be unhinged from the overlong sea voyage, a shipwreck, and attendant privation, as well as the influence of too much "square face," also known as Geneva or Holland gin.

So he continued staring at one particular drip, just below the inverted lip of the cup. As he did so, he was taken back to that time nearly ten years before, when, as a young man, almost unique in his lack of beard—for he shaved religiously seven days a week—he was sent to the court of Shogun Iemitsu by his commander. Iemitsu was troubled, his legendary equanimity disturbed. Christian rebels were defeating his invincible army. Bands of starving peasants, worshippers of the officially proscribed Christ and his mother, the Virgin Mary, were about to defeat the Tokugawa forces. True, the traitors were forced to retreat and take refuge in Hara Castle, but his army had suffered unthinkable losses, numbering in the tens of thousands. The insurrectionists were about to break out. If they were successful, the fires of anarchy would engulf Japan, leaving in its wake smoldering ashes. If they succeeded, there were sufficient numbers of hidden Christians in Japan to overthrow the Tokugawa shogunate.

Iemitsu, a strongly built and dour but handsome man in his thirties, was not the image of his godlike grandfather, Ieyasu Tokugawa. Ieyasu, while powerfully built, had a lamentable tendency toward corpulence, which he insisted on being faithfully portrayed in all images and portraits. His love of truth and realism in politics as well as art pervaded his every act. His son, Hidetada, and grandson, Iemitsu both loved Ieyasu. On occasion, Hidetada tried to outdo his father, Ieyasu, with predictably poor results. Hidetada's son, Iemitsu, had fewer difficulties living up to Ieyasu's legacy and was nearly as skilled in steering the ship of state as his grandfather was. Prior to the Shimabara Rebellion, courtiers and generals avoided comparing the three Tokugawa shoguns.

Shiro Amakusa, the leader of the uprising, was a stripling. He was slender of frame but tall and statuesque, with a face that shone so much that there were adherents who thought of him as the Christ incarnate, something Shiro repudiated vehemently. His victories on the battlefields of Amakusa Province, a land devastated by drought and laid waste by the ensuing years of famine, inspired his fanatical followers to great deeds of valor, threatening the samurai monopoly on Bushido. Farmers with feet as horny as turtle shell from hard labor in the fields and paddies—armed only with a few cast-off swords, pole arms that were no more than converted farm tools, and here and there a scattering of matchlock guns—were defeating the invincible samurai, who were mounted on superb armored horses, dressed in costly armor, and armed with the finest swords, bows, pole arms, and guns.

Iemitsu had been only too aware of the complaints of his courtiers, but they always complained—that was their function. If his generals were discouraged, that was another matter entirely and one that demanded action. Circumstances had reached that point. Only the day before meeting with

Hendrik, Honda Tadakatsu, the son of Heihachiro Honda and hero of Sekigahara, had come to him to caution him. No one, not even Honda, dared warn Iemitsu that the war, which the shogun always referred to as a rebellion by traitors to the shogunate, was causing a crisis not only in the thinning ranks of the army but in the staggering losses that were beginning to affect the members of the high command whose courage was not in question.

Hendrik was a Hollander, but given the dire circumstances, that did not matter, one gaijin was the same as another. Japanese found their personal habits and clothing outlandish and offensive. They were barbarians. Iemitsu had always despised the gaijin, especially the unclean priests in their filthy black robes who befouled the purity of the Land of Tears and the Buddha with their strange practices, pagan rituals, and, above all, their body odor—a sweetish stench of the grave; an obscene, putrid rot. When Iemitsu's father sealed the final Edict of Expulsion in 1622, Iemitsu was ecstatic. The next year, Hidetada had abdicated in his favor but had remained as regent. All *gaijin,* except for one or two at court, were forced to leave Nippon on pain of death. Their temples and churches were burned, and all trade was prohibited except for Holland and China. The Hollanders were permitted to dock at a small man-made island in the harbor.

Nippon was at long last Buddhist and Shinto once more, the Kirishitans, who had flourished—supported by the Dictator Oda, tolerated by Hideyoshi, endured by Ieyasu—were vanquished. All Nihonjin were required to perform the *fumi-e* ceremony once each year. The ritual consisted of stepping on an image painted on copper of the Kirist or the Virgin Maria and a public declaration that they had no connection to the Kirishitans.

Hendrik knew Iemitsu was scrutizining his every gesture and each nuance of his body language, especially how he held the cha cup.

der, his soul all but shattered by the never-ending tableaus of bursting heads, bodies, detached flying arms, legs, hands, living men, women, and saddest of all, children made into corpses as he watched. He was almost beside them thanks to Lippershey's invention. He could see the Tokugawa army ride into the castle through the immense breaches in the massive stone walls. Their banners bore the three hollyhock leaves of the shogun and were triumphant over the cross of Christ and Shiro Amakusa—thanks to him. The Dutchman could no longer bear the ordeal of his witness and sat, utterly spent, on the breech of a sparking nine-pounder cannon.

His brain teemed with the images of death that he had seen on hundreds of faces, each one telling of a different death agony. It was a continuously moving canvas that was more terrifying than the most graphic hell painted by another of his countrymen, Hieronymus Bosch; only that day's vision of hell was of Hendrik's design. It was not the lustful, foolish, greedy nature of humanity that resulted in the hell of Shimabara but his own political machinations and greed on behalf of the honorable Dutch East India Company. It was not the blood, not the flying limbs, not even the pathetic smashed jelly of what were children only moments before that horrified him the most. The multicolors of death ultimately proved Hendrik's undoing: the red-brown, ropy intestines, the vivid blues, the bright greens, and the deep pinks from deep inside living beings as they splashed on stone, wood, and earth. The horses splattered into steaming piles of bright entrails and the entire spectrum of human and animal frailty, heaving and hideous, were brought close to him by his telescope.

He had seen too much, and it had unmanned him. Hendrik stood and was about to hurl himself into the green sea. To forgive him for this day would put even Christ's capacity for infinite mercy to the test. Yet in the end, he was too tired to throw his body over the rail.

He somehow found his way to his cabin and bolted the

door. As the great guns fell silent, he diligently applied himself to a wedge of hard Leyden cheese, a piece of relatively fresh hardtack, and an entire bottle of gin. Then he fell into a dreamless, stuporous slumber.

Hendrik shook his head to clear it of the hideous memories and concentrate on the task at hand. He spoke in an almost doleful tone as he addressed the Shogun. "No, sire," Hendrik said, "the ashes of Shimabara are still warm." Iemitsu smiled, only this time it was a cruel grin, showing even white teeth and healthy pinkish brown gums.

Ah, Hendrik thought. *Being ruler of Nippon has made him ruthless and cruel. The few years have changed him*. He continued his internal monolog, *No. It's just that circumstances have revealed his true nature—circumstances and absolute power.*

Iemitsu spoke in a voice tinged with venom, probing, feinting then striking to the core of Hendrik's thoughts.

"Perhaps, you regret your role in suppressing the traitors." Hendrik knew he was still in mortal danger. He spoke in a tone so lazy and so unconcerned that even Iemitsu could not possibly mistake his meaning.

"Nothing happens without God's will. He knows the outcome of every matter at its inception. If God willed the destruction of Shimabara, who am I to question his will?"

Iemitsu seemed mollified by this answer. He motioned for Hendrik to rise and, as the European stood, said, "I thank you for your directness. I am aware of nearly everything. Lord Arima is guilty of treason. I am pleased to know that you are not. You have been implicated, but I see you are not a conspirator. Arima's plot will fail. You will keep me informed of the new weapons. My emissary will wait upon you."

Without a further word, the shogun left the room. He did not return the Spanish pistol.

Chapter 4

Oyama Shinbei

Shinbei's eyes opened. They felt inflamed, and as he flicked his eyelids, the eyeballs grated against the inside as if made of sand.

The heat in the dungeon was stifling, made worse by the stinking, malodorous contents of the large night soil jar in the corner. The stone walls were approximately five feet thick and were normally cool, even in August. However, this summer the heat was so uncommonly intense that the stones actually retained the heat of the day and radiated it throughout the night.

The stench of stale urine mixed with excrement was suffocating. The guards often left the unfired, low, round clay pot unemptied, not out of cruelty but out of practicality. In order to empty the pot, they had to carry it, sloshing and often dripping, up a flight of narrow, slippery stone stairs, down a corridor two hundred *shaku* long, out the gate, and another two hundred *shaku* to the latrine behind the barracks. In winter, emptying the jar became even more hazardous. Shinbei had drawn this duty more than once before he himself was shut up in the dungeon. He had always detested the huge pot; it was heavy when empty, and few could carry it without some spilling, which necessitated a bath and change of clothing.

Truly, man's bodily functions are disgusting, he thought. The cells of Lord Arima's dungeons were often vacant, and none of his samurai could understand why the Lord did not employ *eta* to carry out such a task. Night soil, urine, and disposal of corpses both human and animal were an *eta*'s lot in life. Born into the caste, their children would be *eta* as well. Perhaps assigning such undignified duties to samurai was thought to instill humility, but it only bred resentment. However, Shinbei never felt the resentment expressed by his comrades. He was grateful and content merely to be a samurai in the retinue of a great hereditary nobleman like Lord Arima.

He remembered Ashitaka, a samurai who seemed to be forever in difficulty and who had been dismissed by Captain Yamashita for sleeping while on guard duty. Ashitaka had once slipped on the lip of the fourth step while carrying the pot. He had fallen, and in falling, he had flung the jar against the stone wall, where it had shattered, releasing a torrent of noxious fluids and solids to pour over the senseless samurai. Holding his nose, Shinbei had prodded the sodden man with the *saya* of his *katana*. Ashitaka had awoken and shaken himself like a wet dog, sprinkling Shinbei with excrement. Ashitaka had looked so ludicrous that Shinbei laughed, despite his own discomfiture. Fortunately, Ashitaka had fallen asleep on duty the very next day.

Shinbei felt a spasm tear at his bowels. It was sharp and painful but not irresistible. He raised himself from the filthy straw pallet, and standing in the middle of the tiny cell and clad only in a loincloth, he felt the large welt on the crown of his head.

Hideo was entirely unaware of this invisible scrutiny. The only reason Shinbei was cognizant of Hideo's position was his own involvement in one of Lord Arima's clandestine schemes. His involvement was doubtless the reason he had been battered and imprisoned.

"Gaijin, damned filthy barbarians," he said to himself. "They have trapped the lord like a fat pigeon in birdlime. It's the guns. The cursed guns. Dirty, disgusting, ignoble, smelly, undignified, and cowardly." He stopped himself on the verge of screaming.

His aching chest filled with a proud breath. His spirits buoyed with a thought. *With this trial, I prove once and for all to Lord Arima and to my mother that I am samurai. I sit here so my liege lord will not be betrayed. By my suffering, being branded as a traitor, Lord Arima will be saved.*

This comforting thought was immediately succeeded by another idea that was far less pleasant. *What if no one knows? My death serves the lord, true, but my mother will never forgive my ghost, and Hana … I must get a message to Hana.*

He thought he heard footsteps approaching, and he smelled a torch. The darkness was less absolute. He looked at his palm, and now he could see the dried blood from his duck egg. His stomach heaved, and he squeezed his sphincter with all his might, forcing back a strong bowel spasm.

They would not find him squatting on the night soil pot. He would rather die.

Chapter 5

The Stranger in the Bathhouse

As the nearly scalding bath water ran out of his ears and his eyes cleared, Hideo looked to ensure that his swords were in their proper place on the stand. He could see Kobiyashi's naked body bent over them with his buttocks facing him.

"What are you doing to my swords?" Hideo asked, loudly. Kobiyashi started and then stood bolt upright. With his friend standing, Hideo could see that his Yasumitsu *wakizashi* lay on the tatami.

"What the hell are you doing?"

Kobiyashi was both startled and mortified, but he was more mortified than surprised. He bent down and replaced the *wakizashi* on the stand under the *katana* and faced Hideo with the same look a dog has when he is caught doing what he should not be doing.

The expression on Kobiyashi's long face was so doleful that Hideo shook his head and relaxed. Kobiyashi could be counted on to cause some clumsy mishap at least once a day. Hideo saw the bamboo vessel lying behind the sword stand, and everything became clear.

"I see you hit the sword stand," he said in a lightly mocking tone. "Better the sword stand than my head."

Kobiyashi brightened slightly.

"I would much rather have hit your head. Hideo, I am so sorry. I would never harm any sword, much less a Yasumitsu."

"You may find this hard to believe, but I value my head more than my sword," Hideo said. Kobiyashi managed a tiny grin.

"And I value your Yasumitsu more than your head. Hideo, please forgive my clumsiness."

"If you want my pardon then get back in the bath. Your privates are not that attractive, if the truth be known."

As Kobiyashi lowered himself into the wood tub, the deep bass voice from behind the *shoji* screen spoke again.

"Once more, spoken like a samurai. Now if you would mind your own business and allow me to bathe in peace, I will no doubt see you both at the contest. I will tell you that I will be a participant." Kobiyashi half fell back into the bath and, in so doing, strained a muscle in his thigh.

"Arrrh, that hurts," he said, and he massaged the muscle to loose it. "If he is a participant, he must be Nagahisa *sensei*, himself. I long to meet him."

Hideo gave his friend a crooked smile. "You long to meet a sword tester? A man who spends his life cutting corpses?"

Kobiyashi became furious.

"Baca! Keep your voice down!"

In fact, Hideo had barely spoken above a whisper, for he wished to give no offense.

"Now calm down," he said to Kobiyashi, "I can't understand your worship of this man."

"You don't understand anything," Kobiyashi said. "Nagahisa *sensei* is the chief of the Hamano School of testers. His style is peerless, and his inlaid attestations on the tangs of swords, unquestionable. Having Nagahisa test the tang will double the price of almost any sword." He added, "Even your Yasumitsu."

Hideo shrugged his shoulders, "I would never permit such a thing. It would be a desecration."

"Perhaps you're right, but for a modern blade, a Nagahisa test is a blessing."

"All right," said Hideo, "You've convinced me. I'll look forward to seeing him this afternoon. One thing bothers me."

"What's that?" asked the now-mollified Kobiyashi.

"Shinbei," he answered, "There's something wrong, and I can't figure it out."

"We could go see Hana. She would know," said Kobiyashi. Then he added, in a tone mixing jealousy and disgust, "I don't think she squats to piss without him knowing how much."

"And he can't squat to defecate without her knowing all the details," Hideo added in a neutral tone.

"Good," Kobiyashi said, "It's settled."

He clambered from the tub as Genji handed him a clean, white towel and a bathrobe. Hideo remained, luxuriating in the bath.

"Cold, please," he said, and Genji poured an enormous dipper of cool water over his head. Hideo climbed from the tub with a grace that was all the more decorous after his friend's scrambling exit. Hideo took the towel and robe from Genji, who smiled at his dexterity.

The two men dressed behind a small *shoji* screen.

As Kobiyashi adjusted his sash, he asked hesitatingly, "Are my privates really that ugly? I've never heard any woman say so."

Hideo, knowing of his friend's sensitivity, repressed a laugh, though not without difficulty.

"No," he said. Kobiyashi visibly relaxed. "No," Hideo con-

was not pleasing to her father, but as he was still smarting from having banished his son, he grimly tolerated the dalliance.

Iemitsu's spies within Arima's household had reported Mariko's relations with Hideo to their superiors in Tokyo and Kyushu, who had then reported them to Iemitsu's counselors. The shogun was pleased.

Chapter 6

Mariko

Accompanied by Corporal Hankei, Mariko hurried down the narrow stone steps as fast as she could in the flickering, uncertain light of the torch. As they neared the dungeons, the rank odor of excrement and urine struck her like the point of a token in the pit of her stomach. She choked off a powerful urge to retch. Continuing the descent, she gagged several times, so strong was the stench in the heat. Mariko longed for fresh air and to comment on the disgusting stink, but she would die before showing any weakness to the seemingly imperturbable, impassive Hankei. Her father had shown her the dungeons once when she was a young girl. That had been an adventure in winter, and the cells had been immaculate and unoccupied when she had imagined herself a princess locked up by an evil magician, waiting for her prince to come and free her.

In that halcyon time not so very long ago, her mother had still been living; Lord Arima had been happy and content and her brother, Daisuke, had been at home. However, then had come the time of troubles, as Mariko thought of it. Her older brother and her father had quarreled constantly, and evening suppers became pitched battles. Her beautiful, slender, accomplished mother began to lose weight that she could not afford to lose—her cheeks gradually disappeared; her skin, formerly as smooth as a placid pond, became wrinkled; and her strikingly long, lustrous, raven hair fell out in clumps. Arima had sent for Hidetada's own doctor, though the shogun himself had been dying slowly at the time. The doctor had diagnosed a growth in her brain and prescribed draughts of an infusion of gold and tea. These had worked for a time, but the progress of the illness resumed, accompanied by terrifying seizures and horrible, fetid breath. It was the horrid breath, more than any of the other maladies, that had distressed her mother. It was so foul that Mariko could scarcely bear to be at her mother's side. The young girl had known this was a time when her mother needed her most, and she had been ashamed of her weakness but could no more have overcome her aversion than she could have taken wing like a great crane.

Worse, matters between father and son had reached a climax. Enraged beyond all reason, Lord Arima had actually drawn his Nagamitsu blade, threatening to behead Daisuke for disobedience. Without a word, the young man had looked at his father's face, which was contorted with fury and red with budging veins bulging, and had walked out the door and kept going, out of the palace. The astonished sentries dared not stop the young lord as he had continued out of the compound beyond the palisade, where the evening dusk had swallowed him whole. Lord Arima had forbidden any mention of Daisuke on pain of instant banishment. This had applied not only to all his subjects but to his immediate family as well. So that there could be no mistake, dozens of scrolls were posted throughout Kyushu and the palace as reminders.

Soon thereafter, Mariko's mother had died. Her failure

to heal the breach between her husband and her only son had been a source of greater pain than the growth in her brain or the sullying of her once sweet breath. When the death agony actually began, she had embraced it with all the enthusiasm of an ardent lover. She had failed, and death was her just and deserved portion. The doctor had been amazed at the brevity of her struggle.

Lord Arima had been inconsolable. He had really and truly loved his wife. She had been the only human being to whom he could have entrusted absolutely all his secrets, his hopes, and his innermost thoughts. Even Daisuke could not separate them, although she had tried mightily to bring them together. In the end, she had been forced to admit to herself that her son had been more at fault than her husband. She had blamed neither one. The gulf was of a nature that would have required Amida Buddha himself to bridge it.

Mariko could remember the day the trouble had started. Although she had been very young at the time, she could still see the angry look on her father's face all throughout supper. Her father had eaten nothing, even though the cook had made a savory fish soup filled with spices and vegetables so fresh and fragrant that Mariko could not resist it. She had just speared a particularly fine piece from the section along both sides of the backbone. It was flaky and succulent and free of the bones that she hated. Her black lacquered chopsticks had been tricky and oh so slippery. She had only recently mastered their use and was justly proud of her accomplishment.

The tension around the fine cinnabar table, which stood barely one *shaku* above the highly polished, red oak floor, was taut as a drawn bowstring. Then Mariko's mother had dissolved into uncontrollable sobbing, and the dam had burst.

Arima rose from his cross-legged seat on the tatami effortlessly.

"You ingrate! You cowardly bastard! See what you've done!" Accustomed as she was to tales of the Gempei wars and the battles of Nagashino and Sekigahara, to bloody decapitations and executions, she had never witnessed any serious discord in her family. Mariko's piece of fish—the special, delicious backbone piece—slipped from her chopsticks and dropped onto the bright cherry blossom embroidered on her favorite silk kimono in a splatter of fish broth and fish fragments. She burst into tears, which redoubled Arima's fit of rage.

"Bastard!" He thundered, "I curse the day you were born. Unnatural spawn of the devil! I'll give you one month. Not one day more to be my son. Otherwise …" The *daimyo* did not finish, because his wife had slumped to the mat as if she were dead.

Less than two months after this wrenching family tableau, Diasuke left the palace. Soon after that, her mother died and Mariko was left alone with Lord Arima. Despite numerous offers from other *daimyos*, seeking to secure advantageous alliance, her father refused to remarry.

Although she could not very well inherit the Lord's domain or title, Arima raised Mariko as if she were both son and daughter, schooling her in the samurai arts as well as music, dance, and manners. Early on he could see she preferred a sword to a *samisen* and a bow to a plectrum. This gave him untold joy, although Mariko's calligraphy was more appropriate to a private soldier in the barracks than to the daughter of a *daimyo*. He had been so deeply offended by what he saw as Daisuke's effeminate qualities that he made only a pretense of disappointment at his daughter's incompetence in the feminine arts.

As she grew to womanhood, Mariko gradually won her way into her father's confidence, though not so completely as her mother. With her death, Arima had lost forever his trusted and indomitable life partner. Still, Mariko was all he had. Her affair with Hideo came as a relief, because at times—watching her skill with the bow or galloping on a spirited stallion bareback—he worried that his personal problems with his son had spoiled his daughter for any future husband.

After all, Lord Arima thought, *Oda is a fine samurai, and his grandfather ruled over all Nippon, even over Ieyasu.* Arima had other ideas for Hideo, who was completely unaware of them.

Arima knew of Iemitsu's plan to marry one of his young sons to Mariko and thereby gain Arima's domain for the Tokugawa. The shogun did not know that Arima had sworn a blood oath before the family shrine to all his ancestors, reaching back to the time of the Taira and Minamoto wars that he would rather die than see his daughter married to a Tokugawa.

He loved his daughter far too much to take her completely into his confidence, so she was also unaware of Iemitsu's machinations. Arima was equally aware that Iemitsu's talk of marriage was an elaborate feint to draw out the lord. The shogun wished for any sort of alliance between the families, knowing that policy alone had led the previous lord to fight on the side of Lord Ishida Mitsunari and the Western Armies at Sekigahara.

Shortly before Hideo's arrival in Kyushu, Mariko had dismissed all her ladies-in-waiting except for Hatsui. She'd had the retainer cut the long, lovely hair she had inherited from her mother and shape it in the style of a young man without a topknot. This allowed her a remarkable degree of freedom, which freedom was known and countenanced by her father. Mariko was watched but from a considerable distance and at discontinuous intervals. When Hideo had first seen her without a head covering, he was astonished at her hair. The combination of her male appearance and her feminine charms had excited him into a sexual frenzy, and he had found it more alluring than the voluptuous curves of Hana, the fairest flower of the Fragrant Blossom.

Lord Arima played a game of Go in three dimensions, using Mariko and Hideo as pieces, employing a strategy so complex that neither of the two lovers could ever figure out whether the lord merely turned a blind eye, actually disliked the relationship, or secretly fostered it. Sometimes guards would materialize at inopportune times, and at other times, they would be unchaperoned when by right, they should have been closely observed. The elaborateness of Arima's thought was such that, from day to day, even the lord himself lost the thread of all its subtleties. Only by this means could he hope to outwit Iemitsu's efficient and all-pervasive spies. The lord could not trust anyone in his household, as the shogun had unlimited resources with which to compromise any man or woman, and if riches were insufficient, he had the ultimate power of life and death over all Nippon.

At last came the ultimatum to either marry Hideo and be a common soldier's wife or break off all relations except those in the natural course of Hideo's duties. Arima played this card with such consummate ability that no one, including the lovers, suspected or saw anything amiss. Kobiyashi questioned why the Lord would permit the man who had dishonored his daughter to remain in his service, but Hideo thought—rather foolishly—that he was only one in a long line of such affairs.

If the truth were known, she was neither as wholly innocent nor nearly as experienced as palace, and especially barracks, gossip would have her be. There were those in the barracks who staunchly defended her honor, while others disparaged it with equal vigor. Although Hideo was the most stalwart of her defenders, he thought it wise to stop short of dueling with the author of any given calumny. Except for a few coarse and vulgar men, most of Arima's guard valued their positions as highly as they did their honor as followers of Bushido, and they refrained from comment on their liege lord altogether. Samurai courtesy and bedrock loyalty to their lord were strong enough to cow Mariko's detractors in many instances. Palace talk was kept to a minimum for fear of losing one's position as well as fear of Mariko herself.

Though slight of build, she was tall for a woman, accustomed from childhood to the exercise of martial arts and consequently deceptively strong. Her figure tended toward the sinewy and lithe—small of bosom and long of leg. Archery was her best martial skill, and she could best most of her father's retainers and had proven as much to many a samurai's chagrin. She was truly her father's daughter and, since Daisuke's exile, his de facto son as well.

Perhaps it was the duality of roles that she was required to fill that made her so unpredictable. One afternoon, she would let a direct insult or negative comment about a very personal matter, such as her hair, from a servant girl pass without notice or even with a laugh. Another morning, a far more innocent remark would result in the perceived offender receiving a stinging slap on both cheeks, one after the other or, even worse, a peremptory dismissal. Not even her closest attendant knew precisely where she stood with Mariko at any given moment. This quality inspired fear in those closest to her.

Most of the time, Lord Arima was delighted with Mariko, and she knew it. She was the son he had lost, the daughter he loved, and enough like the wife he missed so badly. He missed her even after more than a decade, and his heart still ached at the sight of a particular tea bowl she had cherished or a scroll she had loved. He turned down several attractive and very beneficial marriages, using Mariko as an excuse when his own feelings were offended.

This very powerful man, so calculating in nearly all of his actions that Iemitsu himself respected him as a potential threat to his rule, kept the memory of his wife sacred from all the worldly advantage that discarding it would have brought him. Not even Mariko understood this, since Arima wisely kept no shrine of gilded wood with ever-burning candles nor offered munificent gifts to temples in her name. Instead, he had erected a magnificent edifice to her in his heart. There the candles always burnt brightly, and the offerings he made were

a drowning man to breathe. Each person has some fear that is equally irresistible; many simply never come into physical contact with it.

Shinbei listened as the blood froze in his veins. He assumed someone was being tortured and that he might be next. He had a morbid fear of torture, though not the pain. He particularly feared for his testicles and his penis. There were specific methods for manipulating both organs that he refused to dwell on.

There was just enough light for Mariko to have seen the gray snake of the rat's tail drag across the tips of the corporal's toes. Between his clumsy efforts to relight the torch, his manful attempts to retain his dignity, and the scream, she could take no more. She burst out laughing and was helpless to stop it.

Shinbei could not believe his ears. Mariko's laughter filled the air, increasing moment by moment. He could not imagine a woman in the dungeon at such an hour. There were only two women who could possibly have come. Hana or Mariko, but how would Hana have access? She could have prostrated herself before Lord Arima, but not at this late hour. As the lord's sometime calligrapher, Shinbei was familiar with Arima's routine, and it would have taken an invasion by a neighboring *daimyo* or a messenger from the shogun for his personal guard to disturb the lord after midnight. A distraught teahouse girl, however beautiful, wouldn't have a prayer.

Mariko wiped the tears from her eyes and could see Hankei's flint pouch lying near the red eye of the torch end.

"Corporal," she said calmly, "please allow me to strike the light."

She struck once, and the torch blazed to reveal a thoroughly ashamed Hankei, who hung his head as if waiting for the axe to fall.

"Corporal, you are very brave. My father is still grateful for your courage with that stallion. I will inform him of your courtesy in accompanying me at this late hour. You may leave me now."

Hankei did not want to leave Mariko alone with the prisoner, but he had no specific orders, and the lady had been extraordinarily merciful to not only overlook his shameful behavior but to speak of his courage rather than his disgusting cowardice.

"Lady," he said in a voice filled with self-loathing, "Lady, I apologize—" She interrupted him sharply.

"Corporal, I see nothing shameful to discuss," she continued, "I said you may go. I thank you for your company." Her tone was commanding, and Hankei obediently and gratefully ascended the stairs as she held up the torch for him.

Chapter 7

The Interview

"If only you had listened to me, none of this would have happened," Mariko said, looking through the rectangular iron bars at the bloodied and bedraggled Shinbei. He had tried his best to clean some of the filth and blood from his clothes, face, and hands, but the water he used was foul, and he succeeded only in rearranging the stains.

"If I'd listened to you," he said bitterly, "I'd be dead, and my mother dying."

"Asamu has been dying now for months, if not many years now," she said angrily. "I think she'll outlive us all."

"You selfish bitch," Shinbei said furiously. "You don't know what it is to love a mother or a father."

Mariko withdrew into a rage so cold she could have killed Shinbei without a moment's regret.

"How dare you! I won't deign to answer such slander. You deserve to be here."

Shinbei realized that he had made a serious error. Had he only imagined that Mariko had tried to seduce him? He had surely not dreamed that she had opened her kimono when they were alone the night before the night of horror that had landed him here. Or was it merely the unbearable heat that had prompted her actions?

Certainly, he had taken money. His mother needed expensive medicine. She would die without it. Mariko had given him the money. He had been thoroughly searched upon leaving the palace by Captain Yamashita and two formidable samurai he didn't know.

His memory was indistinct. He had been drinking with Hana. He touched the duck egg on his head, and a bolt of raw pain shot down his spine. Arima had asked him to list the contents of a gaijin ship, a long catalog of unfamiliar munitions. There were strange guns and pistols he had never heard of. *Yes,* he remembered now, *there was a barbarian, Hendrik.* He had seen him once with the lord was but not introduced. The *gaijin* and Mariko had seemed to know each other. It was all too strange.

I should have never left my village, he thought. *Once a peasant, always a peasant. To think I was happy when Arima singled me out to assist him.* Shinbei slapped his face hard, so hard that the blow shook the duck egg. He winced. *What an idiot. Baca! To think that Arima and his mannish daughter have ever looked at me as a man. No, they only see a son of a lucky farmer with manure between his toes. Blood will tell.*

He could go to the shogunate police with what he knew. But what did he actually know? He had made a list of contraband weapons. He had seen a barbarian with Lord Arima. If only he'd made a copy of the list. But then the shogunate might have decided to use him as a traitor to divert suspicion from Arima. Besides, everything may well have the blessing of the shogun, because little occurred in Nippon without Iemitsu's knowledge, and rare was the enterprise so foolish as to act independently of the shogunate. The worst part of the fiasco was that Asamu would be disappointed.

"After all her hard work and sacrifice, I have brought disgrace to the house of Oyama. I wish I were dead." Shinbei uttered this last thought aloud without realizing it.

"Be careful what you wish for," Mariko's voice lashed his ears. She continued, "You forget yourself. You have been badly treated, and I am sorry for that. I thought by giving you my purse, I was helping you, but I see now I was being watched."

Shinbei felt ashamed. He knew that Mariko's mother had died when she was a child and that her brother had been banished shortly thereafter. Or was it shortly before? He couldn't rightly recall the sequence of events, but he did know that his words were deliberately hurtful and completely unworthy of a coarse, crude water buffalo driver, much less a samurai—even a second-generation one like himself. That the insult was directed at the daughter of his liege lord made it utterly disgraceful.

"Forgive my ugly words," Shinbei said in a voice filled with shame. "I am ashamed of myself. There's no excuse. Now I really do deserve to die."

Mariko was as quick to forgive as to condemn. She only needed some cause to completely reverse her opinion. She saw in Shinbei a quality of nobility. He was taking full responsibility for his cruelty.

"If my father desired your death," Mariko said, "you would be dead already. I do not want you dead. I don't know why you were arrested."

"Ask your father."

"I asked him as soon as I heard about it. He said it was for your own safety." Shinbei pointed to the duck egg, which looked even more frightful now that much of the dried blood and jelly of hair oils mixed with lymph had washed off.

"If this was for my safety, I would hate to think of your father's idea of punishment."

"Surely you don't think much of such a scratch, "Mariko laughed.

Actually, Shinbei thought he had a concussion, because his mind was wandering and his vision was blurry, but he said nothing about either.

"You were gracious to give me your purse. Yamashita seized it." Mariko pulled the purse from her kimono sash and handed it through the thick bars.

"I return it to you. This time try not to lose it!"

As Shinbei and Mariko were having their clandestine tryst in Lord Arima's dungeon, Hana was working into the early morning hours at the Fragrant Blossom teahouse. Her mouth felt gummy and sticky—the way it always felt after she stayed up all night, forcing herself to drink more sake than she liked to. The sleeve of her best kimono smelled of stale tobacco. It was a smell she hated.

Why do men smoke? she wondered. *It is disgusting, costly, and dirty.*

By far the most difficult task after closing time was always finding and removing scattered ash, tiny strands of tobacco, and ridding the teahouse of the lingering smell. Simple airing was ineffective, so every tatami had to be rubbed first with a damp cloth and sweet vinegar and then dried and rubbed once more with oil of cloves or cedar. Despite the difficulty and cost of cleaning, usually the owner made them pick up each mat, most of which weighed nearly as much as Hana did, and mop the oak floor with more vinegar. The work was exhausting, especially after a sleepless night and knowing that shortly after noon, or so it seemed, the house must be made ready to receive guests and the entire process repeated.

If Hana had her way, she would make a special smoking house where guests could smoke themselves to death with their short, highly decorated silver pipes. Some aristocrats even had bowls and mouthpieces made of pure gold, one of which would be enough to buy her contract, or so she thought. She really

Hana off as a first class at her tender age. Hana could serve tea as well as Makato, play the *samisen* much better, and as much as she loathed tobacco, the owner doubted the finest geisha in Tokyo could fill and light a pipe with more grace and finesse than Hana could.

Oh, Shinbei, Hana thought as she rested on a tatami for a few delicious moments, *I told you to stay away from Lord Arima.* Hana had had quite enough experience with the nobility to know that the best thing for anyone of lesser status was to be polite to a fault and have no intimate involvement. She had never slept with a nobleman, despite numerous and often highly advantageous offers. Many a samurai, including several of high rank, were enamored of her. A wealthy merchant from Osaka had offered to buy her contract, but the owner had had no suitable replacement; Koetsu was not yet of age nor accomplishment, so she was forced, very reluctantly, to decline.

When Shinbei told her that he was transcribing secret correspondence for Lord Arima and spending late evenings in his company, Hana told him in no uncertain terms that if anything should go amiss, his head would be the first to roll. Shinbei had just laughed, showing his even, white teeth.

If only he weren't so impossibly handsome and such a good lover, she had thought ruefully at the time.

Shinbei was indeed good-looking and had a winning way. His comrades liked him in spite of his fine appearance, but they had no idea of his masterful lovemaking abilities. When he came of age, Asamu had given him a pillow book and told the astonished boy to study it until he had memorized everything in it; she would test him, and if he failed, he would get a beating and be sent away. Overcoming his embarrassment, Shinbei had done as he was told. He memorized the book. Asamu never tested him, but the knowledge of technique and the accurate specifics of pleasuring a woman combined with his natural sensitivity made him a truly extraordinary lover.

A geisha was not a prostitute. Not even Hiroko could force

her to open her kimono if Hana refused a guest. For more than a year—to the owner's utter disgust—Shinbei had been Hana's lover. She spent a few nights with others, but they were of no real significance. Knowing of Hiroko's antipathy toward Shinbei, Hana had redoubled her efforts to please their patrons and make certain that the Fragrant Blossom was spotless, making it perhaps the most immaculately maintained teahouse in Kyushu. So Hiroko reluctantly tolerated Shinbei. When Hana told her of his sacrifices to assist his ailing mother, she no longer made hideously ugly faces or insulting gestures with her gnarled hands behind his back. Hana was greatly concerned that Shinbei's relationship with Lord Arima would end in his dismissal or even his death, but these thoughts troubled her less than his proximity to the Lady Mariko. She knew that Mariko was everything she was not: beautiful in an entirely different way, an accomplished *kyudo* artist, wealthy, noble, haughty, and conniving. No one could make smoke drinking more wonderful than Hana could, but Shinbei didn't smoke.

Hana warned him time after time, but Shinbei had always put off her worries with a hearty laugh and a touch that brought the blood rushing to her cheeks and sent a tingle through her nipples and clear down to her privates.

No, she thought, *No, Shinbei is unique.* She paused for a delicious moment, savoring the knowledge. *And he is mine.* She knew that he had been with Lord Arima the previous night, but he always sent word to her or more frequently came in person to spend the early morning hours listening to her play the *samisen* and reclining on cushions while sipping sake. This made his absence alarming.

Yes, another of my Shinbei's good qualities is that he is rarely even slightly tipsy. True, he occasionally drank a fourth flask of sake but never the dreaded fifth. It was the fifth that made men act like rabid apes, smashing furniture and ripping open kimonos. The owner had used Shinbei to escort unruly guests out the door once or twice, but Hiroko usually preferred to do the honors herself. If her tongue failed, which it almost never did, she had an old, retired samurai, named Omi, who worked for food and lodged in a hut on the grounds. In the years that Hana had worked at the Fragrant Blossom, the worst incident came when a samurai tried to rape her. He returned to Edo without his left ear, which the owner had tanned and made into a tobacco pouch.

Shinbei had told Hana of Mariko's attempt to seduce him. It had made her furious at first.

"Why is it that men, even good-looking men, always think women are trying to get them to open their kimonos?"

"Well, it has been very hot even at night. It's just that she was wearing the sheerest, silk kimono. I could see her quite clearly."

"If you're right," Hana had said, "You're in serious danger. If you try to make love to her, she might think you're trying to rape her. But if you ignore her and she is interested in you, she'll take it as a mortal insult. Either way, you're doomed."

Shinbei had laughed, attempting to calm Hana with a kiss and a quick massage of her neck. She drew away angrily, slapping him so hard it stung and left a distinct imprint of her fleshy but shapely hand on his left cheek.

"Fool! Baca!" she hissed, "You think your good looks and charming ways will get you out of this?" She continued, "Curse me for a fool. I should have told you to spill ink on Arima's most precious scroll, overturn the ink pot with your sleeve, drop his finest tea bowl, break his best Ming vase, be a clumsy oaf, and be sent back to the barracks, never to return to the palace. Oh, why are men are such fools?" She had then burst into tears. Shinbei had stood up silently in shock.

In the small quiet voice he had used as a little boy when Asamu raged at him for some boyish blunder, he asked, "Is it really that bad?"

Hana paused, wiping tears and snot from her eyes and nose. She buried her face in Shinbei's well-muscled shoulder.

"It's worse than bad."

Shinbei had the highest opinion of Hana's intuition and presentiments, and his bowels turned to water as her assessment of his position sunk in. He gently pushed Hana away and ran to the screened-off outhouse, simultaneously voiding the contents of his stomach and his bowels.

The feces splashed into the wide-mouthed jar, but his vomit splattered onto the clean earth floor. It took quite some time to repair the damage.

When Shinbei returned, he found Hana cleaned up as well, looking lovely in a fresh kimono, her face bright, all traces of tears effaced.

"So," he had said, "What can I do now?"

Hana had considered.

"Tell Arima that your mother is near death, and you need money for medicine urgently. Tell him you received a message that you must leave at once or you will be going to her funeral."

"But that only postpones the problem," he had said.

"Often a problem postponed solves itself."

"What about Lady Mariko?"

"Of course, the lady," Hana had sneered, and her emphasis on "lady" left no doubt that Hana thought her anything but a lady. "Mariko. Yes, I suppose if you like boyish women who look like boys, she could be seen as pretty. Tell her you're impotent. Have been since childhood. Your secret stalk is never erect. That should cool her ardor."

Shinbei had made a sour face.

"What about you? How do I explain you?"

"Tell her I like girls." Hana had taken Shinbei's face in her right hand, squeezing it like a vise and startling him.

"Listen carefully. I've sacrificed a lot for you. I turned down that merchant. If I hadn't, I wouldn't be flipping tatami mats looking for tobacco ashes or having my breasts pinched by drunken monkeys. Is your manhood so fragile that you can't tell that crabapple-breasted, short-haired weasel that you're impotent?"

Shinbei's eyes had filled with tears, and Hana had kept applying pressure until the corners of his upper lip touched his nose. He had badly needed to sneeze but couldn't. When she had finally let go, he shook his features back into position. His upper lip hurt, and he sneezed four times.

Pulling his injured lip left and right against his large, smooth front teeth, he had said, "There's more to it than you think."

Far from calming her, this only increased her anger.

"Like what?" She had spoken hard and fast.

"I can't say. It's too dangerous."

"How could it possibly be any more dangerous?"

He paused and looked around to make certain they were alone.

"Come outside," he had said and motioned in the direction of the privy.

"After you've been in there?" she had said. "No, thank you."

Moments later they were in the outhouse, which was still fragrant with Shinbei's effluvia.

"Arima is planning something with the barbarians. Mariko doesn't know all the details."

"You could go to the shogun," Hana had said after contemplating that.

Shinbei had turned pale.

"That's dishonorable. I am no traitor." Hana had kissed him long and hard, but their pleasure was diminished by both the lingering stink and the fact that she'd crushed his upper lip.

She had tasted the remnants of vomit in his mouth, and as she broke off the kiss, she had handed him a cinnamon stick to clean his teeth.

"I love you, Shinbei."

Now Shinbei was missing. She damned Lord Arima, his whore daughter, and all gaijin to the lowest depths of Emma-o's hell, there to be tormented for all eternity and never to be reborn.

No, she thought, *If they've harmed my Shinbei they don't deserve a second chance.*

Two great, round tears emerged from her lovely, large brown eyes, trailed down her red, rosy cheeks, and as the first one fell into the perfect bow of her upper lip, the other fell from her left cheek and buried itself between two reeds of the tatami mat.

Chapter 8

Festival Morning

Refreshed by their long bath, Kobiyashi and Hideo stepped out into the suffocating heat. Their freshly washed kimonos sweated through immediately, sticking to their backs.

The sun glared menacingly from just above eye level and beat down without mercy on the dozens of carpenters, peasants, hawkers, and merchants scurrying hither and yon. By shogunate decree, a three-day holiday had been declared throughout Kyushu Province.

Every inn was filled past capacity, and temporary shelters were being erected everywhere to meet the needs of arriving travelers. Already the sellers of food and drink were doing a brisk business, and runners were sent to other towns in search of fresh provender. The festival took on a life of its own, and those in attendance fought off the heat with water from the shallow river and countless parasols, tent fans, and for the wealthy, the lightest of silk clothing.

Unfortunately for Lord Arima and his invited and uninvited guests, the very last of the ice cut from frozen lakes the previous winter had melted in the darkest recesses of the castle only a few days earlier. That the supply of ice usually lasted the entire year was yet another indication of the severity of the heat that August.

Kobiyashi untied his *jingasa* in frustration with the heat.

"This stupid helmet is making things worse, not better."

Hideo untied his as well.

"It was your idea."

"No," said Kobiyashi, "It was yours."

"You have the memory of a sieve."

"Where can we leave them?" Hideo asked.

"Let's leave them at the bathhouse," said Kobiyashi. He continued, "We'll need a bath by this afternoon, anyway."

"We'll definitely need one if we go to the shooting range."

"I don't care if we shoot or don't shoot," Kobiyashi said. "Guns are too filthy for a samurai. If we shoot, we'll certainly need a bath."

"Well, I'm going, so there."

"Fine." Kobiyashi looked at him. "I'm a better marksman than you are."

"It's true you did do better than I did the last time."

"And I'll do better than you this time."

Hideo was quite content to agree, because he wanted to buy a new Kunitomo gun and wanted Kobiyashi's opinion. As much as his friend hated guns, the best were made by swordsmiths, and Kobiyashi knew his swordsmiths. Though Hideo would never admit it, he valued his friend's opinion in such matters. Kobiyashi was passionate—even maniacal—but his judgments were remarkably objective and frequently more accurate than those of more experienced *experts.*

Walking away from the bathhouse bareheaded under the broiling sun was only briefly better than walking under a *jin-*

gasa. Despite their luxuriant hair, which was tightly bound at the neck in the traditional knot, they were sweating.

"I think maybe," Kobiyashi said ruefully, "we should have worn our *jingasas*." This further exasperated Hideo, whose mind was in many places: thinking of Mariko, Shinbei, and the Kunitomo gun he desired.

"Of all the stupid things. Now you want to go get our helmets? I have an idea. Let's forget everything and just walk back and forth to the bathhouse all day until the Fragrant Blossom opens."

"That's madness. The heat is getting to you." Kobiyashi had a lamentable tendency to take everything Hideo said at face value, either deliberately or innocently ignoring any sarcasm or other nuances.

"You really think I am going to spend the rest of the day walking back and forth?" Hideo couldn't help himself. "You think the heat has affected me?"

"Well," Kobiyashi said, "first, we get our *jingasa*. Then we leave them. Then we get them. Then we go back and leave them. Then you say we should go back again and—"

"I didn't say we should get them," Hideo cut him off.

"You did. You specifically said a moment ago, 'I think maybe …' Yes, that was it. You said, 'maybe we should have worn our *jingasas*.'"

Kobiyashi looked at Hideo quizzically. "I didn't say that. You did."

Hideo forced down an almost irresistible urge to bash his friend hard in the nose. Then he turned this urge aside and thought of Mariko. He softened immediately.

"Kobiyashi, my friend, I think this heat is affecting *you*."

"Of course it is. I think it's hot enough to temper a sword without a forge. You could just apply the clay, use the *burin* to create the pattern, and leave it out in the sun all day."

"It's hot," Hideo said, "but not that hot."

Kobiyashi was incredulous.

"You don't think it's hot? You are crazy. It's so hot, I can't stand it."

"If it's so hot," Hideo said, "you should get your *jingasa*."

"That's what I said in the first place."

Hideo was about to say that he'd said it in the first place, but he decided that if Kobiyashi went back to the bathhouse, he would lose his mind.

"Let's get some cool water, and I'm hungry, so let's eat," he said.

"How can anyone be hungry in this heat?"

"I haven't eaten a thing, and I'm starving."

Kobiyashi considered this carefully and listened to the growing rumblings in his belly.

"I agree. Let's eat."

Hideo heaved a sigh of relief. Now that the *jingasa* debate was finally settled they walked to the refreshment stands, which had only just opened for business. There were already considerable lines in front of many of them.

"Who wants to stand in a line in this cursed heat?" Kobiyashi asked.

"Hey, there's no line over there." Hideo pointed to a stand near the river with a brightly colored banner that proclaimed the surpassing excellence of its sweet bean cakes. "It says they were actually served to the emperor two years ago."

"You actually believe that?" Kobiyashi asked. "You are so gullible. You constantly get taken in."

This was actually not the case; it was invariably Kobiyashi who was fooled into believing nearly everything he heard, and he was even more vulnerable to any written claim. Hideo decided that he would choose his battles given the intense heat.

"Somehow, I think that if they were so good, there would be a long line," said Kobiyashi. For once, Hideo could not argue.

"You may have a point," he said. "Besides, I really want something more substantial than a few bean cakes."

Kobiyashi suddenly had a craving for a sweet bean cake and some cold water. He was not that hungry, and it was too early to have grilled fish. Then again, someone had already-begun to grill fish, and the delicious aroma of fresh fish and seasonings drift through the food stalls, making Kobiyashi ravenous, dispelling all thoughts of bean cakes.

"I must have some of that fish," he said to Hideo.

"It smells wonderful. Maybe they serve it like my mother does, with lemon." He licked his parched lips. Hideo eyed the long line, but he was willing to wait for something substantial.

Seated cross-legged on a hummock of tall grass, Hideo and Kobiyashi feasted on charcoal-broiled fish and sweet bean cakes. Drinking from cool glasses of water, they refreshed themselves.

"Is the fish as good as Reiko's?" asked Hideo.

Kobiyashi was so engaged in expertly filleting his fish using the *kozuka* and *kogai* usually tucked safely in the *saya* of his *wakizashi*, just protruding from the *koiguchi* he didn't hear Hideo's question. Instead he asked, "Who made the blade in your *kozuka*? I forgot."

"You forgot?" Hideo asked incredulously. "You forgot something about swords? I'm shocked."

Hideo was surprised, especially as Kobiyashi had praised the *kozuka* blade, in spite of its diminutive size and the fact that the edge was only one-sided. It had been forged by Myoju Umetada, who was revered throughout Japan as a renowned swordsmith of matchless skill. Hideo could never have afforded a *wakizashi* by Myoju much less a *katana*, but *kozukas* were very small knives, so they were relatively inexpensive. The abbot had given it to him as a parting gift, so Hideo might recall him with fondness, which he surely did every time he used it. He handed the knife to Kobiyashi, who glanced at it.

"Myoju," he spat out, disgusted with himself. "It must be this heat," he said as he handed it back.

"What about the fish?" Hideo asked once more.

"It's excellent. Buddha forgive me for saying so, but it's better than my mother's," Kobiyashi replied. "I'm sorry," he continued, "I'm just not myself."

Hideo looked concerned. Kobiyashi was the most even-tempered person he knew, and apart from holy Buddhist priests whose sole concern was the attainment of serenity, he was the most reliably good-tempered person he ever met. For Kobiyashi to not be himself and speak of it was as rare as a snowfall in summer.

"I'm your friend. You can tell me." Kobiyashi sighed and a single, large tear formed in the corner of his right eye and slowly descended the curve of his broad, flat, thoroughly honest nose. This was even more out of character than his moment of introspection.

Hideo tried to lighten his friend's melancholy.

"Did you find a *ha giri* in your *katana*?" Such badinage would ordinarily result in a good hour of spirited defense of the great resistance Bizen blades had to cracking. This time, however, Kobiyashi not only failed to rise to the occasion but sat silently as another tear formed and chased the first down his nose.

Hideo rose in one graceful, fluid motion and knelt just in front of Kobiyashi, placing his right hand on his shoulder. Kobiyashi shook his head, and the two tears fell on Hideo's wrist. Kobiyashi looked at Hideo's noble features and stared into his guileless, gray eyes.

"I don't know. It's just everything is so confused. First, Shinbei and this damned heat. I can't stand it."

"Shinbei," Hideo said, "What about Shinbei? You said you knew nothing about him."

"I heard something. But I was sworn to secrecy." Hideo looked into Kobiyashi's swimming brown eyes. "I wanted to tell you. I hate secrets, but I promised."

"Who'd you promise?" Hideo asked.

Kirishitan thought came out of his mouth, resumed its regular rhythm.

"I was speaking of Adams—Will Adams, Ieyasu's barbarian pilot—his love for a beautiful Nipponese girl."

"Yes," said Kobiyashi, and his voice grew husky with a powerful emotion, "Yes, and he married her as I will marry Koetsu."

Hideo cursed himself silently. He had allowed his Kirishitanity to show, if only a little. Many times he had thought to share his faith with Kobiyashi, so beautifully did Jesus and Bushido compliment each other, but he always decided against it. To do so would increase the danger to both of them. Hideo was no coward—he was, in fact, the furthest thing from it—but to die like a criminal would betray his ancestors, and to be responsible for Kobiyashi's execution would be unbearable. Kobiyashi was too enthusiastic and would be unable to keep the secret.

Of course, Jesus taught that one must spread the gospel, but—and this was one of Hideo's greatest personal griefs—to do so under Tokugawa rule was nothing more than suicide. There would be no glorious public martyrdom that would make more converts, only a lonely protracted torture followed by an equally lonely decapitation. He seemed to be losing his self-possession, as if his hidden Kirishitanity was taking on a life of its own, pushing through the dark of his unspoken faith toward the light of—God forbid—some public witness.

Thank God for Will Adams, Hideo sent up a fast prayer of thanksgiving. His slip was a very strong warning. He resolved to pray more at night and spend less time at the Fragrant Blossom. Spending time in the Buddhist Temple rarely caused comment, and any comment it might evoke was extremely favorable. The more devout the samurai, the more commendable his worship, and Hideo was well aware of this attitude. He knew there must be other *kakure* Kirishitans in Lord Arima's service, but the danger of revealing one's faith was simply too great to risk the slightest public or even private expression. Hideo's mother had drilled into him that his Kirishitanity must be locked away in his own skull until such a time when the Tokugawa shogunate fell or tolerated the religion once more.

I must keep it locked up. God will understand and forgive me, he thought to himself.

Kobiyashi was blissfully unaware of Hideo's lapse. His moon face was transfigured by a daydream in which he and Koetsu were married and had one little moon-faced boy, who sat at his father's feet, listening as Kobiyashi told him the story of Masamune and Samonji, the wicked apprentice.

Alas, thought Kobiyashi, *I will never be able to afford her contract.* Just then an idea occurred to him that he had never thought of before. *If Hideo marries Mariko, he will be rich. He could lend me the money, and I would repay him with my service. Lord Arima would surely give me to his daughter.*

"Why don't you ask Mariko to marry you? Then you wouldn't spend your life pining away over her."

Hideo had proposed to Mariko, but she had laughed at the idea and said that she could not possibly leave her aging father. Although he was an older man, Arima was still formidable, and could best practically any samurai in his service at any one of the martial arts. He was also a master of the *cha no yu* and a finer calligrapher—when he wanted to be—than Shinbei. Hideo had heard about Daisuke, though Mariko had never spoken of her brother. He ascribed Mariko's refusal to the insurmountable disparity in their social positions.

If only my grandfather were alive, thought Hideo, *she would rush to accept me.*

"What are you vaporing about?" Kobiyashi asked.

"Mariko refused me. Besides, I am in her father's service."

"I know," said Kobiyashi, "it was only that if you married her, you could lend me the money to buy Koetsu's contract."

"My friend," said Hideo, "If Mariko married me, I would give you the money. That is, if she would lend it to me."

"You are a good friend to borrow money from your wife for my sake," said Kobiyashi.

"And you too," said Hideo. "Now let's go before the sun bakes our brains."

Chapter 9

Nagahisa

The midday sun was a force to be reckoned with. Its rays beat down on the milling crowd like so many wooden sticks. Here and there the sweating bodies parted as people—especially old men and women and a few frail children—fell victim to heatstroke. Lord Arima had hired a number of farmers that were out of work due to the drought to thread their way through the throngs of spectators, carrying buckets of cool river water to revive the fallen. All agreed that the lord's foresight was admirable.

At the most important venue, long sections of split bamboo, pierced with numberless tiny holes, were filled with water. Attendants with bellows forced the water out under pressure creating a refreshing fine rain that cooled the air under the tremendous awnings and parasols. Arima's prestige and honor depended on the success of the contest and festival, and he had not neglected any opportunity to ensure it would be a triumph.

Chapter 10

The Kaishakunin

His detractors said he had inherited the title and the office from his father. Of course, most of those who knew him or of him had inherited their offices and titles from their fathers, so he found this humorous rather than insulting. In fact, he did owe the opportunity to his father, but if he were not both a consummate diplomat and one of the greatest samurai in Nippon, no right-thinking shogun—much less the astute Iemitsu—would have appointed him. He was now well into middle age, wealthy, and still powerful both physically and politically, but his office was all too familiar to him, and he longed for a younger man to take his place. Iemitsu was aware of this, but an ideal replacement had not been found.

He was still handsome—tall and spare of build, all sinew and muscle as if all fat had been chiseled away. His arms were long, and the definition in his forearms was a frequent subject of art students who used his much-reproduced official portrait as a model. His face was likewise spare, with high cheekbones, small, shell-like ears with attached lobes, a well-shaped, small nose, and thin lips, which were usually compressed. His hair was perfectly coiffed, shot through here and there with streaks of gray.

Yet it was the eyes that no one could forget. Some said that they were the eyes of Amida Buddha in a human being; in their fathomless brown depths, they could see boundless compassion. Others said that they were terrifying; in them one could see a void of infinite nothingness. It is said that no one, not even Iemitsu had ever stared him down. The eyes were not wide so much as deep. They were brown with a particularly black pupil and an iris flecked with pale gold. Whether one saw compassion or the void, all agreed that his eyes were beautiful. His handsome and somewhat forbidding face was forgotten whenever anyone looked into his eyes.

His birth, his youth, and his parents' tragic deaths were the subject of folk tales and teahouse songs. Suffice it to say, he mastered the sword at an early age and rapidly achieved such a reputation of perfection of style as well as strength that he succeeded to his father's position during Hidetada's regency. He learned his considerable political skills from Tokugawa Ieyasu himself during the long days of protracted illness that preceded the shogun's death. His own father was dead, and the young man—for he was very young at the time—had looked upon the corpulent Ieyasu as a surrogate father. Where another, lesser man might have seen a rival in this relationship and cause for jealousy, Iemitsu saw only an opportunity.

The office of Kaishakunin, or official shogunate executioner, was perhaps the most important in all the Bakufu government. All real power was vested in the shogun, but the shogun's power depended on the lords of each individual province. These hereditary feudal fiefdoms were ruled by *daimyo,* such as Lord Arima, who frequently quarreled among themselves over land, marriages, and taxes. At one point, Ieyasu had only been *daimyo* of Edo province, a relatively unimportant fief until he distinguished himself at Nagashino and was brought forward by Dictator Nobunaga. His descent in the Minamoto line permitted the emperor to name him shogun following the death of Hideyoshi Toyotomi, the Taiko.

The surest means of control over the fiercely independent *daimyos* was the power of life and death. To guarantee their fealty, Ieyasu instituted a system by which each *daimyo*'s family would live in Edo for much of the year as a guest of the shogunate, but of course, given his legendary thrift—some said miserliness—the stay in Edo was at the *daimyo*'s expense. The cost of having to maintain two palaces often hundreds of miles apart left many *daimyos* poor or even close to insolvency. Without money, the shogun reasoned, it would be impossible to hire mercenaries, and poor *daimyos* were no threat to the government. The Kaishakunin served as the mediator between the shogun and his *daimyos.* A particularly troublesome *daimyo* could, as a last resort be "invited onward," which was a polite way of being ordered to commit *seppuku*, or ritual suicide. This state of affairs was rare, but there were occasions when not even the most careful diplomacy prevailed. Sometimes a difficult succession required that a claimant to the title of *daimyo* be bodily removed.

As the shogunate had a compelling interest in maintaining order, the Kaishakunin represented the shogun at what was essentially a state-sponsored execution. The affairs were elaborately choreographed to the last detail. The executioner stood to the side of the suicide, and at the exact moment the *daimyo* or offending official finished slicing his abdomen with a *tanto*, the Kai Shakunin swept his head from his body, which would always fall forward in a decorous manner, as the immaculate white death kimono remained tucked beneath the dead man's knee. Any deviation from the prescribed ritual was a disgrace to the shogun, and woe betide the executioner who allowed a single lapse in the ritual.

Lord Ishido had presided over a number of executions, and his peerless sword—an *ubu* (unaltered), perfect Mitsutada *tachi,* perhaps two polishes removed from the original—had never failed to perform its office.

There had, of course, been incidents, including the extraordinarily shameful succession after the *daimyo* of Harima unexpectedly died of apoplexy. A troublesome claimant, who was a first cousin of the late lord, was "invited onward," but at the penultimate moment, he had stabbed Ishido in the leg. The wretched man had pierced Ishido's calf muscle but fortunately missed the artery. Off balance and falling, Ishido made a slashing stroke across the claimant's back, severing the spine, but blood spattered on the tatami, and worse, the man's mouth opened and a gargled curse was heard, which had horrified the spectators and witnesses. The episode was shocking in the extreme and a great disgrace, but it was one which accrued not to Iemitsu or Ishido but to the Harima family. Iemitsu had ordered the new lord to remit double the annual assessment for a period of five years, which effectively bankrupted the province for that time.

All who knew of the affair agreed that Ishido's conduct was not only blameless but exemplary and a credit to Bushido. Pleased that this near catastrophe and debacle was publicly seen as meritorious, Iemitsu at first awarded a percentage of the Harima tribute to Ishido. Suffering remorse over the extravagance and feeling that he was too generous, the frugal shogun later reduced the figure by half, but it still made Ishido a wealthy man. The *tanto* used in the suicide was a Masamune, which Iemitsu thought to award to Ishido, but at the last minute, he couldn't give it away and kept it for himself as a reminder of the weaknesses of Harima Province.

Aside from a long, thin, white line on either side of his calf, Ishido had suffered no lasting harm.

By all the gods, it's hot, thought Ishido. *This infernal black kimono is no help; why is Nagahisa taking so long? He's gotten fat*

ing in his beautiful, carrying, bass voice—the same one that had so intrigued Kobiyashi in the bathhouse.

"This *tachi* was forged by Umetada Myoju. At high noon, I will demonstrate the Yamada *tameshigiri* technique as I perform the Kurumasaki cut across the belly."

Nagahisa held the Myoju blade out to unconcealed cries of admiration from the crowd and whispers and murmurs of desire for such a sword from the benches. The introduction over, he put aside his weariness and the feeling that he was living in a repetitive nightmare life in which he was doomed to perform the same routine for the same crowd to people over and over until death overtook him.

Now, he thought, *I can't even enjoy my rice.*

But the feel of the Myoju, so heavy and fat, and the accolades of the excited assembled people had their inevitable effect, and he felt young again and became as enthusiastic as he had been at his first public test. He remembered it as if it were about to happen. He had been given an unsigned blade attributed to Sanjo Munechika, which, if genuine, was worth as much as a province, but the Honami and the *daimyo* who owned it were not on good terms, so the Honami refused to authenticate it. They also refused to condemn it and requested that the *daimyo* have it tested by the Hamano School and then resubmit it after testing.

Swords were tested on the corpses of criminals, which, given the efficiency of the Bakufu secret police, were usually plentiful. The *dodan*, or scaffolding that holds the body in position, never varies. Nagahisa was to perform the same cut he would make that noon. When the silk covering was removed, he could see the body was rather dried and looked old, though usually the bodies were fairly fresh to avoid putrefaction and offense to the tester and his witnesses. They were entirely exsanguinated by *eta* trained in the technique prior to the test. The Munechika was a good blade to be sure. It was very ancient but deeply curved, which made the cut more difficult. It had been polished many times, so it was quite thin, having lost much of its *niku,* or "meat." Nagahisa had examined it carefully prior to the test, looking for fatal flaws such as *ha girl,* cracks which could be disguised by an unscrupulous seller or polisher. The *daimyo* had confided to him that he was not certain of the sword's history and that he had purchased it from a samurai on a trip to Tokyo. The samurai had fallen on hard times, or so the old man had said, and the daimyo had purchased it for a few gold *ryo.*

This had not been good news for Nagahisa. He had told his *sensei,* but the master had said that the school was paid to test swords.

"Some will pass, and some will fail. Our task, or rather your task is to make the perfect cut with your mind first, and then the sword will do its work with its abilities. You cannot make a false sword true, but you can fail and make a true sword cut falsely."

With these words echoing in his head, he had steeled himself to make the cut. Emptying his mind, he had cut through the desiccated corpse and awoken as though from a trance. His master was nodding his unspoken approval with uncharacteristic animation. The body had been severed.

Nagahisa had held up the sword and seen with dismay that it had bent in two places a *shaku* apart and nearly 70 degrees to the right. It was also bent at the *habaki.* A numb feeling swept through his body as he tasted the bitter brew of failure. The *sensei* had taken the blade from his nerveless fingers and looked into his eyes, which had been swimming with tears.

"I congratulate you on a perfect cut. The more so as the body was imperfect; I feared the blade would stick in the backbone. It didn't. You are now a master of the Hamano School."

The supposed Munechika blade had been returned to the *daimyo,* who had received the wrecked sword with more embarrassment than anger.

The heat in the center of the stage was torrid. Nagahisa had no parasol and no chingasa, much less the bamboo troughs filled and refilled with cool water. He did have one of the greatest swords he had ever examined in his strong right arm. For the moment, this made him the equal of his old friend, Ishido, whom he smiled at. His smile was returned.

He's gotten old, Nagahisa thought, *It's been years since I've seen him. I hope power hasn't ruined him completely.*

Nagahisa could rest assured that Ishido held him in the highest esteem. This knowledge gave the tester great pleasure, for the two had once enjoyed exciting times and adventures together, though mainly of the teahouse variety. Neither had served at Shimabara. Putting down a peasant uprising by a nineteen-year-old Kirishitan boy was not to their liking. To die facing such a foe was hardly a true, honorable samurai death. Nagahisa would have liked to see the siege and the mighty cannon of the gaijin navy in action, but that was as far as it went.

At first, Ishido had been disgusted by Iemitsu's employment of a foreign navy to bombard Shimabara, fearing it would be interpreted as a sign of weakness by the *daimyos.* After due consideration, however, he could see the genius in Iemitsu's use of a Kirishitan navy to annihilate a Kirishitan army. It showed the *daimyo* that their shogun used barbarians to destroy the followers of a foreign religion thereby saving Nihonjin lives. It also demonstrated that the gaijin were clearly ignoble adherents of a false doctrine whose teachings of brotherly love were betrayed by their wicked actions. Having thoroughly learned the lessons of Nagasaki and the San Felipe from Ieyasu and Hidetada, Iemitsu had no intention of make martyrs of the Shimabara traitors, and what better way to avoid the trap than by having them killed by their fellow Kirishitans? He was his father's son and his grandfather's grandson. Using one wolf to defeat another wolf was a tried and true Tokugawa strategy.

Seated next to the guest of honor, Lord Arima looked at

the Myoju with decidedly mixed emotions. He was enough of a sword aficionado to understand its greatness, but his feelings for Iemitsu and the Tokugawa colored his appreciation. He found it difficult to separate the blade from its owner. Iemitsu had everything. He had sons; he had the Myoju; he even had Ishido, who, after all, was as much the shogun's possession as the beautiful sword.

And, he thought, *equally deadly and dangerous. I really should kill him while I have the opportunity. Before he kills me. I know he has instructions to invite me onward after the contest. The whole festival's nothing but a façade, and I have to pay for it.*

Unlike Iemitsu, whose thrift was the subject of much jesting, Arima was not parsimonious. But to pay for the entire festival, when it was all a feint, serving as camouflage for Iemitsu as he took over his fief, was a bitter pill to swallow. Nevertheless, Arima's pride and honor ensured that the festival must be magnificent in the smallest details, and no expense was spared, because it bore his name.

If Iemitsu had put it on, everyone would die of heatstroke before the contest begins. The food sellers would serve garbage at stupidly high prices and be forced to pay a large percentage to Iemitsu. So typically he makes a daimyo *pay for everything. If the festival is a success, the shogun takes credit. If it is a failure, we are blamed by our own people and denounced by the shogunate. By Buddha, if Iemitsu were in Ishido's place, I would kill him myself.*

Ishido could sense Arima's hostility. When the *daimyo* smiled, he could see the intensity of loathing that lay just beneath the surface of a forced welcome. Of course, Arima knew what had brought him to Kyushu. It was an open secret that Lord Arima despised the Tokugawa and Iemitsu in particular, believing that he would be a far superior shogun. Lord Arima wanted Japan to be governed by a meritocracy rather than the hereditary dynasty of the Tokugawa clan, whose tyrannical rule would surely degenerate after Iemitsu died. True, the sho-

elaborate, pantomimed apology, which the great sword tester accepted with a gracious nod of his powerful head.

Then the sound of gunfire further shattered the stillness. Nagahisa bowed low to the nobles and directly to Lords Arima and Ishido. He badly wanted to wink at Ishido, but propriety and the presence of Lord Arima prevented him. As he rose from his bow and received the nods from the benches, Ishido broke his impassivity with a distinct wink of his left eye. Nagahisa could not completely repress a smile, though it ill accorded with the solemnity of the situation. Ishido acknowledged it with a second wink.

Nagahisa felt compelled to reassert his dignity and turned to Musashi.

"These damnable guns. Barbarian filth. They'll be the ruin of Bushido. First, Bushido, and then the empire itself! Only evil comes from the gaijin. Guns are ignoble instruments—base in function and purpose. Any fool can use them. They stink like hell itself." This was said with considerable passion and some bitterness. Musashi, who understood Nagahisa's aversion to the gun, felt compelled to reply.

"*Sensei*, Nagahisa *sama*, not all barbarian innovations are cursed. They brought tobacco and *namban tetsu*. Why even Yasutsugu *sama* is signing his swords 'made with *namban tetsu*,' and he is Iemitsu's personal swordsmith."

Nagahisa groaned.

"Yes, I know all about Yasutsugu. We've tested enough of his blades. I admit they are uniformly excellent, but that is as much due to his temper and construction as the barbarian iron."

"And the tobacco?" Musashi couldn't resist saying.

"Yes, you know better than anyone that life would be difficult without my pipe in the evening. I still say the gaijin are vile, disgusting creatures, and their guns will destroy both the samurai and the way of Bushido. Eventually, they will ruin all concepts of honor."

"But *sensei*, guns gave Nobunaga the victory at Nagashino. And even Ieyasu used hundreds of *ashigaru* at Sekigahara."

"Yes, and I find it abhorrent. In war, one must make use of anything, but it doesn't make it right. Hidetada used the Dutch to batter down the walls at Hara Castle, but mark my words well, Musashi, the day will come when foreign cannon will batter down the Tokugawa if they are not careful. Guns have their place, I suppose, but then so does night soil."

Hideo and Kobiyashi heard the firing, as did everyone at the festival.

"The target shooting has begun," Hideo said. "I never told you, but if I can find one, I want to purchase a good Kunitomo gun with silver dragonflies inlaid along the barrel." Hideo's statement came as somewhat of a shock to Kobiyashi.

"Guns are an ignoble weapon. They are good for peasants who cannot master the bow. They are smelly, awkward, stupid mechanical devices. The bow is clean and beautiful. I can't believe you want one. You are so traditional, such a lover of Bushido."

"No," said Hideo, "Listen here. You have a tendency to see yourself reflected in everyone you know, including me. I am no such traditionalist as you paint me. Now, Shinbei … he is a traditionalist."

"Maybe you're right. I do tend to be overenthusiastic. I wish you hadn't mentioned Shinbei. I actually forgot all about him for a time. Now you have to go and talk about him."

"I forgot about him, too. I'm sure he's just fine." But Hideo thought, *I wish I knew. Maybe Kobiyashi's right. Maybe he's dead.*

Then, inevitably, Hideo's thoughts turned to Mariko. Her body always reminded him of a bow, so taught, so balanced, and so ready to be drawn. An involuntary thrill passed through his groin. Hideo was experienced in the ways of women, but no one had ever aroused him like Mariko, and though many months had passed since he had loved her physically, hers was the image that filled his mind and fueled all his erotic fantasies. There were times when he found this annoying, but no teahouse girl or even another *daimyo's* daughter could replace her, and it was not from lack of trying. Now she was associated in his mind with Shinbei.

In his heart, he cordially disliked him. Not only was he a better calligrapher who had the confidence and intimacy of Lord Arima, Hideo had to admit that Shinbei was devilishly good-looking in his peasant way, and perhaps Mariko did see him as a lover. Part of him wished that he actually were dead, but the Kirishitan part of him urged him to love and protect Shinbei. Hideo was cordial and courteous to Shinbei as he always was to the people he most disliked. If Shinbei were in trouble or danger, Hideo would risk his life to save him.

Kobiyashi knew that Hideo regarded Shinbei as a rival, and he was no longer surprised at the solicitousness with which Shinbei was treated.

"Listen," said Kobiyashi, "I happen to know that Nagahisa *sensei* is famous for procrastinating over a test, especially an important one, and this is certainly the most important one of this year."

"And maybe any other year," said Hideo.

"Right," said Kobiyashi. "Let's go to the shooting grounds."

Hideo was very surprised.

"I thought you had your heart set on seeing the test."

"If I know anything of Nagahisa, he will want an enormous lunch before anything else. Besides, the guns will take my mind off Shinbei. That, and I want to help you choose the right gun."

Hideo wrinkled his nose.

"You know about guns, too?"

Kobiyashi smiled knowingly.

"Who do you think makes the best gun barrels?"

"I haven't thought about it."

"Many fine swordmakers are forging gun barrels. Iron is iron, and steel is steel. The best barrels are folded just like a sword."

"Truth?" asked Hideo.

"It's definitely the truth. I happen to know that Okisato himself has made a barrel for Iemitsu's hunting gun."

"How do you always know these things?"

"I talk to people, and I don't spend half my life praying." He added quickly, "Not that devotion to the Lord Buddha isn't admirable, I just can't do it all the time."

"So the great and glorious Okisato deigns to make gun barrels. I never would have believed it."

"He certainly does. That's why you need me. There are so many forgeries of Kunitomo guns coming from Osaka. Samurai have been killed and injured by them bursting. They are called 'noodle guns.'"

Hideo rubbed his right cheek.

"Can you imagine this face ruined by a burst barrel? Buddha save me from a noodle gun."

Hideo imagined the concussion of the powder's explosion and the pain from the iron fragments ripping and tearing through flesh and bone. He had seen men with blue-black marks on their hands and faces where grains of unburnt powder had buried themselves under the skin and remained unabsorbed.

The design of the gun made it essential for the face to be next to the explosion of the powder in the pan and the primary charge in the breech. If the barrel were to rupture, serious injury and even death could result. Some sort of disfigurement was inevitable. Hideo was glad that Kobiyashi knew so much about guns. A scar from a blade was a mark of honor, even if the cut was accidental. A powder burn was ugly and brought the wearer no honor.

"On second thought," Kobiyashi said, "let's wait a few moments. I think something's happening. Look over there."

to tell him of Ishido's friendship with Nagahisa. This bore all the hallmarks of one of Iemitsu's beautifully contrived coincidences.

Ishido turned from the lord to greet his old friend with pleasure—his first real pleasure of the day, and quite possibly the last. The executioner's habitually impassive face was wreathed in an almost ecstatic smile.

"Nagahisa *san*. It's been a long time, much too long."

Nagahisa was equally pleased to see Ishido treated still him as an equal despite the vast difference in their respective ranks. He acknowledged Ishido's courtesy with a delicate deference.

"Ishido *sama*, I am pleased to see you looking so well."

Then, as in the old days at the fencing academy, the two dispensed with all etiquette, and in full view of Lord Arima and many others and careless of the trappings of social rank and dignity, embraced each other with a peasant's heartiness.

Kobiyashi was shocked at this disregard for social distinction.

"How disgusting. You'd think they were two toothless old women at a reunion of retired geisha. Such a lot of hugging and kissing and carrying on! What about samurai dignity? If I didn't know better, I'd think both of them had escaped from a Kabuki troupe." He hocked loudly and spat on ground between his feet. "Disgusting."

Hideo saw his chance and seized it.

"Listen, only a moment ago, you were extolling their virtues. 'Nagahisa is the greatest tester; Ishido is the greatest fencer.' Now you're telling me they're like two old geisha. Which is it?"

"That's the problem," said Kobiyashi. "They are truly great, and they act so disgracefully. It makes me sick."

"You're telling me that Ishido is an executioner, and Nagahisa is a sword tester. Well, I think you and I could defeat either of them in a fair fight."

"Quiet, you fool, they'll hear you. You may be a fine swordsman, and I'm not bad myself, but a duel is something serious. You may be a master at slicing green bamboo or cracking a buffoon's skull with a *boken*, but killing a man is different."

The thought of his Yasumitsu slashing through the black kimono studded with the symbol of the government that had killed his mother was uppermost in Hideo's mind. Standing only twenty *shaku* from Ishido with no height and only a few men between them, he could feel the blood pumping in his ears like the rush of a flood-swollen stream. His right hand convulsively clutched the handle of his *wakizashi*. The words of the Christ were drowned out, and he knew only that the man near him represented the men who had taken away and no doubt tortured his beloved mother. Settsuko would be avenged.

Hideo never knew whether he would have acted or not. Each time he thought of the penultimate moment he came up with a different conclusion and scenario.

Hideo's body was about to make the decision independently of his mind when he was distracted by a sudden, sharp, piercing pain in his right shoulder blade. Astonished, he looked and saw an iron *jita*, a weapon carried by the shogunate police, marking him. He heard the four words no one, even a samurai, ever wanted to hear in the Tokugawa police state. They were uttered in a silky but totally flat tone without the least emotion.

"You are under arrest."

Hideo slowly turned his head to face the officer. It was the eyes he would always remember. They were almost golden with large black pupils and flecks of hazel in the retina. They were quite round, uncharacteristically so, almost like gaijin eyes he had seen in old scrolls depicting foreigners. They seemed almost merry and twinkling in stark contrast to the deadly seriousness of the voice.

He must have an interesting ancestry, Hideo thought to

himself. He was not one to shrink from any encounter. That day, when the official had ravaged his home, had burnt away all fear except his fear of the Lord God.

Hideo drew back, and the *jita* was withdrawn. Instantly. Hideo drew his *wakizashi*, and the man in black smiled as if he were highly amused.

"You insolent bastard," said Hideo.

The official didn't move a muscle. He only kept smiling at the young samurai and the shining sword. Drawing a blade on a shogunate official was punishable by crucifixion or impalement.

"You will die for this," he said, using exactly the same unaccented tone. Hideo felt compelled to answer the challenge, but some part of him resisted, and his answer was unconvincing even to his own ears. Then again, they were so filled with a rushing noise that he could not be certain exactly how he had reacted when he recalled the incident. His voice came out thin, high-pitched, and reedy.

Kobiyashi could not believe either his ears or his eyes, so quickly had the quarrel erupted. All three men were oblivious to everything around them as if nothing else existed.

"But you will precede me," Hideo said.

Sensing that Hideo was about to strike. Kobiyashi grabbed Hideo's wrist and looking into the round eyes of the man who stood motionless holding his jita upright in a classic defensive posture, said in a loud voice, "Great shogunate official, let's stop before things get out of control. I am a witness. Hideo, here, did not draw his sword in anger. We were overly excited by the presence of Nagahisa and the upcoming contest. I asked him to show me the blade. It's a sho dai Yasumitsu." The official resheathed his *jita* and continued to observe the two men.

"Why, you insolent puppy. This is a conspiracy. You're both under arrest."

Lord Ishido had been observing the entire incident from a few paces away, as had Nagahisa and Lord Arima. Of the three men, only Ishido recognized the policeman. He was dumbfounded.

Why is he here? Ishido's thoughts raced. *Iemitsu said nothing to me about him. By all the gods, things must be more serious than I thought.* He was confused as to how he should address the policeman. Obviously, he had to do something, but what? To act as if nothing had happened was, unfortunately, impossible. Both Nagahisa and Lord Arima were staring at him as if seeking guidance. As the senior official, he had to demonstrate his authority, but faced with this man with the gold *mon*, he was temporarily at a loss. The same *mon* adorned his magnificent kimono. They served the same government, the same shogun. *Why is he here?* The thought ran through his mind over and over again, unanswered.

Best to be impaled for being a buffalo as a goat, he thought.

In his most severe official voice, Ishido addressed the man, "Policeman, what is the matter? Why are you disturbing the festival with your antics?" The official replied in a subservient tone, looking Ishido directly in the eye the whole time as if to say, *Just follow my lead and all will be as it should be.*

"Great Lord, this young ruffian was about to attack you. Either you or Lord Arima."

Nagahisa, seeing something special in Hideo, wanted to diffuse the situation and protect Ishido as well.

Interposing his bulk between Hideo and Ishido, he said, "What about me? Am I too unimportant to assassinate?"

The policeman took full advantage of this timely interruption.

"Perhaps I am mistaken. May I see your *wakizashi*?"

Relieved at this astonishing and happy turn of events, Hideo once more drew his short sword and decorously handed it to the man upright, with the edge toward himself.

Nagahisa and Ishido crowded close to have a better look while Lord Arima looked away, beckoning to one of the many spies he had hidden in the crowd. The spy signaled assent, a gesture ignored by all except for Arima. The man held the blade up to the sun, and the blade seemed to catch fire as the temper leapt from the body of the sword.

Ishido couldn't help himself.

"Excuse me, may I see the sword?"

The man handed the sword to him. Ishido pointed the flat of the blade away from the sun—no easy task as it was almost directly overhead. He sighted down the flat, his eyes bright with excitement.

"Damn this sun, it's hard to see the *utsuri*. It must be fantastic in candlelight." He looked at Hideo with something approaching deference. "A fine sword. Would you consider parting with it?"

Kobiyashi held his breath. Never in his life did he dare dream of being in company with samurai like Lord Ishido and Nagahisa. Lord Arima was his liege lord, so even though he was a great samurai, it was different, somehow expected.

Hideo had no wish to give offense, but he was conscious of the fact that he might well have murdered this man only a few moments before. He searched for the perfect reply. He treasured the Yasumitsu, and it would be dishonorable to see it pass into Tokugawa hands.

"My Lord, the Yasumitsu was my father's blade. As much as I would like to give it to you, I feel it is not mine to give."

"And why not?" Ishido asked, with disappointment in his question. He was not happy with his position, because once again his love for swords had placed him in the position of a supplicant, a beggar.

Hideo sensed that Ishido would not insist.

"The sword belongs to my unborn son, who I pray will carry it with honor in the service of his shogun." Hideo winced internally as he spoke, but as much as one part of him hated his words, another part of him accepted them. After all, he had almost damned himself for all eternity by taking earthly vengeance.

Ishido was disappointed. He had thought the young man would be eager to please him. He had had some hope of success when Hideo had said something about giving him the sword. He would never have accepted the Yasumitsu as a gift; he would have insisted on paying the full price. The price would have been high, and a part of him was relieved, because he was very interested in some expensive land at the moment. The *wakizashi* would have required him to delay acquiring the land, and the owner had told him if he did not want it he had another buyer.

Ishido turned to Lord Arima and Nagahisa with a smile. He managed to erase his disappointment from the reply.

"What a fine young man. Lord Arima, you are fortunate to have him in your service. What is your name?"

Hideo was nervous. How could he not be? Two powerful lords, one of them his liege lord, and Nagahisa, as well as the mysterious policeman were all looking at him. His future, as well as Kobiyashi's, depended on him answering all questions without any error of fact or form.

This is worse than any duel, he thought. *One mistake, and we are doomed.*

"My name is Oda Hideo, son of Shintaro and Settsuko, my Lord."

This revelation astonished Ishido and Nagahisa.

Ishido thought, *Now, I understand why Nagahisa is here. Arima has a descendant of Nobunaga in his service. Nothing escapes Iemitsu.* Ishido had to confirm his suspicion.

"You're related to Nobunaga?"

"Yes, Lord. I am a grandson by one of his concubines. A very minor, unacknowledged relation."

The policeman caught Ishido's eye and flashed him a look of approval that said, *You're doing well. Keep going.*

Ishido looked at Hideo.

"Introduce me to your friend."

This was the greatest moment in Kobiyashi's life. Everything suddenly seemed possible. Even Koetsu's contract might be within his reach.

"Kobiyashi Takei, son of Toshi and Reiko, my Lord," Kobiyashi said, with honor mixed with the appropriate seasoning of deference.

Lord Arima looked on silently but seemingly pleased to have two such stalwart, young, promising samurai in his service. Both Hideo and Kobiyashi looked at their liege lord for approval, and Arima nodded. Inwardly, he was seething and furious.

Damn Ishido, and damn this stupid policeman. How stupid does Iemitsu think I am? This man is no policeman. Clearly, he has gaijin blood somewhere in his background. If he's a policeman, then I'm a gaijin. Ishido knows exactly who and what he is, and I don't. When I'm shogun, the sun will never see either one again.

Ishido was clearly more interested in Hideo than in Kobiyashi. By asking for an introduction, Kobiyashi knew he was merely being polite. Kobiyashi bore Hideo not the least bit of ill will. In fact, he was Hideo's greatest admirer. He was awed by Hideo's grandfather and couldn't understand Hideo's extreme reluctance to trade on the name.

Yet, Hideo's reticence was an integral part of his very nature. It was rooted in his secret Kirishitanity and his natural humility. He was so successful at hiding his parentage that many soldiers in the barracks were unaware of the Oda living among them, or so it seemed.

In reality, everyone knew, but they liked Hideo so well that they rarely made mention of it.

Chapter 14

Shigemasa

Shigemasa was very pleased with his handling of what could have been a public relations failure of the first magnitude.

Iemitsu had had his agents brief him thoroughly before his journey to Lord Arima's domain. One of the most interesting subjects of the briefing was Oda Hideo. Ieyasu had carefully monitored all descendents of the dictator and the Taiko, eliminating all legitimate heirs. The illegitimate children were watched from birth, but Ieyasu had not considered them to be dangerous to the shogunate.

One of the many duties Shigemasa had undertaken was to protect Ishido from Lord Arima. He had been watching Hideo and Kobiyashi when he saw Hideo's right hand on the *tsuka* of the finely mounted *wakizashi*. The abstracted look on the young samurai's face was far from the look of a professional assassin. Shigemasa knew the look well; it was the expression of a man who might carry out an attack for purposes of revenge

his service. Your words bring honor to him." He added, "And to you."

Nagahisa deliberated on Hideo's honorable speech, and an idea came to him that would dishonor Lord Arima, whom he would never forgive for that one contemptuous look, and honor Hideo at the same time.

The masseuse in the bathhouse had given him a purge of eucalyptus leaves that was acting powerfully on his bowels. A griping pain below his navel warned him that he would soon need to relieve himself.

The cut he was about to make was a difficult one, even for him, and perfection would be expected. To fail with the shogun's hereditary treasure in the first contest of the festival was not something he cared to contemplate. The repercussions would be immediate and injurious, possibly even fatal. Here was the perfect solution: He could have his longed for movement and shift all responsibility for the test. After all, who would blame an inexperienced tester? Nagahisa pressed his abdomen and loudly broke wind. Ishido wrinkled up his nose at the sulfurous cloud. Nagahisa smiled hugely.

"Gentlemen, I fear I shall shortly be discommoded. You see, this morning I took a purge." He turned his grin on Hideo. "Have you ever made the Kurumasaki cut?"

Seeing where his friend was going, Ishido said, "You can't be serious. If you can't do it, use Musashi."

Nagahisa looked from Hideo to Ishido.

"Do you really think the shogun would be pleased if Musashi used the Myoju? No, I think this man, who is, after all, a direct descendant of the dictator, would be much better." He looked at the Kaishakunin with an appraising eye. "Of course, my lord, if you would deign to make the cut …" Nagahisa paused. Ishido pursed his mouth.

"I didn't come here to participate, only to officiate." He added, "Besides, necks are more in my experience than trunks."

At this, both he and Nagahisa doubled up with laughter, leaving Hideo wondering at the joke.

Hideo looked first at Nagahisa, who was still sputtering, and then to Ishido, who regained his composure.

"My lords, may I speak my mind?" he asked.

"By all means, do," Ishido said.

"You can't be serious," Hideo said to Nagahisa.

In an instant, the sword tester changed from a large, good-humored older man to a deadly serious, even dangerous person.

In a cold, flat voice, which was all the more menacing given the laughter of the previous moment, Nagahisa said to Hideo, "I am as serious as death itself. Are you man enough to attempt the cut?" He paused before continuing, "Or is that lovely sho dai Yasumitsu simply for show? In which case, you would do the sword a favor by selling it to Lord Ishido."

Hideo was angrier than he could remember being. At the same time, he realized that Nagahisa was in the right. When Hideo belittled their skills earlier to Kobiyashi, he never dreamt that he would be standing face to face with the two greatest samurai in Nippon. The truth was that either one of them was a very deadly adversary fully capable of cleaving him in two without a further thought. As for Lord Ishido, his abilities were legendary. Hideo understood that most of his anger was directed at himself, and until he proved himself, he really had no right to stand in the same circle with these men. Suddenly, he wanted to be respected by them more than he wanted anything in the world, more than he wanted to be with Mariko, even more than he wanted to avenge his mother's death.

Hideo dropped to his knees on the dusty ground, under the pitiless sun.

"My lords, please allow me to make the cut."

Nagahisa looked at Ishido, who nodded, and Nagahisa raised Hideo, taking his right hand. He drew the Myoju from his belt and handed it, still in its *saya,* to Hideo. The heavy blade was like no sword Hideo had ever hefted. It was massive and very long. Hideo felt an energy surging up the handle and into his hand. As valuable as was Hideo's Yasumitsu, the shogun's Myoju was priceless, the finest work of that masterful artist.

Hideo now knew that his *kozuka* blade was a fake, but he didn't care. With a sword like this, he could cut through a stone lantern, and he hadn't yet drawn it from the *saya*.

"I thought you had to relieve yourself," Ishido said.

Nagahisa could see the reflection of how the sword felt on Hideo's face, and he liked what he saw. Obviously, Hideo was responding to the spirit locked inside all great swords, a spirit felt only by those worthy of them. Nagahisa was comfortable with Hideo performing in his place. The real contest would take place much later, and he could easily forgo the preliminary bout. His gut twisted in spasm, and Ishido noted the grimace on his face.

"Well," he said, "I'm going, but I must first introduce the lad."

Nagahisa led Hideo back to the platform, and the two climbed the steps side by side, watched with interest by a gathering crowd. The benches were nearly full of sweating noblemen. Ishido took his customary seat, noticing that Arima had not returned. He scanned the crowd and saw it part like a tree in full leaf before a strong wind. The lord walked through the dense pack of people, heedless of the press around him as if he were man taking a solitary walk in the forest. Even the constant buzz of voices, like a hoard of locusts, died down as he passed. He came up the back steps near the riverbank and took his seat next to Ishido. The lord was slightly out of breath but otherwise self-possessed.

"You missed the excitement," Ishido said. Arima was about to make a reply to the effect that the excitement had not yet begun when he noticed Hideo with Nagahisa.

"What's this?" he asked.

"Wait but a moment," said Ishido, "You will see."

He spoke subtly but with deliberate calculation to give just the right amount of offense. Ishido had decided to provoke Arima sufficiently to put him off his guard but, of course, not enough to offend decorum. Arima seethed inwardly, but his face was serene. When he spoke, his voice was equally unaffected.

"Good. This should be interesting," he said. To himself, he said, *Whatever it is, it is nothing to what you will see shortly.* He added, *You self-righteous imbecile.*

Nagahisa motioned to the crowd, which fell silent. His sonorous bass voice launched itself over the assembly like a great arrow penetrating to the furthest reaches of the festival.

"Gentlemen, I find I am called away on a most urgent matter."

A mild groan of disappointment passed through the crowd like the sighing of the wind on a summer night.

"I shall return for the contest later. The cutting test I was to perform will be made, instead, by a retainer of our most esteemed host." Nagahisa paused a moment to achieve greater effect and, in a more powerful voice, called out, "Lord Arima." This was very well executed, and those who were disappointed began to cheer their liege lord. Arima looked to Ishido and smiled as if to say, *There, you see, my people love me.*

Ishido noted the crowd's enthusiasm, because it was neither staged nor feigned but was an expression of their delight in the festival, which was indeed spectacular. Even the deadly heat didn't dampen their enjoyment, and the water bearers, the magnificence of the contest, and the fair prices charged by the concessions all reflected most favorably on Lord Arima.

"Oda Hideo will be seconded by my own apprentice, Musashi," Nagahisa said, "The sword is by Myoju Umetada, a precious treasure blade of our beloved shogun, Iemitsu."

The shogun's name was not greeted with universal enthusiasm. Actually, it was well received but not in comparison with the reception given to the mention of Lord Arima.

Ishido forced down a scowl. *Soon this insubordination will come to an end*, he said to himself. *The sooner the better.*

Lord Arima was ecstatic. He decided to add fuel to the fire and rose. As he did, the people fell silent once more.

"My people, fortunate residents of a great province, let us thank the shogun for his protection and the prosperity his enlightened rule brings to all."

The response was immediate and powerful. A roar like a tsunami swept the festival grounds. Not a single family did not appreciate the advantages of peace or failed to remember horrors from the wars that had ravaged the land for generations.

Lord Arima bowed to Ishido, who stood, his Tokugawa *mons* flashing in the sun. Arima did not bow as deeply as he should have, though this discourtesy was noticed only by the nobility and passed unnoticed by all others. Ishido took the insult with good grace and bowed deeply to Lord Arima, who once again addressed his people.

"Let the contest begin."

Musashi took advantage of Lord Arima's speech to prepare Hideo. As the cheers of the crowd faded, he asked Hideo, "Excuse me, sir, have you ever tested a sword before?"

"No," said Hideo, "I will need your assistance."

"Always remember that the tang is of soft steel and bends easily. Also, some men have harder bones than others."

"I know that," said Hideo. He continued, "I have some experience cutting green bamboo." Hideo had considerable practice cutting bamboo and enjoyed it very much.

"That's very good," said Musashi. "And how were your cuts?"

"*Sensei* Yamagata Yagu said they were excellent for an amateur. He judged them 'very precise.'"

"Good," said Musashi. "When you approach the *dodan*, bow first to the bench with Lord Arima, then to the crowd, then once more to Lord Arima. Then your mind must enter the Zen state. You must be one with the Void. If you cut through the corpse with your mind, the blade will do your spirit's bidding. If you cut only with the strength of your body, you will fail."

Hideo had complete faith in the peerless qualities of the Myoju *tachi* suspended from his sash. It felt like a living thing.

"And the Myoju?"

"The sword is possibly the finest I have ever seen," Musashi said. "Nagahisa said it was the finest sword he has ever seen. I am amazed he is not going to test it himself, but as of late his bowels have been bothering him. He will be fine later for the contest. It is a great honor to test such a blade."

"I understand."

"I hope you do. The sword is perfection and cannot possibly be blamed for any failure. You will use the *tsuruchi do* style. It will make everything easier."

Hideo was unconvinced that anything would make things easier. His own bowels were in an uproar. He cursed himself for a fool.

Why did I agree to this? If I fail, I will be forever disgraced. Worse, I'll be a laughingstock, a buffoon. Remembered forever as a puffed-up fool, a spineless offshoot of the great dictator. Yes, there's one way out. He turned his full attention on Musashi.

"Musashi san, I am unworthy of this honor. I am presumptuous. It is you who should make the cut. I resign."

Hideo's relief was brief. Musashi was not flattered by his ploy. He replied with force.

"Impossible! Nagahisa *sensei* has given instructions. You must make the cut. Of course, if you wish to explain yourself to the people," he continued wickedly, "I'm sure Lord Arima would understand."

Hideo knew that Lord Arima would look upon any refusal as cowardice and an insult, but he would see failure the same way. He was trapped by his own pride. It was the pride of the dictator, whose blood ran through his veins. Hideo knew he could call on Nobunaga's courage when needed. He had called upon it that day during the fight with the *boken*.

Christ said he 'brought a sword,' and the sword is the soul of the samurai. This crystallized his thought, and he drew the *tachi* holding it with the edge to the crowd, which was on its feet. Its roar pounded in his head, mingling with his Oda blood. The steel of the blade looked like it was on fire with reflections of the bright yellow sun, which beat down from above. Hideo faced the *dodan* just as Musashi was about to remove the silk drape. Hideo felt like a *kabuki* player in a dream.

Then a silence began behind him. Hideo turned from the *dodan* to see an astonishing sight. Four retainers wearing the Arima crest on their kimono carried a man on their shoulders. Hideo did not recognize any of retainers.

The man they carried had his arms and legs bound. His head was bandaged completely, leaving only a small opening under the nose. The cords holding him were visible under the black silk cloth that disguised everything except the head. The man struggled but was very much a prisoner.

A shocked silence fell over the entire festival, and for the first time that day, the song of birds—those few who had braved the midday heat—could be heard. The crowd parted for the samurai as if they were sickles and the people so much ripe grain. A solar eclipse would not have had a greater effect. The retainers mounted the steps and walked to the *dodan*. They dropped the man to the floor and untied the bundled corpse from the crosspiece of the *dodan*.

The living bundle attempted to move like an enormous caterpillar, twisting all the while. One of the samurai kicked him hard with a calloused right foot to the right temple of the head; the twisting stopped. Laying down the corpse, the men turned their attention to the motionless man.

This amazing, wholly unexpected, and unprecedented

event was observed by Shigemasa and Kobiyashi. They had returned from their examination of Shigemasa's sword and were seated with the other samurai.

Ishido watched the proceedings with great interest, as did Lord Arima. Hideo and Musashi had the best view of all. They stood dumbfounded, and Hideo sheathed the Myoju without thinking.

Time seemed suspended although the actual events took place very quickly.

Within moments, the bandaged man hung suspended from the frame of the *dodan*, his arms and legs firmly attached. The man began to struggle once more but quickly realized the utter futility and hung limply. The sun blinded Hideo for a few moments, and when the white spots faded, he could see the bandaged man's torn and bloodstained kimono.

Hideo examined the man and, as he looked at his feet, he almost fainted. Yes, it was the hem of the kimono. It was hand-embroidered with cherry blossoms that were minute but definitely visible. Hideo recognized them as the handiwork of Hana, who despised needlework. She had sewn them as a mark of favor for her lover. The body hanging from the *dodan* was Oyama Shinbei. There could be no mistake. Shinbei was proud of his lover and proud of her needlework.

"Hana wanted the Fragrant Blossom to go with me," Shinbei had said to a number of samurai in the barracks.

Seeing a live body in the *dodan*, Ishido was torn between outrage and morbid curiosity.

Now we have a real test, he thought.

Lord Arima was disappointed. He had thought that Ishido would be sufficiently angry to stop the test and incur the anger of the people.

Hideo swayed as the heat and the horror combined. He would have fallen if Musashi had not grabbed his shoulders. Hideo came to himself.

"I can't cut a living man, I can't."

Musashi frowned.

"It is highly unusual, but there are times when a living criminal receives justice, and his death is of use to the Hamano. It is a painless death," he added, hoping to reassure Hideo, whose face was turning as yellow as a squash.

"You don't understand. I just can't," Hideo repeated in a monotone like a chant.

Musashi was tempted to slap him, but their difference in status made such a thing impossible.

"The people are waiting. Lord Arima is waiting. You have no choice. No choice at all."

What would the Christ do? Hideo thought. His mind raced through the scriptures, and then it stopped on the statement, *Be anxious for nothing. Yes, it is all in the hands of God, and I must be anxious for nothing.* Comforted by this thought, Hideo summoned up all of his Zen training and contemplated the Void.

Musashi saw that Hideo had recovered from his shock and smiled approvingly.

Like a man in a trance, Hideo once more drew the Myoju, which flashed in the sun like a beam of quicksilver.

Ishido could see the dragons as they coiled down the blade. He could see Hideo enter the state required for success under such circumstances. The Kaishakunin knew it better than perhaps any samurai in Nippon save one.

Shigemasa watched as Hideo collected himself after being completely scattered by Arima's surprise. He did not yet know all the reasons behind this turn of events, but he was confident that all would reveal itself in a short time. For a moment, Shigemasa wished he were in Hideo's place, not because he was bloodthirsty, but because the sword had taken hold of him as well. He knew that Iemitsu treasured the Myoju as much as he did any material possession, and Shigemasa would have liked to report that he had personally tested the shogun's *tachi*. That would have pleased the shogun, who was notoriously difficult to please. It would have impressed the Dutchman, Hendrik, as well, although Shigemasa had no real need to impress the gaijin. The Dutchman simply had a high opinion of firearms, and Shigemasa felt that this foolish belief was partially due to Hendrik's experiences at the siege of Hara Castle and partly due to his lack of experience with a truly great sword.

Kobiyashi could also see the cherry blossoms on the hem of the kimono, and he was frantic with anxiety for Shinbei and even more for Hideo.

What is going on in his mind? Kobiyashi wondered. He dared not give voice to his terror with Shigemasa.

To go from joy to such horror, he thought, *it is the way of this life and the way of the wheel.* This was cold comfort, but at least Shinbei would be separated from this life by a mighty and peerless blade. It would be a true samurai's death.

Later, Hideo could not remember the actual stroke, try as he might. He recalled the sound of the crowd, which was as loud as thunder, and then the hot spray of blood coating his face, warm and sticky, smelling sour and sweet at the same time.

Musashi's face went white as if in shock. The lords were on their feet cheering, but cheering what, he had not the slightest idea at the time.

Mechanically, Hideo resheathed the Myoju, which was stained red and had fragments of bone clinging to the edge. He drew it out again, whirling it around 360 degrees, the inertia flinging bits of bone and blood to the floor, which ran red with pools of blood. Hideo resheathed the sword and began to fall. Musashi raced to support him. Then, for a moment, everything turned black.

When he opened his eyes, he blinked several times. Lord Arima and Lord Ishido stood by him with ecstatic looks of approval.

"What happened? Did I make the cut?" His voice sounded distant but familiar. To Ishido, Arima, and Musashi, it sound-

tonight. If his *kami* appears in my dreams, he is dead. I don't think it will come."

Hideo felt relief, and the twitching in his bowels subsided.

"We will meet later at the Blossom."

By way of reply, Hana squeezed his hand and left him.

Chapter 15

A Chance Meeting

Mariko woke late. Seeing that the sun was quite high, she called to her attendant and ordered a hot bath. Goki, one of her few remaining maids, sweetly said that she had the lady's bath waiting. Mariko rose naked from her futon.

Peasant girls sleep naked, Goki thought, *but here is the lord's daughter, who could have the softest sleeping robe, and she sleeps with nothing on.*

In Mariko's defense, the heat was oppressive, so much so that Goki wondered why anyone wanted a hot bath. She looked at Mariko's body.

She is slim as a young boy. Her back is broad and her waist narrow. Her breasts are like small apples, but her nipples are large and long. She thought for a moment. Goki had four older sisters and often saw them naked. Her sisters would often sleep with her for warmth in winter, but Mariko never asked her to do the same.

My lady is strange, very strange, Goki thought without continuing. She would have liked to sleep with Mariko, to feel the long sinewy arms around her and smell her sweet breath.

Only a few months before, she had dismissed nearly all of her servants and bodyguards. Goki was a witness to the disagreement that this had caused between Lord Arima and her lady, but the lord threw up his hands and never mentioned it again. Goki had learned quickly that in any quarrel between the lord and his daughter, Mariko was usually victorious. When she had entered his service, Lord Arima had asked her to spy on Mariko and report any unusual meetings with men directly to him, but this had stopped after she had told the lord about Mariko meeting with the gaijin.

Goki had never seen a barbarian before, except in woodblock prints, which showed them with long filthy beards, bizarre clothes, and huge, round, staring eyes. This gaijin, while frightening, wore a kimono, was beardless, and had strange golden hair and very round eyes. She only saw him twice, and when she had detailed the meeting to Lord Arima, he had given her a silver coin and told her that if she ever even breathed a word of what she saw to a living soul, she would spend the rest of her life in the deepest dungeon cell, surrounded only by rats. The threat had worked and Goki had never said anything about the gaijin, even to her sisters.

Mariko rarely said anything about her personal life to Goki. This was surprising, because Goki understood that most great ladies took their maids into their confidences. Mariko was different, but Goki would very much have liked to kiss her lips and taste her mouth. She sighed, watching Mariko's lithe figure step into the steaming tub.

Mariko luxuriated in the hot water. She let all the tension of her early morning meeting in the dungeon leave her body. She crushed eucalyptus leaves in her hands, bringing them to her face, inhaling the pungent fragrance. Flinging them into the steaming water, she burst out laughing at the thought of Shinbei.

He had looked so bedraggled and forlorn, smeared with dirt, blood, and Buddha-knows-what-else, standing with a large knot on his head. When she first saw him in the flickering torchlight, she hadn't known whether to laugh or cry. Knowing men's egos are as easily bruised, like an overripe peach, she decided that tears would go over better than laughter. Tears would give Shinbei an opportunity to console her, as if she needed consoling.

Yes, she thought, *it's always best to let men think they are being strong for a woman.*

The only young man for whom Mariko had any respect was Oda, and much of that was due to his birth as the grandson of Nobunaga.

Hendrik, the Dutchman, intrigued her. She knew of Ieyasu's gaijin, the needle watcher Adams, and a liaison with a barbarian would make her famous. She had lost count of the times that she had entertained this fantasy. Hendrik was almost a match for her in self-possession, and both of them knew that their liaison would be as brief as the fall of a cherry blossom. It was the novelty. Hendrik's light brown pubic hair fascinated her, as her nearly hairless body and her elongated brown nipples did him. The sex was passionate and satisfying. Strangely, he did not smell sour as she had expected him to. Her father had told her that he was a most unusual gaijin in that he bathed nearly every day.

Indeed, Hendrik bathed every day when he was aboard ship, using the quarterdeck wash pump, even in the frigid waters of the more northerly latitudes. This bathing outraged the ship's physician, who could not understand why Hendrik was still alive considering his constant removal of every trace of laudable fat. All the other Dutchmen, including the commodore, bathed either by accident or once a month at most, and even these monthly bathers were seen as eccentric. Ieyasu and

"I accept your challenge," Mariko said, with cool dignity. "Now draw or die standing."

Hana drew her *aikuchi*, as did Mariko. Mariko was surprised to see that Hana's dagger was of good quality.

"That's a nice blade you have, but it won't save you."

Hana could see that her reference to the Dutch sailor had unnerved Mariko, if only slightly. She pressed her verbal assault.

"You look like a hairy Ainu. Surely your legs have never known wax, much less your hairy privates. Shinbei was right when he said it looked just like a Dutch sailor's beard."

Blood pounded in Mariko's head, but her years of training made her thrusts and feints automatic. She slashed Hana's cheek, cutting to the bone. Hana gasped but gamely fought on; still, her need to protect her bosoms impeded her fierce counterattack. Mariko caught the edge of Hana's blade in the soft steel spine of her own and deftly flipped it up in the air, catching it with her left hand. Instantly, she had both daggers pressed against opposite sides of Hana's throat. Despite the withering heat, Mariko was not breathing heavily, although the fruit bat–shaped sweat stains reached down to her waist. Blood still flowed down Hana's face disappearing into her cleavage. Hana was panting like an overworked dog and smelled no different.

Mariko was always magnanimous in victory. It was one of her more attractive traits.

"You silly girl, you may well have the heart of a samurai but not the technique. Nevertheless, I shall allow you to live."

"You won't kill me?" Hana panted an answer, "But if my Shinbei's dead, I want to die." Mariko then understood that Hana's relationship to the calligrapher was simply love and nothing more. There was no policy, no politics, and no strategy in her love for Shinbei. More important, Shinbei had told her nothing more than a few harmless details. If he had told her specifics, Hana would have sought to blackmail Mariko or her father to save Shinbei.

I'll tell her enough to reassure her. Besides, she thought, *Shinbei's role is over, regardless.*

She sheathed her dagger but retained Hana's and stepped in front of the exhausted girl. Hana was physically spent and emotionally drained. She waited for death as patiently as a domestic animal waits for slaughter.

Mariko looked almost sorrowfully at the slash in Hana's cheek. It would leave a thin, white scar for the rest of her life, but then, geisha wore makeup so it wouldn't show. Mariko disdained makeup, refusing to wear it even at the court of the emperor, which was why she had never been presented.

"Listen to me, little sister," she said to Hana, almost kindly. "Things are almost never what they seem to be. I am no heartless monster, despite what you hear. Shinbei desired me but I refused him."

"You lie."

"Think, girl. What reason do I have to lie? You owe me your life."

This fact was undeniable and made Hana pause.

"But if my love is dead, my life is over. Take it!"

"Trust me, little sister, your life is not over."

Hana looked in Mariko's eyes and she saw fearlessness and truth.

Despite her tender age, Hana had known many men and more than a few great noblemen. She was familiar with the far-seeing intensity of a real follower of Bushido, and she knew then that Mariko would not lie about such a thing at such a time. Mariko handed the *aikuchi* back to her, offering it with the edge facing herself, holding the point erect. At this generous gesture Hana made her decision.

"I would never sell my sword even to ransom my Shinbei's life. You have spared mine. I beg you to keep it as a token of my esteem."

Mariko was deeply touched at Hana's graciousness, and she made her decision. First, she bowed deeply to Hana, as deeply as she would have bowed to an equal. There was crusted blood on Hana's cheek, but the bleeding had already stopped, so clean was the cut and keen Mariko's dagger. Mariko tenderly cupped Hana's rounded chin and looked into her eyes.

"Would you like to move into the palace as my adopted sister?" she asked. "I am often lonely by myself."

Hana's eyes filled with tears. Never in her wildest dreams had she thought that such a chance would come her way. But alas, it was impossible.

"I'm sorry, but I can't," she said, tearfully. "The teahouse owns my contract."

Mariko smiled. This presented no obstacle.

"I will buy your contract. You will be my younger sister."

Hot tears streamed down Hana's face, dissolving the dried blood and tingeing her tears pink. Heedless of the damage to her kimono, Mariko embraced Hana as she would her own sister.

Unbeknownst to the two women, Shigemasa had observed the entire fight.

When they embraced, he moved noiselessly on down the riverbank in the direction of Lord Arima's castle.

Chapter 16

The Shooting Range

All the way to the shooting range, Hideo and Kobiyashi answered each other's questions and told their stories. By the time they reached the structures, they were once more sweating through their kimonos, and each one had more questions than answers.

"Was it really Shinbei?" Kobiyashi asked for what seemed to Hideo to be one too many times.

Hideo had washed in the river before donning Hana's kimono and scouring his skin with gravel had removed all of the blood and vomit. His skin was chafed raw by the rough stones, but he felt much cleaner. He had also washed his own kimono and removed all blood, bone, and vomit. It had dried quickly in the sun, and he was able to change out of Hana's garment before arriving at the range.

Hideo was almost desperate for information about Shigemasa; he saw that Lord Ishido's attitude toward him was posturing and that Shigemasa was obviously far more important than he appeared. Hideo even wondered if Shigemasa weren't really the shogun in disguise. Kobiyashi scoffed at this idea and then admitted that he'd never seen the shogun.

Kobiyashi had told Hideo about the fight between the two peasants.

"You know, after the fight, Shigemasa said something funny." Kobiyashi was taking his usual long time to come to the point, rubbing his moon face with his fingers.

"He said something like 'Remember, the shogun is your benevolent father, not your enemy.' The way he said it sounded almost like he was talking about himself and not Iemitsu. Like I said, it was strange." Hideo considered this.

The firing range consisted of little more than a series of rudely constructed, low tables one hundred *shaku* from a raised earthwork backstop.

Mizukami, the rangemaster, was Lord Arima's armorer, who was responsible for cleaning and maintaining the lord's extensive collection of personal firearms as well as the military muskets used by his retainers. The lord permitted Mizukami to supplement his meager salary by selling a few matchlocks on the side. These guns were all individually licensed by the shogunate and very carefully tracked. Anyone found in possession of a gun without the appropriate government license, which described the measurements of the barrel, was subject to a large fine if he were a samurai and summary execution if he were not.

Hideo was still contemplating whether or not Shigemasa was actually Iemitsu when he saw Mizukami.

"Mizukami, I am pleased to see you."

Mizukami was a short, wiry samurai whose father had been a musket man at Sekigahara and whose grandfather had been a musket man at Nagashino. Rumor in the barracks had it that Mizukami used gunpowder to season his food, so closely associated was he with guns. He endured a considerable amount of abuse from samurai who viewed firearms as a threat to Bushido. They didn't understand, like Mizukami did, that if other *daimyo* had guns, Lord Arima must have them as well. Mizukami would have been perfectly happy if all guns could be banned throughout the empire, but as long as others had them, he was determined that Arima's would function perfectly.

Mizukami believed in samurai virtue and the code of Bushido as fervently as Hideo or even Kobiyashi. He had heard of Hideo's achievement with the shogun's Myoju blade, but he had no idea that the test victim might have been Shinbei. He beamed at Hideo.

"I understand that congratulations are in order. Nagahisa *san* may be looking for new employment."

"It was stupendous," Kobiyashi said. "A perfect cut made by a matchless blade. The cheering crowd—"

"He leaves out the part where I vomited like a sick dog and disgraced myself," Hideo interrupted.

Mizukami appreciated Hideo's self-deprecation as a manifestation of samurai humility, and he knew that in Hideo's case the humility was sincere and all the more praiseworthy given his ancestry. Seeing the look on Hideo's face, Mizukami changed the subject.

"You gentlemen care to shoot? It's very hot, so be careful between shots. Make sure you swab out thoroughly before pouring powder in the muzzle. I don't want any premature discharges. A samurai needs his hands, not to mention his face."

With that he handed Kobiyashi a plain but serviceable musket, a bag of lead balls, a flask of powder, and a length of burning match. He was about to hand Hideo the same type of gun when Hideo said, "I've been thinking of buying a gun. Something nice by Kunitomo, with dragonflies inlaid on the barrel."

Rather than being pleased as Hideo had expected him to be, Mizukami looked crestfallen.

"I had one like that only this morning. Kunitomo barrel with gold dragonflies in *hira zogan* and a nice, small bore. Perfect for hunting ducks."

Hideo was not happy.

"What happened to it? That's just what I want."

"Why didn't you tell me?" Mizukami said.

"I really decided only this morning."

"Damn," said Mizukami. "I wish I'd known."

"I don't suppose the buyer would be interested in selling for a profit?"

"No," said Mizukami with disappointment. Then he brightened.

"Listen," he said, "I have another on order, a beautiful Kunitomo with silver dragonflies and a Tokugawa *mon*. I can have the Oda crest inlaid on the breech instead. There's still time."

"Hideo doesn't want some Osaka noodle gun," Kobiyashi chimed in. "His head is very valuable to him." He started laughing.

Mizukami wondered if Kobiyashi was being serious; if he were, Mizukami should be seriously offended. He took pride in his judgment, even though he had no love for guns. He decided it was a joke and laughed.

Hideo looked over the practice muskets and then asked the rangemaster to choose one for him. The two men carried their guns to the stands.

The sun was directly overhead, and it beat down with great fury. Both Hideo and Kobiyashi took great care to avoid a premature discharge. They were grimy with burnt and unburnt powder, and the stench of burning saltpeter was literally choking them.

"Imagine being an *ashigaru* at Nagashino with hundreds of these stinking guns, the smoke burning your eyes like fire, and then having to reload and shoot so fast. Aiyee, it must have been hell. My poor grandfather. I never really appreciated him, until now. Then again, your grandfather was a genius. After all, he won the battle."

Hideo had only managed to get off one shot and was struggling with his piece. Kobiyashi was tempted to laugh at his usually unflappable friend, but seeing him wrestle with the unwieldy weapon—his face nearly black and his hands filthy—he had mercy.

"See," he said, "I told you these damned guns are both filthy and smelly."

Just at that moment, the match cord of Hideo's gun made a hissing sound and some molten saltpeter dropped onto the web of soft skin between Hideo's thumb and index finger, burning him painfully.

"Damn it to hell," Hideo exploded. "I swear these barbarian guns come straight from Emma-o himself. They even smell like hell."

Kobiyashi smiled wryly.

"I admit they are not spiritual."

Hideo was not finished expressing his frustration.

"They are vile trash. Prince Yoritomo had no need of such ignoble weapons."

"Your grandfather would disagree," Kobiyashi said.

"They are part of the curse of modern times," Hideo raged on. "The sword, the lance, and the bow—they are the foundation of Bushido. This … " he held out the gun, which still had the burning cord in its serpent. "These are … "

Words failed him, and he silently loaded a charge, rammed it home with the wooden ramrod. He carefully primed the pan and sighted down the round barrel, found a block of wood, and pressed the brass button trigger. The brass serpent snapped down into the pan, but the fall snuffed out the match.

"Shit," he said.

Kobiyashi was shocked. Hideo rarely swore, and *damn* was a very strong oath for him. For Hideo to use the vulgar *unco* he must be at his wits' end.

"I can't believe this dung ever happened to my grandfather. I must be doing something wrong."

Mizukami had been watching Hideo—master of the sword, bow, and lance—fail miserably with the gun, silently taking some satisfaction in his failure.

"Would you like some assistance?" he asked, walking up to Hideo, who held the gun upright like a dead rabbit.

"Yes, I would," he said, handing the gun to Mizukami. "This devil's anus doesn't work. Each time the hammer falls, it extinguishes the match. I don't see how anyone manages to fire one." Hideo ignored the fact that Kobiyashi had already fired his musket a number of times.

Mizukami took the gun, blew on the match until it glowed and hissed, opened the pan cover, sighted carefully, and fired at a breastplate. He handed the gun back to Hideo.

"They work better when you open the pan cover," he said quietly.

Hideo looked at him sheepishly and then felt compelled to speak.

"It doesn't matter. The fact remains that guns are devilish and ignoble."

"I agree completely," Mizukami said. "If all guns were destroyed, Bushido would be that much stronger."

He left Hideo standing with the musket and returned in a few moments with the stout iron breastplate, which had been-pierced through, leaving a mushroom of jagged iron jutting out of the back. Kobiyashi, having successfully fired his piece once more, walked over. The three men examined the armor.

"See," Kobiyashi said with authority. "A fine breastplate shot through both sides." Looking at Hideo, he continued, "You couldn't duplicate this shot with a bow using an arrow forged by Myoju Umetada himself. Admit it."

"I certainly do admit it," Hideo said as he fingered the bullet hole. "That's the whole point. The weakest peasant, even a toothless old woman, can do this with a gun and kill the best-armored samurai. What will become of Bushido if such weapons are permitted?"

He looked at Kobiyashi, whose face was nearly unrecognizable, so covered in powder residue that he looked like some devil in a *kabuki* play, and then at Mizukami.

"You speak the truth," Mizukami said. "That's why the shogunate has restricted all guns. And even so, I worry about them."

Chapter 17

A Disturbance

Although many found it hard to believe, the afternoon sun made the morning's searing heat seem mild in comparison. Still, the crowd seemed to increase, as did the activity of the water bearers. Most of the spectators drank hot tea as an anodyne to the sun.

Hideo and Kobiyashi, seated on tripods, were watching closely as a magnificent eight-plate helmet made in the Kamakura style was lashed to a *honoki* wood stand on the platform, where Hideo had made his cut with the Myoju earlier. The bowl of the helmet was not lacquered but made of russet iron studded with domed rivets.

"See," said Kobiyashi, "The helmet has its own *dodan*. No sword can cut it. The rivets will deflect the blow."

"I am not so sure," said Hideo, "Nagahisa told me he will use his *kasane gesa* style to cut through the very top, using the sweat hole as the point of entry. You can see the *tehan* is of soft metal. He will use it to catch the edge and direct the force down through the body of the *kabuto*."

"A good strategy," said Kobiyashi, "Nagahisa is no fool. There are no rivets at the top. But remember, Okisato uses gaijin steel. His breastplates are matchlock proof."

"Does that mean you would wear one and let Mizukami fire at you?"

"No," said Kobiyashi, "I am not such a fool."

"I didn't think so. I will admit that Okisato is great, but sometimes these claims are for publicity."

"By the way," said Hideo, "Koetsu asked about you last night."

After all the talk of Shinbei, the cutting test, Mariko, Shigemasa, Nagahisa, Lord Arima, and Lord Ishido, Hideo's mention of Koetsu was sweet music to Kobiyashi's ears.

"She was asking when you were going to visit the Blossom and favor her with your presence."

"I would go tonight, but I am short of money. The end of the month is coming, and we will have our pay."

"I will give you an advance of your pay. Besides, you said earlier we should go to the Blossom this very evening."

Kobiyashi gave Hideo his most ovine look then said in a sheepish tone, "You know that my tongue often outruns my reason, especially when it comes to money. You have no idea what it is like to be poor."

"How can you say that to me? You think I'm rich? If I were, I would have Mariko."

Kobiyashi sighed deeply, and a tear rolled down his round cheek.

"I'm sorry. This constant lack of money is frustrating to me. Besides, you said you were going to buy a Kunitomo gun. That takes a year's pay. That's why I said what I said."

Hideo put his arm around Kobiyashi's shoulder.

"I might as well tell you. I am going to sell my Myoju

kozuka to Captain Yamashita. He wants to give it to his father as a present."

Kobiyashi shook his head.

"But you know it's a school piece with a fake signature."

"Of course, I know. Remember, you told me all about it."

"That still won't pay for a good gun."

"I know that, I was going to take a loan from a moneylender."

Kobiyashi gave Hideo a horrified look.

"A moneylender? If you failed to pay for any reason, you would be disgraced, forced to resign your commission, even turn *ronin*."

"Yes, but I have faith. Nothing in this world of illusions is ever as it seems to be. Everything is in the hands of …" He almost said God, which would have been the second serious slipup of the day. He thought, *I have been leading the hidden life for many years and now my Kirishitanity somehow refuses to be secret. God help me.* Hideo was really worried. He abruptly changed the subject. "Exactly who and what is Shigemasa?"

Kobiyashi's moon face looked perplexed.

"He didn't tell me."

"He must have told you something about himself," said Hideo.

"No, not really. But there is something strange. He left, and I looked away from him for a moment to find you—it couldn't have been more than the time it takes to blink—and when I looked back, he had vanished."

"That's impossible."

"I know what I saw. I am sober as Lord Ishido."

Hideo considered Kobiyashi's words for a moment.

"Maybe he is a ninja."

"I don't believe in ninja. They are a tale invented to frighten naughty children into behaving."

"Believe me, Kobiyashi, they are more than legend. They exist. My grandfather used them, and so did Ieyasu."

"But no one has ever seen them."

"That is because no one has ever seen them and lived to tell about them. Using your logic, you could say death is not real because no one has ever seen it and lived to tell the tale."

"I just can't accept men in black kimono with supernatural powers."

"Then explain how Shigemasa disappeared."

"I can't. That's why I told you."

"Both of us have seen a Buddhist priest shoot an arrow and then split the next six on each other's shaft. It is an impossible feat."

"But everyone saw it. It happened."

"Of course. It was a public demonstration of the power of faith. Shinto teaches us that there are *kami* all around us; the world itself is alive. We must learn to accept our limitations and strive to see behind the veil."

As Kobiyashi digested this information, a conch shell sounded three times, echoing over the festival grounds.

"We must hurry," said Hideo. "That is if you want a good seat. The contest you've been waiting for is about to begin."

They made haste, practically flinging their muskets at Mizukami, muttering their thanks, and running off.

Okisato Nagasone, the greatest armorer in all Nippon, a child prodigy revered throughout the land, mounted the platform to make last-minute adjustments to his helmet. He was still young, of medium height with a narrow, intelligent face, and deep black eyes, which, it was said, knew every secret of iron and steel. His black hair hung down long and was tied at the back with a cord. Using his hand as a shield against the merciless sun, he stepped back and smiled at the gaily decorated helmet as if it were a favored child. Mingled in his face were love, affection, and wonder.

Lord Arima, Ishido, and Nagahisa were seated with their backs to the sun, fanning themselves as the bamboo dripped water on their sweating faces. The cries of hawkers selling hot, green, bitter tea, sweet bean cakes, and skewers of grilled fish mingled with the murmurs of the crowd. No birds dared to sing, and even the locusts and cicadas were silent in the phenomenal heat.

Musashi knelt at one end of the platform, taking care as he removed the cover of a long sword box emblazoned with a large, single Tokugawa *mon* in raised gold lacquer.

Watching him, Lord Ishido commented to Nagahisa, "I see this will be a true *tameshigiri,* even though you are using a helmet instead of a body."

Nagahisa smiled a thin cruel smile and looked at Lord Arima as he said, "Or a live person for that matter."

Arima knew this was meant as a slight.

"What are you implying by that remark? This is my province, and I control what takes place here." He looked at Ishido, who was obviously intent on remembering every word and continued, "With the shogun's approval, of course. Lord Ishido has commended me already once this day."

"Your province is in almost every way exemplary, my lord," said Ishido. He had taken Nagahisa partially into his confidence, and the remark was designed to goad Arima, but it did not succeed as well as Ishido hoped.

Arima gestured at Musashi.

"Your assistant is most accomplished. If I remember rightly, those robes are the Noshime Asakamishimono that must be worn as he attends to the Ondogu box."

"You are most acute, my lord," replied Nagahisa with great enthusiasm, "Musashi is not the only man who is accomplished."

"Speaking of accomplishments, I have been charged by the shogun ..."

Here it comes, thought Arima.

Ishido thought, *At last, the final moves in this game are beginning, and I have a countermove prepared for any eventuality.*

"My mandate is to continue to investigate the smuggling of new and dangerous weapons." Ishido paused, "Barbarian weapons. Lord Arima, you are doubtless aware of the San Felipe incident of evil memory."

Arima nodded.

"The shogunate believes that a gaijin ship is anchored in Your Lordship's domain. The ashes of Shimabara are still warm. I've said enough."

Lord Arima smiled at Ishido, inwardly relieved. *Obviously, Iemitsu has no idea of my plans. For once, his spies have failed him.* He decided to throw Ishido even further off track.

"Guns are not the weapons of a samurai. They are infamous gaijin filth, contrary to Bushido itself."

Ishido smiled thinly.

"Nevertheless, you keep your arsenal well stocked with these filthy devices."

If only he knew just how well stocked and with what, Ishido would runaway and hide himself under Iemitsu's skirt, but he'll never get the chance. This day will be his last.

Out loud, he said, "Ishido *sama*, I am not a fool. If other lords have guns, I must have more and better. A *daimyo*'s first task is to protect his people and his fief. A weak lord is useless to the shogunate."

Ishido had to admit this was well said.

"I salute you, Arima *san*. You are wise. Shogun Iemitsu has no use for fools or weakness. Your father guarded Ieyasu's left flank at Sekigahara and helped defeat the traitor Hideyori at Osaka Castle. I spoke only in general terms and not of you."

Nagahisa rose from the bench reluctantly. He was very much enjoying his role in Ishido's carefully rehearsed drama, as well as Lord Arima's bamboo water contraption.

"Gentlemen," said Nagahisa, "If you will excuse me. I must don my Noshime."

Suddenly, a figure wearing a basket on its head leapt clear of the milling throng close to the benches of the nobility and leveled something at the end of an arm. There was a sharp explosion, and the nobles, who had remained seated for an instant, looked at each other all still seated and shouted loudly as Ishido and Lord Arima stood and followed the progress of the basket through the crowd.

Shigemasa had also witnessed the incident and had done nothing to interfere with the basket's mission. However, he now moved quickly to the commotion as the basket drew another hand gun, and the crowd fell back as the basket threw off the head covering to reveal a tall, black-haired man dressed all in black. His face was the color of dirty snow. He brandished the pistol wildly to force the mass of people into retreat as frightened children began wailing. Men, women, and children were falling into one another in their frenzy to get away.

Shigemasa stepped into the cleared space, and the wildly staring man leveled his gun at Shigemasa's chest. There was a blur of bright steel, and almost his entire right arm, from above the elbow, fell to the dusty ground, still holding the gun. The pistol discharged. A silver scream echoed above the wails of the children as the lead ball pierced a young woman's calf and exited, leaving a clean wound. The would-be assassin's face grew whiter as he stared down at his arm, heedless of the fountain of blood that pulsed from his shoulder as it sprayed the crowd with each beat of his heart.

Shigemasa carefully avoided the gushing blood and removed the gun from the nerveless fingers as well as another one from the man's sash. The injured man was in a state of shock and stood motionless. The crowd began to murmur and grow angry and would have fallen on the man and torn him to pieces but for the arrival of Lord Ishido and Lord Arima. The throng drew further back, and the silence was broken only by the moaning of the woman who had been shot as she was quickly taken away by two of Lord Arima's water carriers.

The basket man began to shake violently as Lord Ishido approached. The sight of the three hollyhock leaves emblazoned in heavy gold thread all over the official's kimono brought the man out of shock.

In an unearthly but clearly audible voice, he screamed, "Long live Shimabara. Long live Shiro Amakusa." Then he fell heavily on top of his severed arm, like a tree whose trunk has been cut through.

Shigemasa looked at the two lords and spoke in a firm voice. "Clearly, the assassin was extremely disciplined. Such fortitude is very rare in these modern times. Before Nobunaga reduced the Enryaku-ji and Hongan-ji at Osaka there were many such stalwarts in the Tendai and Ikko sects."

Ishido raised his fine black eyebrows.

"Buddha defended us against those fanatics," he said. "I thought they were all dead."

Shigemasa bent down. "Let us see."

He looked up at Lord Arima, who looked down expressionlessly.

"Hand me a cloth," said Shigemasa, testing the lord's reaction as he omitted the honorific.

Arima handed him a cloth without demur. Shigemasa's gold collar tabs shone in the bright, blinding sun as he carefully wiped the face of the dead man. His skin was unnaturally white, partly from exsanguinations, but he was still too pale for a Nihonjin. His features were regular, and the man was young. His hair had been dyed black, and the blood soaked off the dye above the high forehead, where the hair showed through as a light shade of brown. The man's eyes were closed, and despite his horrific death, his face was peaceful. Shigemasa lifted the eyelid of the right eye, and although blood pooled inside, Shigemasa could see that the iris was green. Now he was certain and said to the two lords, "The assassin is a gaijin dressed as a Nihonjin with dyed hair. Clearly this is conspiracy."

"A conspiracy against whom?" Lord Arima asked icily.

"Please hand me those pistols," Ishido said. Shigemasa handed both guns to him.

"Might I see one?" asked Lord Arima.

"I do not wish to give offense, but we are in public." Gesturing to the silent faces pressed around as closely as they dared, Ishido shook his head. Having made his point, he turned his attention to the lifeless body.

"My lord, you will please have the corpse placed in a jar with all the necessary preservatives. I am taking it back to Edo with me." Ishido's tone was one of absolute authority, utterly lacking in the customary formality. Clearly, he expected unquestioning obedience.

Lord Arima spoke with as much deference as he was able to summon.

"It shall be as you wish."

Shigemasa turned to two of Lord Arima's water carriers. "Tell the herald to sound the horn." He looked one last time at the blood-smeared face. Then he looked at Lord Arima.

"My lord, the contest must continue."

Arima was only too happy to have time in which to assess the attempted assassination of Lord Ishido by a barbarian.

Or was I the intended victim? he wondered. *Could Hendrik be playing a triple game? No,* he said to himself, *gaijin are not that subtle.*

Another far more unpleasant possibility occurred to him. *Gaijin are not capable of such subtlety, but Iemitsu is.* Arima pursed his lips in a scowl. *Caught between Shigemasa and the shogun's dog, I must be extra vigilant.*

The lord of Nagasaki was very displeased. He could easily kill Ishido, Shigemasa, and all of Ishido's retainers, but without actual gaijin soldiers and their deadly cannon, the best result he could hope for was a rebellion like Shimabara, with young Oda taking the place of Shiro Amakusa under his direction. Ishido had not come all that way for the festival, and that was a certainty.

In all likelihood, it was shogun Iemitsu himself who had arranged the attempted assassination of Lord Ishido, which would serve as a pretext for the annexation of his province, his arrest, and suicide because everything was his responsibility alone. A barbarian attempt on his own life would accomplish the same purpose. If it were successful, he was still without an heir. The death of either Ishido or Arima would result in Iemitsu gaining the province. More than anything, Arima detested being impotent, the more so because, in almost every way, he knew he was anything but. Though unless Hendrik actually had the Dutch East India Company land soldiers from Batavia, he was reluctant to commit himself to actual rebellion.

Of course, there were the Spanish who directed the Franciscan Kirishitans; they had already delivered a quantity of munitions, and far more were on a nearby ship at anchor, but Arima did not trust the Spanish any more than Iemitsu did. Hendrik had told him stories about the Aztec king of Mexico, Montezuma, and the Inca king, Atahualpa, and how they had been betrayed and subsequently died at the hands of the Spanish. Arima's father had told him of the San Felipe incident and how the ship had run aground with gaijin munitions. Tortured by Ieyasu's officials, the pilot had confessed that the Franciscan priests, who had still been tolerated at the time, had been sent to prepare the people for the Spanish army that would surely follow.

Then again, Arimareasoned, *my position could only gain by gaijin overthrowing Iemitsu and the Tokugawa*. All things considered, Lord Arima greatly preferred the Dutch to the Spanish.

But surely, Hendrik could not be so clumsy as to send a Hollander to kill Lord Ishido and fail. He had had no contact with Hendrik for all too many days. He knew the rajahs and sultans still ruled in Djakarta under the watchful eyes of the Dutch. He was aware that Hendrik had been in Tokyo, but that was all he knew.

Yes, he said to himself, *I have no other choice. The timing could not be worse. Ishido lives, and Shinbei is now useless.*

Buddha forgive me, I must send Mariko, perhaps to her death. Iemitsu's cursed spies are everywhere, and now this evil Shigemasa dogs me. He sighed. *All life is illusion, even my lovely Mariko.*

Unconsciously, Arima began to breathe the Prana in and out in the Pranayam, immediately tapping into the fifth chakra. He saw all life from birth to death, with all of its joys and tragedies as nothing more than a way of opening himself to his higher nature. Whether his grand design failed or succeeded meant nothing. As his exercise ended, he felt calm and purposeful once more. The ultimate significance of human actions was one thing; essentially, they had none.

Notwithstanding the grimness of his situation, Arima couldn't suppress a smile, which caught the attention of Ishido.

I prefer to win, he thought.

For his part, Ishido could not help but admire the man, while cordially disliking him. Nagahisa sensed the conflict between the two lords, and though his sympathies were solidly with Lord Ishido, his attentions were focused on the russet iron, rivet-studded helmet that stood proudly on the platform, visible to all.

Chapter 18

Kotetsu

Seated on the bench, Ishido was uneasy. Iemitsu had sent his own personal *tachi* for the test over Ishido's strenuous objections. He had told the shogun that the outcome was uncertain, that there was a greater than even chance that the blade would crack or even splinter into fragments. This would be seen by all as an evil omen for the Tokugawa. The sword was the soul of the samurai. In a real sense, Iemitsu and his sword were one. That the helmet belonged to Lord Arima did make the contest more exciting, but Ishido had vociferously protested that it made the contest into something very serious. The prestige of the Tokugawa was being placed at risk.

"Yasutsugu was a superb swordsmith but not known for supreme sharpness," he said. "If the blade fails in any way, it will be seen as a failure by the shogunate, endangering my real mission." He had literally begged Iemitsu to send a massive sho

Shigemasa chortled. "Arima's power play failed most miserably."

Chortle as he might, Shigemasa was concerned about the two killings—the death of the would-be assassin far more than the man cut in half by Hideo. The assassin was certainly a gaijin. That he was a gaijin with dyed hair and kimono passing himself as a Nihonjin was unsettling but hardly surprising, given the fact that gaijin were not permitted to travel unescorted.

The truly disturbing fact was his discovery of a cross with the crucified Kirishitan god on a gold chain around the man's neck. Ieyasu had mistrusted the Kirishitan priests as had Hidetada; both had suppressed them. Iemitsu directed more of his attention to snuffing out the smallest embers of the Shimabara conflagration than anything else in the realm, except, of course, for tax revenue.

Lord Ishido had taken responsibility for the corpse, and that was fine with Shigemasa.

It couldn't have been Hendrik, he reasoned. *He has nothing to gain if Ishido dies, but everything to lose, including the concession to trade. His death might benefit the Spanish by eliminating the Dutch if they are suspected. Arima's death would be of no benefit to any gaijin.*

If Iemitsu wanted to kill Arima, who has no heir, he would have told me. Shigemasa paused in his musings. *Then again, sending Ishido was excellent strategy, as was sending me. Having a Kirishitan gaijin kill Ishido would incite anti-Kirishitan sentiment, which would please Iemitsu and provide a pretext to repress any remaining Kirishitans.*

Shigemasa was a very patient man and willing to wait. Iemitsu was a famous gambler but only in circumstances when he knew the outcome in advance. It was time to place a bet. He saw an empty seat near Lord Arima, and he walked to the platform, the gold Tokugawa insignia granting him passage through the crowd and the officials. He took his place in time to hear some of the wagering.

"I will bet fifty gold *koban* on the helmet," Ishido said with confidence. He was confident because the money belonged to Iemitsu, and the shogun had ordered him to make the wager. Arima was astounded.

"You're betting against the shogun?"

Ishido smiled.

"All is fair in such contests. The helmet is indestructible; anyone can see that."

Lord Arima thought for a long moment. *I can't very well bet with Ishido, backing Iemitsu is the last thing he'd expect.*

"Ten gold *oban* on the Yasutsugu," he said.

This very large sum was more than either the sword or helmet was worth. If Ishido met the bet and lost, Iemitsu would be displeased, even if he gained Arima's province. To the shogun, land, peasants, and rice were one thing, but gold was another. Arima was thoroughly enjoying Ishido's discomfort. He would be betting against Iemitsu, and the sum would be far more than he could afford.

Abandoning good manners, Arima twisted the knife, "If that's too rich for you, make it five *oban*." Arima's mocking tone made Ishido reach involuntarily for the Mitsutada, but this was neither the time nor the place.

Your time will come soon enough, he thought, and then he spoke words he would soon regret, "Not at all, enough of these paltry sums. Two hundred gold *oban* on Okisato's helmet."

Now it was Arima who gasped. Two hundred *oban* was an enormous sum of money, nearly a quarter of the annual income of his entire province. It would necessitate some sacrifice to raise it. Losing such a sum would be crippling but not fatal. It would most certainly bankrupt Ishido, and Iemitsu would die before giving him such an amount.

Where would he get such a sum? Arima wondered. It was

unthinkable for any samurai, much less Lord Ishido, to default on a debt of honor.

"Two hundred gold *oban* it is," said Lord Arima in a voice loud enough to be heard by Shigemasa and the other nobles, loud enough to be heard by Nagahisa and Musashi, loud enough to be heard by Hideo and Kobiyashi. So there would be no mistake, the lord of the province repeated, "My Lord Ishido, that is two hundred gold *oban*," with an emphasis on *oban*.

"Did he say two hundred gold *oban*?" Kobiyashi asked Hideo.

"Yes. Think of it. Many *daimyo* never see that much in their whole lives," said Hideo.

"One gold *oban* would buy Koetsu's contract," said Kobiyashi in a velvety voice that was heavy with love.

"I can't believe Lord Ishido has that much money. Lord Arima, I believe. Lord Ishido would have to sell everything he owns and then some to raise such a sum."

"I wish I had money to bet," said Kobiyashi, "I'd bet on the helmet."

"Gentlemen's bet," said Hideo. "I'll take the Yasutsugu."

"I thought you liked the helmet."

"I thought you liked the sword."

"The thought of two hundred gold *oban* being bet makes me like the helmet," said Kobiyashi.

"I'll take the sword. There's nothing like taking the offensive."

"Unless the defense is invincible," said Kobiyashi.

"We'll soon see," said Hideo.

Bets were being made all over the festival, and the wagers on the sword were almost equal to the bets on the helmet. It was Lord Arima's province after all, and the Okisato helmet was his.

The nobleman seated to Shigemasa's left offered to bet twenty gold *koban* on Lord Arima's helmet. Shigemasa politely declined, saying that he had too much respect the shogun as well as Lord Arima to wager against either one. When Ishido raised his wager from *koban* to *oban*, Shigemasa nearly fainted. Among a myriad of concerns, it was his business to be on intimate terms with the financial condition of every one of Iemitsu's closest advisors so as to guard against corruption. Ishido's entire worth would fall far short of paying the loss. Iemitsu wouldn't dream of backing such a substantial play.

Ishido couldn't believe the words had come out of his mouth. Yes, he disliked Lord Arima, and, yes, he wanted to retire and leave the worldly arena. But to risk everything he had worked for—a lifetime's labor—on a festival contest? He knew it was far more than a festival entertainment, but if he lost, nothing would compensate him. Iemitsu would consider the money part of Arima's estate, and the shogun would want the gold from him as surely as he would want it from Lord Arima, as surely as the sun was hot.

Ishido wiped his sweating face.

Why did I do it? he thought, and it was almost a curse. *The damned heat, Arima's sneer, this one last mission*, Ishido shook his head. Regardless of the outcome of the contest, Ishido seriously considered leaving the festival and taking his good mare back to Edo, leaving the Arima problem to Shigemasa, whom he knew was more than capable. Iemitsu could appoint a new Kaishakunin, and he could retire. His wife would be overjoyed. She always complained that she saw too little of him. Part of this, he attributed to her barrenness, but he never held it against her.

Ishido was content that his line would die with him. *Karma*, he thought, *Karma for all those invited onward*.

Now, with the stroke of a sword, he would either be rich beyond his dreams and that land would be his as well as a beautiful house, or he and his wife would be reduced to beggary, and his illustrious name synonymous with disgrace.

What is it the Kirishitans say? "He who lives by the sword dies by the sword." Strange that I should think of that.

Actually, he thought about Kirishitanity a good deal since finding the crucifix around the dead gaijin's neck. He knew that there were brave Kirishitans; the martyrs at Nagasaki had proved that beyond any doubt. Shigemasa had given him the amulet to take back to Iemitsu along with the clay jar containing the body—one more martyr to the cause of the man they called Christ. It seemed strange to him to not only worship but die for a dead god. Then again, if he remembered right, Christ wasn't dead but only killed that he might rise from the dead, reborn. The fact that Christ was reborn as himself, without change proved that he had achieved enlightenment, as had the Buddha. What Ishido couldn't understand was the Kirishitan celebration and commemoration of his death rather than his rebirth.

No Buddhist dwelled on the death of the god but on his rebirth as himself. It was evidence of his godhood that he was able to escape from the endless cycle of birth and death common to all living beings. It was an enigma, and one he knew he would never solve. He only knew that he would certainly suffer death and rebirth, because enlightenment was an infinite number of incarnations beyond his present earthly existence. His role as Iemitsu's executioner had more than likely adversely affected his karma, in spite of his Zen posture, which made him almost completely dispassionate about his deeds, which would hopefully minimize the production of negative karma.

On the stage, Nagahisa drew the Yasutsugu and handed it to Musashi for a final inspection, which included several applications of *uchigamori* powder from Musashi's *uchiko* puff. After the powder was sparingly applied to the shining sword, Musashi wiped it off in a single stroke, beginning at the base and ending at the point. He then sighted carefully down both sides of the blade, looking for any imperfection—no easy task in the hot, dazzling sun. He did not look happy.

"Master," he said in a low voice, "the *uchiko* ball is not the very finest. We used the last of the very best on the Myoju." He was deeply apologetic. "I should have brought extra. *Sensei*, I have failed us."

"I fear we will need more than *uchigamori* powder to defeat Okisato's helmet," Nagahisa said kindly. "His armor is proof against muskets. Iemitsu's Yasutsugu blade is peerless, and our Hamano cuts are perfect, but the heat gives the helmet an even greater advantage, because the iron is softer, making the sword more likely to stick."

"But then, isn't softer iron more easily cut?" asked Musashi.

"We will soon see, won't we?" Nagahisa said, grimly "Musashi, you didn't bet on us, I hope."

"You can't expect me to bet against myself," Musashi said.

"How much?"

"Two silver *koban*."

"So much?"

"Remember who is making the cut. If Hideo were making it, I would bet everything I have in this world on the helmet."

"So would I," said Nagahisa.

Taking the sword from Musashi, Nagahisa sighted down each brilliant edge, reassuring him of its perfection. Raising the Yasutsugu over his head in the classic *kasane gesa* stance, Nagahisa paused, breathing Prana in and out. Both arms back over his head, his veins stood out on his neck like thick ropes from his bulging muscles. He concentrated all his physical strength and mental energy, slicing through the helmet with his mind.

The festival grounds grew silent. Only the twittering of a solitary finch broke the heat-deadened stillness. All eyes were on Nagahisa as they waited for the downstroke.

Suddenly, Okisato, whose eyes were also on Nagahisa,

cried out, "Wait! Pardon me. The *kabuto* is slightly off center."

He bowed politely to Nagahisa, walked over to the helmet, and adjusted two of the cords. He bowed once again and assumed his position in the corner of the platform.

Nagahisa once more gathered up all his resources for the masterstroke, bringing his massive arms over his head.

Nagahisa's "Yah" echoed through the festival, scaring children and making many spectators jump with fright. Nagahisa recoiled, as if he were cut, at the tremendous clangor of steel on steel.

As he raised the sword from the helmet, everyone was horror-struck. The shogun's sword was missing an entire section of the edge, one *shaku* back from the point. The missing piece was as long as a man's thumb and reached nearly to the ridgeline. There was an easily seen bend in the steel as well. The sword was completely ruined.

The helmet was cut more than halfway through the bowl. Anyone wearing it would have had their skull cleaved past the eyes. Nevertheless, under the rules of the engagement, the helmet had won.

The initial shock wore off quickly, and it was replaced by a deafening buzz as the crowd recovered its wits and people began paying off bets.

Several nobles, as well as Lord Arima, Lord Ishido, and Shigemasa rose and congratulated Okisato and Nagahisa.

Nagahisa bowed low before Okisato.

"Okisato *sensei*, a superb *kabuto*," he said. "Matchless quality. I have never seen the like. My congratulations."

Okisato received the compliment with an even lower bow.

"A truly noble effort. A thunderous, irresistible stroke," Lord Arima said to Nagahisa.

Ishido said nothing. He had bet everything he had or ever dreamt of having and won. But he sensed something was amiss and contented himself with nodding his approval, first to Okisato as the victor and then to Nagahisa. Musashi stood apart from the others and dissolved in tears, which rolled down his face in a slow, unceasing flow.

Shigemasa couldn't take his eyes off Okisato. He had never seen such a powerful emotional conflict take place so clearly on any man's face. The master armorer seemed about to explode, like a volcano prior to an eruption. Okisato's face was ashen pale. He was sweating profusely, more profusely than Nagahisa, who seemed calm in comparison despite having just undergone such an awesome expenditure of energy and will.

Okisato fell to his knees before Nagahisa in a gesture of supplication more appropriate to worship of the Buddha than to a living man. He stammered, his words coming through pauses in the bitterest, soundless weeping that anyone present had ever witnessed. A damned soul in hell could not have expressed greater suffering.

"My lords, I must confess or die right here. I am low. Lower than the lowest hairy Ainu. Lower than the most despised *eta.* Lower than an infected corpse during a plague. I deserve to be buried alive in a jar of excrement. Buddha may forgive me, but I will not forgive myself."

Arima, Ishido, Shigemasa, and the others looked at him with the greatest consternation. Musashi even stopped weeping and stared at the shaking man prostrated before Nagahisa. Okisato's behavior was unprecedented. He looked up at Nagahisa, who towered over him and continued in a voice that indicated that his spirit was completely shattered beyond repair.

"When I saw you raise the shogun's Yasutsugu, I knew you would slice right through my helmet like so much green bamboo. This worthless dog deliberately destroyed your concentration. The helmet needed no adjustment. Please use the sword I ruined to take my life. I know I don't deserve such an honor. I will understand if you refuse."

Nagahisa was thunderstruck at the naked display of self-abasement before such an august company. For a time, he was at a loss for words.

Finally, he said, "Okisato *san*, your most excellent tactic was nothing more than a legitimate ruse of war and perfectly permissible given the circumstances. I am sure Sun Tzu and the lords here would agree. I failed to sever your *kabuto*. You are blameless."

Arima, Ishido, and the others, including Shigemasa, all murmured their assent. Okisato rose to his feet and, slowly but deliberately, removed all of his clothes, beginning with his outer kimono until he was completely naked except for a small loincloth. The merciless sun beat down on his exposed, sweating flesh. He removed his handsome gold ring and handed it to Nagahisa.

"Your noble words and gracious actions make my cowardly self-seeking behavior that much more unbearable. I have murdered a great sword to gratify my own vanity, and the sword is the soul of the samurai."

Nagahisa tried to return Okisato's ring.

The inconsolable artist waved him off, continuing, "You, who are so noble, can't possibly appreciate or imagine the depths of my depravity. First, I must cleanse this vile body in the snow of Fujisan. After I am reborn in the sacred snow, I shall turn priest to make certain my vainglorious soul is clean. From this time forward, I shall never again make another armor. I will make swords to demonstrate to the iron spirit that I understand the gravity of my offense."

"But I repeat," Nagahisa said, "you are blameless. You won the contest."

"I will humbly dedicate the rest of my life to washing away this disgrace by taking the name Kotetsu."

Kotetsu turned to Lord Ishido, "Please tell the shogun of my disgraceful behavior. I will forge for him such a blade as will please him if it is my last act on earth. Please allow me to take the Yasutsugu as a pattern." The naked swordsmith fell to his knees once more, this time before Lord Ishido. "Please accept my apology, Ishido *sama*. Either that or dispatch me at once with your Mitsutada, although to die by such a blade is far more than I deserve."

"No, Kotetsu, as the representative of the glorious shogun, I extend to you the hand of friendship." Having said this, Ishido raised him. "On behalf of our illustrious and benevolent shogun, I accept your gracious offer to remake the Yasutsugu. Now enough of this humility, the contest was like no other. Let us shake hands and drink a flask of sake together. This sun is far too torrid to remain standing here."

Ishido wiped his head once again. He longed for his seat on the bench under Arima's dripping bamboos.

Kotetsu smiled, but his look was wistful and full of sadness at the loss of something beyond all price, namely, his honor.

"Alas, my lord, I wish I could, but I cannot. I am without honor until my rebirth. I am an unclean soul unworthy to touch the hem of your kimono, and until I exorcise the demon of my vile pride. I am unfit to associate with men, much less men of honor. I bid you farewell. I beg you to excuse me."

With that, Kotetsu removed his loincloth and left the stage as naked as the day he had been born. He walked through the astonished, speechless crowd. Without sandals, he trudged through the dust, carrying the irreparably damaged Yasutsugu blade, his right hand clenched around the body of the sword near the missing section. He trailed bright red drops of blood that mingled with the brown dust, throwing up tiny, quivering globules as he walked.

Hideo and Kobiyashi watched Okisato's self-imposed walk of degradation with open mouths. Not all of the dialog had been audible from where they had sat riveted to their folding stools. Other samurai, made desperate for refreshment by the broiling sun, had left, seeking shelter and water, but Kobiyashi had stood and advanced to the edge of the platform. Hideo had followed until they had been able to hear all of Okisato's confession, or at least most of it.

Both samurai watched the solitary the figure as he trudged through the dust toward Edo and Fujisan. The important events of the festival were over.

Neither spoke a word, so dumbfounded were they at everything that they witnessed. Finally, Kobiyashi felt compelled to break the silence.

"That was the most unbelievable thing I have ever seen in my life," he said.

Hideo shook himself like a dog waking from a dream.

"After the cutting test," he said, "I knew I'd fallen into a nightmare life, and what I just saw confirms it." A thought came to him. "What if none of what we did and saw today was real and soon we will wake up on our *tatamis* in the barracks and find out that all of this was nothing but a very long dream?"

"I could see that, but do you ever remember sweating this much in a dream?" He wiped the large beads of sweat from his neck, where his black hair lay damp like grass after a long, hard rain.

"No, I don't," said Hideo. "It was just a thought. Everything seems so strange, so unreal."

"It's the heat and this cursed sun. Let's hit the bathhouse, then the Fragrant Blossom."

"What are you going to use for money?"

"How about your offer to lend me one month's salary? Or did you forget because this is all a dream?"

"Now I know this is no dream. I agree to the loan, but you're buying."

Kobiyashi laughed and then broke off almost immediately.

"Okisato made me forget about Shinbei. How can we face Hana?"

"Hana thinks Shinbei is alive," said Hideo, and driven

by his truthful nature, he added, "Or at least she has a strong feeling he is. Why do you think I haven't been more distraught?"

"Because you are a good Buddhist?"

"I thank you for that. I try to be," said Hideo. He thought to himself, *A good Buddhist and a Kirishitan. I hope I never have to choose one or the other, but there really is no choice. I am a Kirishitan at heart.*

"I need a bath," Hideo said, brightening.

Kobiyashi sniffed with his large flat nose, and as he did, he sensed a faint aroma of vomit.

"Yes, I think you do."

The festival was nearly over. The crowd had dispersed, seeking shelter from the sun.

Workers were busily dismembering the stands, cleaning up every discarded scrap of wood, cloth, and paper for later use. Nothing was wasted; everything would be reused. Urine would tan leather, and feces would nourish vegetables.

Shigemasa was depressed. He always felt this way after a fair or event. At the beginning the events took on a life of their own, then they grew old and tired, and then they died. Afterward, there was nothing left but the remains, and then even they were gone, leaving nothing behind but memories, and with time, even these would fade and vanish, leaving only Prana.

As he continued to muse, he looked at Ishido, who gazed into the distance, following Okisato's every step.

Now that he is so wealthy, Ishido will surely retire. We will need a new Kaishakunin. He thought of Hideo but, just as swiftly, dismissed the notion. Iemitsu would never permit any relation of Oda—no matter how far removed—to have even a little power within the shogunate.

Still, he mused, *still, he would be an ideal choice. It's always best to have a young man.* He looked at Ishido's face, still handsome in middle age. *And there's still Arima to settle*, he said to

the process several times. She would need the Prana to succeed with this formidable old woman.

"Mistress, you are far too modest. Your house is perfection. The Fragrant Blossom is indeed fragrant and as lovely as a cherry blossom."

Hiroko was pleasantly surprised by Mariko's demeanor and tone. She had expected nothing but arrogance and abuse from this woman, who looked like a beautiful young man to her eyes. Mariko's graciousness and politeness disarmed her but only slightly. She had suffered much from the nobility and hated them passionately.

"To what does my humble house owe the honor of my lady's presence?"

"I am here for Hana," Mariko said, having nearly exhausted her limited capacity for pleasantries.

Hiroko clasped her crocodile-skinned, liver-spotted hands together in a gesture of supplication to heaven.

"My daughter, my beautiful only daughter. That is what my Hana is to me. I am but a poor teahouse owner, and her uncle brought her to me as a young girl. I taught her everything—everything—and raised her as my own." Hiroko forced big tears to roll down her sallow, flabby, wrinkled cheeks.

Mariko was sickened by this shameless posturing, but she let Hiroko go on.

"You ask me to give up my child? This is all too cruel, as you have the power to compel me." After delivering this impassioned lie, Hiroko began sobbing. The sobs were too much for Mariko.

"One does not beat their daughter like a naughty servant. Enough of this deceitful acting! Even with good cause, no one beats her daughter bloody."

Hiroko stopped crying. With a considerable tincture of the vulture in her voice, she said, "That's a lie. The girl lied to me again. You can't believe your own daughter these days."

"Would you like to call your daughter in?" Mariko replied

in a tone that would freeze hot water. "We can look at her and see the truth."

Hiroko left off acting, and a sly smile quickly replaced her carefully constructed look of grief.

"No. That won't be necessary. If you had children of your own you would understand that they need discipline above all other things."

Mariko was acutely aware of her childless state. If she were to have a son, there would be no question of a proper succession with or without her brother. Arima reminded her of this whenever they had one of their frequent disagreements. As a result, she was exquisitely sensitive on the subject. It was like an infected wound that caused great pain at the lightest touch. Whether Hiroko made the reference intentionally or not, Mariko neither knew nor cared. She only knew the jolt of pain that shot through her heart, stomach, and bowels.

She would have killed Hiroko under different circumstances. As it was, she contented herself with aristocratic loftiness. Looking at Hiroko as if she were the dirt under her feet, she used a tone that dripped with disdain.

"I detest this sort of stupidity. One need not experience things in order to express a valid opinion." She paused and smiled a thin, cruel smile so as to leave no room for doubt, "Executions, for example."

This was no idle threat. A word from Mariko to her father that Hiroko had spat on the name of Arima would certainly cost her her life. There was more than one person who could attest to Hiroko's hatred of the nobility. The old woman was thinking of all the men and women who could betray her. The list was long, far too long. Surrender was the only sensible course. The vulture vanished and the honey flowed as she said, "My lady, please accept my profound apologies. I am growing old and apt to allow my tongue to run away with my reason. Of course, my lady is right. I am nothing but a foolish old woman."

Having clearly won the argument, Mariko was, as always, gracious in victory. The ice melted.

"I accept your apology. We all make mistakes. Exactly how much is Hana's contract?"

Hiroko relaxed, she had been very close to the precipice. She decided that she would forgo the pleasure of a protracted negotiation.

"I paid Hana's uncle one hundred—"

Mariko cut her off. She had no intention of relinquishing her position.

"You lying old lizard, listen to me and listen well."

She lay down two rice paper packets of gold. The jet-black calligraphy and the clean whiteness of the crinkly paper was a perfect compliment to the deep red of the cinnabar table. Hiroko was enchanted but tried to look disinterested.

"There is two hundred *koban*, payment in full as of now. If you utter a word of complaint you will be arrested for sedition, and the Fragrant Blossom will have a new owner."

"Gracious lady, forgive a stupid old woman's love for her daughter."

She handed a lengthy contract to Mariko, who tore it into shreds, which drifted like falling leaves to the spotless *honoki* wood floor.

"Hana is now a guest in your house," she said haughtily. "Treat her as such."

Hiroko decided that she preferred death to being scorned in her own house.

"Lady," she said with as little deference as she dared, "it is unseemly to abuse me in my own house."

Realizing that, by going too far, she was being inconsistent with the Buddha and her own dignity, Mariko relented.

"Very well, I will go to her myself."

With that, she swept out of the room, leaving Hiroko to gloat over the gold.

Chapter 20

Lord Arima's Study

Lord Arima paced back and forth in his study but found no answer to his problem.

His study was large; the floors were polished cedar, a natural red, and fragrant. The walls were also cedar as were the shelves and even the ceiling. The frames of the oiled rice paper doors and windows were cedar as well. A particularly large and fine-gilded, wooden Buddha stood in one corner facing out, the beautiful, sinuous fingers of its right hand touched and were raised in benediction. Candles and oil lamps flickered, and jasmine incense burned in Ming porcelain burners. The walls were mostly bare, with only two scrolls of calligraphy. Even they were elegant in their simplicity; each showed a single Buddhist Sanskrit character. The shelves were filled with scrolls in carefully labeled categories—Shinbei had spent many hours organizing and writing labels in his lovely brushwork, which had been much to his liking, because he disliked what he regarded as busywork and sought solitude for his art rather than Lord Arima's company. In the middle of the floor were four *tatami* mats of the finest quality and a long, low table of shining black lacquer, bare except for a superb *suzuri bako* of magnificent gold lacquer that had a single gold horse, perfectly rendered, which seemed to prance across the cover.

"Where the devil is Mariko?"

He had left the palace earlier after giving her clear instructions to meet him in his study after the final contest. He worried that she might think that he actually had executed Shinbei. He knew from the guard that she had visited him early in the morning, but he also knew from her maid that she had gone to bed just before sunrise. If she thought that he had killed Shinbei, she would be very upset, even though he was certain that she was not having an affair with him. Lord Arima knew that she blamed him for sending Diasuke away and for making her break off her relationship with Hideo.

Faced with the situation as it now stood, he thought that the second may have been a false move. It might have been much better to encourage her, even allowing them to marry. Of course, such a union would constitute a very serious threat to Iemitsu. The Oda name still had currency with many samurai, and the embers left by the Shimabara insurrection still smoldered, even in Arima's own province. He had no notion of Hideo's devotion to the Kirishitan faith. If he had, he would have almost certainly blessed the marriage.

Arima very much wanted to share the truth about Shinbei with Mariko. His selection and grooming of an heir was taking far too long, and the presence of Lord Ishido indicated that Iemitsu had made a decision. His hand was being forced.

Two men were already dead, and it was increasingly likely that many more would die before the sun set that very evening. Arima was determined that they would be Tokugawa men rather than his own. If only he had a commitment from the Dutchman, he could arrest Ishido and his retinue, detain Shigemasa, and mobilize the province.

Seeing his samurai backed by gaijin forces with their iron cannon and quick-firing muskets and weapons impervious to rain, other dissatisfied *daimyo*—and there were many—would flock like so many crows to the Arima banner. Oda Hideo was no more than an emergency strategy if Hendrik failed him. Lord Arima had all but given up on the Spanish. The assassin was almost certainly Spanish. The elaborate crucifix was evidence of that. Then again he could have been a Dutchman who simply wore the talisman to deceive were he to fail or be captured.

No, he thought, *he had to be a Spaniard. No Dutchman would kill himself. They did not have it in them. Their skin was too pale and their blood too cold.*

Killing Ishido would send a message to the *daimyo* that the shogunate was too weak to protect even its most valued officials.

But, Arima said to himself, *I am also responsible for the personal safety of all officials in my province attending my festival.* Initially he had considered the possibility that he had been the intended target but had immediately dismissed the idea. Now he was not so sure. It was getting late in the day, and there was no word from the damned Dutchman.

He stopped pacing and sat cross-legged at the low table. Looking at the prancing horse, he debated whether to write but found himself too agitated. He reached under the table where he kept his smoking pouch and silver pipe. Lord Arima disliked smoking, so much so that the habit was forbidden within the palace. He looked on it as a weakness that was inconsistent with Bushido, a womanish vice that sapped a samurai's strength and dignity.

"Do as I command, not as I do," he said ruefully.

He had taken up smoking to calm his nerves during Shimabara. Then he had quit and resumed; it was a yearly pattern. Hendrik had sent him a packet of surpassingly fragrant and strong tobacco called Latakia some months before, and it was black and moist as he filled the tiny bowl. He took a rush over to a lamp and lighted the pipe, discarding the burnt reed. He drew the powerful smoke deep into his lungs and exhaled, blowing an almost perfect smoke ring, which hung in the air before the Buddha.

The strong tobacco had an immediate loosening effect on his bowels, and for a moment, he thought he might have to defecate, but the feeling passed, and he drew another equally deep draught of smoke. This time he held his breath for a long while, and the tobacco made him lightheaded and dizzy. Then as he breathed out, it seemed that all of his thoughts were blown out through his mouth to hang in the incense-filled, heated air to be regarded by the smiling face of the Buddha.

As he relaxed, he once again examined his motives.

Why even bother? he wondered. *All physical things are only illusion. My body, which is decaying, is an illusion. The very process of decay is illusion. If I should succeed in becoming shogun, it matters nothing. Or if I die tonight, it matters even less. If Daisuke were here, that would be something, but still an illusion.*

Then he thought about the man he had ordered to be dressed in Shinbei's filthy kimono and killed. Hendrik had sent him as a messenger about the danger of dealing with the Spanish. The small, wiry Nihonjin had also carried a sealed instruction ordering his own death. The man's name was Yamazaki,and he was a Kirishitan. Not only did he make no secret of that fact, but he proudly told an astonished Lord Arima that it was his duty to "spread the gospel"—or words to that effect. This made the sealed order entirely superfluous.

The man was obviously mad, and Arima wasted no time before throwing him into a windowless cell and gagging him so that his dangerous teachings would not infect his guards with the contagion of Kirishitanity. He would have embraced Hideo as Krishitan despite his deep distrust of Kirishitans in general in order to bind the Spanish to his rebellion, but certainly the Lord would never permit any dissemination of the doctrine among his soldiers. The madman's death would undoubtedly be put on a long and detailed list of negative actions that adversely affected his karma. Arima was quite resigned to the fact that he had accumulated sufficient bad karma to ensure that he would be reborn as either an *eta* or something worse.

Yamazaki had not protested when he was seized. Quite the contrary. He said something like, "I am blessed to be tortured as was my savior, and if I die in his service, I will not perish but have life everlasting." Now he was dead, cut in two by the shogun's Myoju.

Lord Arima refilled his pipe and relit the half-burnt rush. Puffing deeply, he continued his meditation. Although he was overjoyed by the public destruction of Iemitsu's Yasutsugu, he was less pleased by Ishido's forbearance in regard to the enormous gambling debt. Naturally, he was immensely relieved to not lose such a sum, but he hated conceding the moral high-ground to the man who had, in all likelihood, come to invite him onward, failing some solution that he could not conceive of himself.

What did it all amount to in the final analysis? Very little, he mused. Suddenly, Arima was struck by the similarity between the little Kirishitan samurai's talk of rebirth and Okisato's, or rather Kotetsu's, need to wash away his transgressions in the pure, cold snow of Fujisan. One could hardly imagine two more entirely different people, yet both would experience rebirth: one through physical death, and the other through a spiritual death of the self that he had been for decades.

Well, he said to himself, *Yamazaki already knows what it is to die*, and then some part of him badly wanted the odd little Kirishitan Nihonjin spy to have his heart's desire come true. He sincerely wished that he would be in paradise with his gaijin savior. Then as he looked through the holes in the smoke rings he was blowing, he wanted to be with Kotetsu, high up in the snows of Fujisan, taking off all his clothes, washing away the accumulated bad karma of all the years as lord of the province and in that thin, cold, sacred air, experiencing his own rebirth.

He could almost feel the cold air on his face when he awoke with a start. He had nearly fallen asleep on his feet.

"Now where in the name of Amida Buddha is that daughter of mine?"

Lord Arima carefully put his pipe down on a small blue underglazed dish and struck a copper gong. Immediately, a powerful samurai walked into the study. Ignoring the smoke, which stung his eyes, the soldier looked at Lord Arima impassively.

"Ah, Sato," said Lord Arima. "I was going to send you to find my daughter, but on second thought, I will not seek to alter her karma. You may withdraw."

Sato withdrew, walking backward until he was through the entrance. *The lord seems very preoccupied. It must be the festival and this accursed heat. It's making everyone mad. Besides, since she dismissed her guards, no one follows Mariko anymore.*

Lord Arima walked to a small, heavily ironbound, *honoki* wood chest. He placed a long iron shim lengthwise in the cylindrical wrought iron lock. Reaching into the chest, he pulled out a brocade silk bag that was intricately tied with a purple silk cord. He untied the cord, opened the sack, and drew out a dagger mounted in a simple wooden storage handle and scabbard. The appraisal, beautifully written on the *saya* in large brushstrokes, had been given by one of the more reliable Honami sword appraisers. The two characters chiseled into the tang would have been instantly recognizable to any samurai.

He reseated himself and drew the blade from the *saya*, which he laid on the cinnabar carefully so as to leave no mark. The blade was thick and almost chubby with an exuberant temper in the Soshu style. The blade was pierced through with two slots that ended near the base of the blade in a sort of half-moon. The steel was a bluish color. The peg holding the tang in the handle was of black horn and fitted very tightly.

Lord Arima would have preferred his Nagamitsu *tanto,* but now that was in Lord Ishido's sash. But then again there was something poetic and altogether fitting and proper about using a blade whose very possession was punishable by death. Not that Lord Arima cared, but all swords signed by the swordsmith Muramasa had been declared illegal by the Tokugawa shogunate. All blades so signed were required to have the offending signature removed or defaced. Ieyasu's uncle had committed *seppuku* with a Muramasa, and Ieyasu had been badly cut with a Muramasa sword, so they were thought to be unlucky for the Tokugawa. The previous Lord Arima had borne no love for the Tokugawa and Ieyasu and never disfigured his dagger. Lord Arima grew up knowing about the *tanto,* but he had kept its existence secret, even from Mariko, knowing her as he did. She would flaunt it at the first opportunity, bringing trouble on their house.

The Spanish ship was laid up in a sheltered cove where Arima had played as a young boy. He had loved the creatures that lived in the shallow tide pools. The young lord had never ceased to be delighted by the bright colors of the anemones, hermit crabs, and starfish. He had liked nothing better than to poke his finger into a fat anemone and feel its tentacles curl around his finger. The sea in the cove was always cold—sometimes shockingly so—and there was a deadly riptide that had once carried one of his samurai far out to the open ocean where he had drowned.

No, he thought, *I can't betray Nippon to the Spanish, no matter how much I hate the Tokugawa. I know that now.*

He had paid an immense sum in gold for modern Spanish muskets and pistols, weapons that did not need a lighted match to fire, only a flint stone. He simply could not permit Spanish soldiers to march to Kyoto and then, Buddha forbid, to

Kamakura and destroy the Great Buddha, replace the temple with a Kirishitan church, and return to humble the emperor. If he did so, even if he were to become shogun, the Arima name would be a curse spat out like poison, synonymous with the word *traitor*. To prevent himself from changing his mind, he had ordered that Yamazaki be dressed in Shinbei's clothing and trussed up shortly before midday.

"Now Yamazaki can tell no one. The Spanish guns are mine, and no one's the wiser."

Hendrik and the Dutch East India Company were a different story. They desired trade rather than conquest. The siege of Shimabara had proved that. The company had turned its great guns on the castle walls and reduced them to rubble—something all Iemitsu's armies had failed to do. Hendrik had directed the navy in the company's name.

Lord Arima thought the Dutchman had even had an affair with Mariko. He liked the genial Hollander as far as a Nihonjin could like a gaijin. There were several obstacles to using Hendrik. One was the friendship between Hendrik and Iemitsu, although the shogun had no friends worthy of the name. The other more serious issue was the disinclination of the Dutch forces to leave their base in Java.

Unlike the Spanish, they did not conquer in the name of their god. Arima understood perfectly that Kirishitans had their sects as did Buddhists, and they could and did kill each other, just as Buddhists did, in flagrant disregard of express commandments against murder. At one time, he had considered an alliance with the Portuguese Jesuits in Macao, but their power had declined over the years. Hendrik and the Hollanders were "the last shot in his locker," as the Dutchman had told him.

Arima was convinced that the assassin was sent by Iemitsu to kill Lord Ishido and give the shogun a very public reason to remove him. Iemitsu was the Nihonjin most able to use a gaijin as a tool of policy. There was nothing that worried the shogun more than the possibility of a Kirishitan insurgency. Arima knew his domain was home to more *kakure* Kirishitans than any province in Nippon. To him, they were a curiosity as well as a possible resource.

If only young Oda were a Kirishitan, then I would have had something, he said to himself. He wondered what it would take to have Hideo publicly announce allegiance to the Kirist and raise the Arima banner. Certainly Mariko would be more than sufficient, and they seemed to love one another. *Yes. I have been a colossal fool to separate them.*

The Arima line was no older or nobler than the Fujiwara, and Oda had made himself dictator of Nippon. Nobunaga would be revered and remembered for centuries. And Arima actually liked Hideo's feat of arms at the festival. Taking the place of that insolent bastard Nagahisa, whom Arima longed to have in his dungeon, was masterful. *It proves that legitimate or illegitimate, blood will out.*

Yes, Hideo has proven himself worthy of my princess. I will remove my bar to their happiness, assuming happiness is possible in this illusory world of sorrow and pain. No, I will not send her to Hendrik. Damn the girl! Where is she?

If Hendrik sent him news that the Dutch had landed on his shores, he would lead his samurai to Edo, sweeping all before him. There was still time, but part of him knew it was no more than a very bright dream that would fade as quickly as a sunset in the dead of winter.

He looked deeply into the steel of the Muramasa. Therein lay death, and the prospect was less frightening than alluring.

Arima had never had a close advisor; his father, the previous lord, had taught him very well. His father firmly believed that if he needed advice, he could consult nothing wiser or more reliable than his own death. He personified his death and instructed his son to do the same, telling him that a better counselor simply did not exist.

Arima had almost committed *seppuku* following the death of his wife, and there were many times when he regretted not doing so. After the final argument with Daisuke, he had taken out the Muramasa. He had even donned the special white death kimono, but just as one part of him had looked forward to the release, another part had still had an interest in carrying on the Arima line and outwitting Iemitsu.

If he had not loved his wife and held her in such high honor, having an heir would have been very easy, but he did, and there was no changing that fact. Staring at the frosty temper line, which rose and fell above an edge that was keen enough to slice paper it merely touched, he realized that he was famished. This made him laugh aloud.

Here I am contemplating my own death, and my body tells me it is hungry and in need of nourishment, he thought. *How utterly absurd! How typical of our ridiculous lives.* He laughed again. Then he struck the gong with his knuckle, and the big samurai appeared noiselessly.

The man saw the Muramasa, its handle wrapped in white rice paper in preparation for *seppuku*, but he said nothing, and even his eyes were expressionless.

"Yamamoto," Arima said, "Bring me a bowl of fish soup, if there is any, and some pickled radish." He thought for a moment. "Yes, and a flask of sake—the good one from the New Year's barrel."

The samurai said nothing, bowing low and retiring. This time, he turned his back on Lord Arima to give him greater privacy.

Chapter 21

A Village

The village was small and consisted of a number of huts arranged along a dirt street. The village was poor but clean. Inside one of the thatched-roof dwellings, Asamu lay on a pallet stuffed with hay on the hard-packed dirt floor. The inside of her hut was lit by some rushes that protruded from a bowl of oil. The only real furniture, besides the pallet, was a large iron pot that hung from forks formed by an iron tripod over a fire pit. The ceiling had been blackened by the smoke of many fires.

The embers in the pit were cooling as a young peasant man entered. He walked quietly to Asamu and gently awakened her. She opened her eyes and, seeing a stranger, blinked but did not stir.

"Young man," she asked in a voice whose strength belied her deep wrinkles, "could you please pour me a cup of water?"

She motioned with a withered, large-veined hand to an earthenware pitcher and rude cup.

"Certainly, mother," the man said, as he did what she asked.

She drank thirstily and then said with a mixture of pride and asperity, "Boy, I am not your mother. My son is a samurai in the service of Lord Arima. He is the lord's scribe. But I thank you for the water." She looked at him carefully. "Do you live in the village? I don't think I know you."

Asamu rarely left her home, preferring that the villagers come to her, which they still did to buy her delectable, homebrewed sake.

"No," said the young man, "I am just passing through."

"You look to be my son's age. He has not come to see me for a long time, but then his duties command him, and this is as it should be. If only you knew the sacrifices I have made for my son."

Shinbei could scarcely bear wearing peasant garb. Captain Yamashita had brought the none-too-clean bundle that morning to his dungeon cell. Shinbei had plied him with questions, but Yamashita said nothing except, "I advise you to flee if you value your life. Go back to your village. Remain there until you are sent for. These are the lord's orders. Say nothing to anyone. You have the lady's purse. Now go."

As soon as he was released from his prison cell, Shinbei had wasted no time obeying the captain's instructions, though it had taken him most of the day to reach the village. He had not seen his mother since her long illness, and he was ashamed of being seen in peasant clothes. He was a good samurai and thought little of either his ill treatment or his strange departure. Life was like that. *One moment everything was nearly perfect. You had Hana, you were trusted and petted by your liege lord, and then without warning, you were arrested, beaten, thrown in a dungeon, not knowing whether you would live to see the morning, only to be given peasant garb and be sent walking to your village.*

All of the way to the village on his seemingly interminable walk, Shinbei had kept repeating the mantra, "Hana was right. Hana was right." If he had listened to her, none of the horrors of the night's arrest and beating, imprisonment, and humiliation would have taken place.

The bird's egg on his head throbbed. He had seen by the torchlight that Mariko had been of the verge of laughing at his sorry state. She had given him her purse because she had promised to assist with Asamu's medicine, and arrogant and careless as she was, she valued her word.

Hana had been right about everything.

The nobility cared nothing for the samurai except to use them as grist for the mill of their personal schemes. When Lord Arima initially learned of his talent for calligraphy, he should have—if he had had any sense—spilled ink on all his work, broken his fingers, feigned a seizure—anything to prove he was no more than a common soldier. Instead, he had made his best obeisance and eagerly accepted the lord's suggestion that he come to the palace and draft correspondence. Everything had seemed to be going so well, and there was the promise of extra pay, which would go to Asamu, who was forced to curtail the food business and lived on what was left of her illegal sake sales.

On hearing of his mother's plight, Mariko had offered her help. Shinbei knew of her liaison with Hideo and its tragic end, as did the entire barracks and all the people of the town. Her affair with Hendrik was known to very few, and Shinbei thought that was the reason for his downfall. What he had difficulty understanding was that not only was he still alive but Lord Arima had inexplicably allowed him to return to his village. Of course, Lord Arima's spies were everywhere, and certainly there were watchers even in Asamu's village.

Shinbei missed Hana, and her absence, coupled with the

fact she thought he was dead, was like a dagger thrusting through his entrails as the distance between them increased.

He hadn't eaten for nearly an entire day. Three times since he had left the lord's dungeon, as the punishing hot sun rose, Shinbei had had to squat by the roadside, shielding himself behind desiccated weeds, blighted trees, and brown grasses, voiding painfully, resulting in nothing more than a watery mucous of pink tinged with blood. The stress of his arrest, beating, and confinement had concentrated in his bowels, and although he had escaped the ignominy of using the clay pot in front of Mariko, he had been seized with agonizing cramps as soon as Yamashita had left him at the outskirts of the town.

After the third episode, Shinbei had thought of a way to get a message to Hana. Doubtless, she had been tormented by rumors of his grisly death, which would have no doubt reached her through samurai privy to barracks talk. She might have heard of his arrest, and knowing her fiery temper well, already tried to accost or even assault Mariko. In spite of all his efforts to convince her otherwise, Hana persisted in the delusion that Mariko wanted to have an affair with him. Shinbei knew he was handsome, and he was certainly not insensible of the looks Mariko gave him from time to time. However, like so many good-looking men, he readily assumed that all women were interested in having sex with him as opposed to merely appreciating good looks as they would a fine gelding or stallion.

Lord Arima had allowed him to see Hendrik, the gaijin, but any correspondence between them was written by the lord, who had kept all matters concerning the gaijin closely guarded. The barbarian was courteous and, to Shinbei's surprise, spoke Nipponese and did not smell. Perhaps he should have reported what he knew to the shogunal authorities, but he did not want to betray his liege lord, and more importantly, he didn't know very much. Besides, Shinbei didn't want to harm Mariko. A part of him, the self-destructive part, considered the possibility of having an affair with her. He was better-looking than Oda, although he admitted that Hideo was a better swordsman. Oda was the grandson of the dictator, while Asamu had been forced to sell food and drink in order to ensure Shinbei's status as a samurai.

So much had happened in a very short time, and here he was face-to-face with his mother, whom he had feared would be close to death.

Mariko's purse felt heavy in his belt. He hadn't even dared to look inside on his way.

His feet were accustomed to long, punishing marches, and the soles were horny with calluses, so he was not crippled by his lack of sandals. His feet were in harmony with his mode of dress, a noblewoman's finely embroidered silk purse was not.

Asamu looked suspiciously at the strange peasant.

"You don't happen to know my son?"

"No," said Shinbei. "A noble lady, Lord Arima's daughter, gave me this purse to bring to you."

He handed the heavy purse to Asamu, who opened the flap and drew out a bright gold *koban*. She bit it and, satisfied at its purity, replaced it, staring at her disguised son. Without further comment, Asamu stood and delivered a resounding slap to Shinbei's jaw, which caused the egg on his head to hurt so badly that he nearly fainted.

"Do you think I am a fool? That I can't recognize my own son's voice! What is the meaning of this? Why are you dressed like some miserable farmer? Was it for this that I ruined my hands and my beauty cooking night and day?" All of this was said in the same tone of voice that had made it a relief for Shinbei's father to slip away into death. Stunned by the blow, he had remained silent. Asamu picked up an iron poker and raised it above her head.

"I send you away a samurai, and you return a peasant? Explain yourself, or son or no son, I will beat you senseless."

Asamu did not realize that she had already carried out her threat, and as she raged on, Shinbei collapsed at her long,

protected from the world until you were born. You owe me your very life, and you talk of loyalty?"

"Yes," said Shinbei, "You and father taught me the way of the samurai, of Bushido."

For the first time since he had entered his mother's hut, Shinbei saw her angry face relax, and she allowed a faint smile to make the wrinkled corners of her habitually downturned, lemon-sucking mouth turn upward.

Asamu went to a corner of the hut, bent down, and pushed aside a very well-worn *tatami.* Underneath was a sort of door made of pine boards. She lifted it up and, rummaging around, drew out a black kimono. It bore the Arima *mon* on the back.

Looking at her son with a gentle expression, she said, "You are still a samurai in the service of the lord?"

Shinbei's avowal that he was and remained a samurai was not enough; Asamu had to hear it again. After the shock of seeing him return disguised as a poor farmer, she could not hear it often enough. With his soft untanned underarm smarting from the hot soup burn, Shinbei wondered why he had come. It was obvious that his mother wasn't dying. In fact, she seemed to be in full possession of her strength. Her blow to his face proved that, as did her sarcastic comments about the doctor and the herbalist. He had sacrificed nearly all of his pay, all of the gold he had been given by Lord Arima to keep his mouth shut about the gaijin. His devotion to her was the cause of serious discord between him and Hana; nearly all of their arguments had Asamu at the core. Already, he was tired of Asamu's physical and verbal abuse, but then, he had nowhere else to go.

"Take off those peasant's rags," she said. "This was your father's kimono. I saved it all these years. I can only hope and pray that you are worthy of it."

Shinbei was reluctant to disrobe in front of his mother, but nevertheless, he shed his ragged clothes and donned his father's kimono. Asamu reached up and touched a stray lock of fine, black hair that had fallen in a long curve across his handsome face. At this unexpected tenderness from his mother, a large tear made its way down his cheek unnoticed.

The intense heat did not diminish with the approach of evening. If anything, it increased as the earth radiated all the stored sun's rays back into the torrid atmosphere.

"Praise Buddha!" Asamu said. "My son has returned a samurai. This is a good day. This heat, which all others spend their time cursing, feels good to my old bones."

She hugged Shinbei, and the rare gesture made him feel like a wooden doll was embracing him, his mother made herself so stiff. Asamu quickly broke away.

"Hoki," she said to the boy, "heat some of the better sake. My son must be thirsty from his journey."

Soon the flask was heating in the embers, giving off a most delicious steam. Though Shinbei knew he was very badly in need of food and drink, the few spoonfuls of fish soup had somewhat satisfied his most pressing needs for nourishment. More food could wait. He was worried almost sick about Hana.

Asamu sensed his anxiety.

"The sake is nearly ready. What's wrong?"

Shinbei was reticent to speak of his concerns about Hana, knowing that Asamu violently disapproved of the affair. There was always the chance that his mother's smoldering temper might erupt. He knew that she had been about to beat him senseless with the iron poker.

"I must get a message to Hana. I left without telling her."

Asamu made a face like she swallowed vinegar.

"Don't tell me you're still lusting after that whore."

"Hana is not a whore," he said, shrinking back and expecting the worst.

"Every samurai should have a whore before he takes a

wife," she said almost gaily. "Hoki," she said to the boy, "Can you find Lord Arima's palace?"

Hoki smiled at Shinbei to indicate that he was on Shinbei's side. Asamu treated the lad well enough; she fed and clothed him and did not beat him too severely. Hoki quickly learned that Asamu's tongue was far fiercer than her cane but that neither was fatal.

"Well," she said to her son, "Don't mind me. Tell the boy what you want, and he will tell it to your precious whore."

Hoki went to Shinbei, who bent down and whispered in Hoki's right ear. When he was done, the lad nodded.

"Remember, the Fragrant Blossom. It is near the festival grounds by the river, ask for the Lady Hana." Asamu reached down and held up one of the shining gold *ryo*.

"Go and return quickly, and I will buy you new clothes."

At this, Hoki shot out of the hut like an arrow speeding to its mark.

Chapter 22

The Cabin

Hendrik sat at his mahogany desk; he peered though the long, brass barrel of his microscope, examining the wing of a particularly colorful butterfly.

As he twisted the finely knurled wheel to bring the exquisite wing structure into clear focus, Hendrik could see God's hand in the beauty and regularity of its color and form. He once more found himself in complete agreement with Leonardo DaVinci, the most renowned Italian inventor and painter.

Only a fool would doubt the existence of God when all nature proclaims his handiwork.

Through the wall of his intense concentration, he thought he heard a tapping sound. He had left the strictest orders not to disturb him under any circumstances.

"What is it? Damn your eyes," he said as he opened the bolted door.

A diminutive midshipman, who was barely ten years old—

Slijkerman, he thought—said in an abashed tone, "Sorry, sir, but there is a Jap samurai to see you. I told him the captain is ashore, but he wouldn't take no. He gave me this."

Gerrit, for that was the boy's Kirishitan name, handed him a massy piece of gold. It was one of Shigemasa's collar emblems.

Safely ensconced in Hendrik's cabin a few moments later, Shigemasa seated himself opposite the Dutchman. He held out his hand, and without a word, Hendrik returned the gold insignia, which Shigemasa immediately replaced on his kimono.

"The little boy was most insistent about your privacy," said Shigemasa, "He finally agreed to disturb you. I wanted you to be certain. There are assassins about."

Hendrik's interest was piqued.

Knowing that Shigemasa spoke fluent Dutch, he did not respond in Japanese.

"Assassins at the festival?" he asked. "Please tell me all about it."

"This afternoon, a Kirishitan barbarian, wearing a large cross with a Christ crucified, attempted to kill Lord Ishido."

"Who would authorize such a thing?"

"I thought you might know," said Shigemasa.

"Lord Arima," said Hendrik.

"Possibly, but that would only hasten the inevitable. Actually, I must confess that you were my first suspect," Shigemasa said genially.

"Whatever for?" said Hendrik.

"That's what I couldn't figure out."

"If you can't figure out my motive," Hendrik laughed, "then I don't have one."

Shigemasa laughed as well.

"I know."

Hendrik thought a long moment.

"A short glass of gin?"

"I thought you'd never ask."

Pouring the gin into a blown-glass beaker, Hendrik asked, "Have you considered the possibility that the intended victim was Lord Arima? I understand the Spanish feel he is not upholding his end of the bargain."

"I thought he already had the guns from the San Cristobal."

"I agree with you."

"Of course, neither of us knows exactly what the Spanish captain agreed or did not agree to."

"What about Iemitsu?" Hendrik asked.

"I seriously doubt he would trust a gaijin agent, and even if he did, he would tell me."

"I wouldn't be too sure," Hendrik said. "I saw him in Tokyo. He has changed since Shimabara. To be honest, he frightened me."

"Iratia princeps mors est."

"The wrath of the prince is death. I compliment you, Shigemasa; you have been studying your Latin. Tell me," Hendrik continued, "That boy, the grandson of Nobunaga, is he aware of anything?"

"You would know better than I would." Shigemasa smiled. "You have Arima's daughter in common." Hendrik looked surprised.

"If I didn't know better, I'd say you were spying on me."

"If I didn't spy on you," said Shigemasa, "I would lose my position."

"Position? Hell," said Hendrik, "You'd lose more than that. So, I repeat, does young Oda know anything?"

"He might know about you. Then again, Arima's daughter has not been seen with him for months."

"I still can't help thinking it was Iemitsu. By killing Lord Ishido, using a gaijin, he has the perfect pretext for seizing Arima's province, all the time inciting hatred for barbarians and Kirishitans. It is classic Sun Tzu. Create an incident, make people fear foreign domination, and label anyone who is opposed to the resulting war as a traitor."

"And if Lord Arima dies," Shigemasa said, "it is equally beneficial in making the people think that the gaijin will use the resulting confusion to invade Kyushu, rouse the Kirishitans, and replace the Buddha with their god."

"Precisely," Hendrik said. "What if both Arima and Ishido were assassinated by a barbarian?"

"Then so much the better for the shogunate," said Shigemasa, "Using your theory of course."

"Of course," said Hendrik.

"Then it's either the Spanish or, Buddha forbid, the shogun," said Shigemasa.

"As I said, civil war is bad for trade, so you can rule out the company, which means me," said Hendrik.

He glanced at Hendrik's mechanical clock.

"I wish there were more clocks in my country," said Shigemasa.

"We make them with Japanese numbers engraved on the dial."

"I know," said Shigemasa, "They're so very expensive. I see it's nearly six o'clock. That's how it is said, ne?" No matter how much he tried to suppress it, Shigemasa could not help attaching the Nipponese expression to many sentences. *Ne* had an almost infinite variety of meanings, from "isn't it so" to "it certainly is" depending on the degree of nuance and the subtlety of who was employing the idiom in any given sentence.

"One more thing before I—" he broke off. "Shimatta, I almost forgot to thank you for the most excellent gin."

"Would you like a bottle?" said Hendrik. "Courtesy of the Company. We might not see each other for a long time."

"You know," said Shigemasa with great cordiality, "You are right. I will most certainly accept your generous gift. And in return, I will give you some counsel. If I were you, I would leave these waters as soon as convenient, and I would not return."

Hendrik immediately understood the implied threat, however genial the messenger. This was the real reason for Shigemasa's visit. Clearly, the shogunate suspected him of clandestine dealings with Lord Arima and even the hated Spanish.

Hendrik was just as happy to leave Japan as to stay. Actually, he was far happier to leave and return to his pepper plantation outside Djakarta. He loved the rich, tropical green of the mountains and the almost infinite variety of lepidoptera. Even aboard ship, the heat made life miserable, and here the fall of night brought no relief. At home, the night fell like a soft, black curtain over the fierce heat of the day, tigers prowled in the cooler air, and the darkness pulsated with the songs of birds and insects. Japan had been dried up by the continuing drought. He could see the results through his telescope, even without setting foot on dry land.

His affair with Mariko had been brief—so short that it was more of an encounter than an affair. She had come to him one night, dressed in the midshipman's uniform he had sent to her earlier. Boarding the foreign ship had been easy for her. The ship was docked with only a skeleton crew aboard. He met her at the gangplank and escorted her without incident to his cabin. He recalled her body—the arm muscles strengthened by practice with the bow, the small firm breasts, and the incredibly large nipples. She was acrobatic and so aggressive that he was almost unable to perform. She was everything his mistress in Batavia was not.

He never saw her naked again. Her cinnamon breath intoxicated him, and he would have left the company and married her if she had asked him to. She had everything he admired: power, grace, and noble birth. They could have been legendary like Ieyasu's Englishman, Will Adams. He had known that she loved a young samurai, who was the grandson of Nobunaga and everything Hendrik was not. Hideo was young, Japanese, handsome, and born of an illustrious, noble family.

Hendrik thought of Lord Arima.

Yes, he is a strange one. All his troubles could be solved by remarriage and a son. Though not of gentle birth, Hendrik understood inheritance and succession. Never would he have dared to suggest a marriage to Lord Arima, but for the life of him, he could not fathom the lord's inexplicable unwillingness to marry. Mariko had told him that her father didn't even keep a regular concubine but insisted on a different woman each time he felt compelled to seek female companionship.

Thank God I'm not a nobleman having to worry about my successors carrying on. In my case, a simple will suffices for all such concerns, thought Hendrik.

Shigemasa waited patiently for Hendrik to answer, comment, or remain silent. He felt certain that he could depend on Kobiyashi to make him aware of any unusual events in Arima's barracks, having sworn him to a secrecy so complete that even Hideo, then again especially and particularly Hideo, would be unaware of anything that passed between them. In return for his allegiance to the shogun rather than to Lord Arima, Kobiyashi would receive the thing he wanted more than his own life: Koetsu's contract. Shigemasa had asked him for his heart's desire, and Kobiyashi had told him. The pact was that simple and straightforward.

At first, the young man had demurred, saying it was contrary to Bushido to go against the interests of his liege lord, but Shigemasa explained to him that by serving the shogun, he was serving the nation, which, during the Tokugawa era, was entirely honorable and in perfect harmony with Bushido.

"Yes," Shigemasa had said. "A hundred years ago, you would have been entirely correct to cleave to Arima, but times change."

Then Kobiyashi had expressed his unhappiness at having to keep secrets from Hideo, but Shigemasa had consoled him by guaranteeing the fact that Hideo had kept secrets about Lord Arima and a barbarian, knowledge that could make Kobiyashi into a *ronin*. In the end, Shigemasa had completely convinced him that right action, in Buddhist terms, consisted of shifting his loyalty from his lord to Iemitsu.

Shigemasa had told him that Captain Yamashita had also decided that the interests of the nation must take precedence over the concerns of an individual *daimyo,* and this had further cemented Kobiyashi's decision.

Shigemasa regretted that Iemitsu hadn't given him any specific instructions about Hendrik, but Iemitsu never gave detailed orders to any of his officials on sensitive missions. They were expected to improvise, and if they failed, dismissal, denial, and consequences would ensue. As usual, the shogun offered Zen parables that could be interpreted in any number of ways. His father, Hidetada, had been more open, and his grandfather, Ieyasu, had actually been loveable, but Shigemasa was biased. Iemitsu was a better administrator than his father and possibly even than Ieyasu. Iemitsu could convolute any problem to his advantage by thoroughly confusing everyone else involved. His orders were specific but always open to interpretation.

When Shigemasa had asked him about Lord Arima, Iemitsu had said, "His father served my grandfather at Sekigahara, and the son will do the same in the present affair." One thing Iemitsu made crystal clear. He had said, "Shigemasa, you must find every gun of the new Spanish design. If you must find the San Cristobal, and then burn it. If you must destroy Arima's palace, destroy it. If you must devastate the entire province, then do so. Not a single gun of this type must exist in Nippon, except in my arsenal. See to it, though it costs me a thousand gold *koban*!"

Shigemasa knew that Iemitsu's comment about the gold was theatrical, his way of saying that the guns were of signal importance and failure was not an option. Shigemasa had two

Hendrik drained, refilled, and drained his own beaker once more. His handsome, tanned face suddenly looked drawn and prematurely old. His nerves were overwrought. Shigemasa's timing was inopportune. For the second time in one day, Shigemasa was taken completely aback by a strong man's singular behavior.

Images of decapitated men and women whirled through Hendrik's mind's eye, as they had a decade earlier through the telescope. Their vividness had not decreased with the passage of years. At any other time, he would have relocked them away in the deepest darkest strongbox of his memory, but he was sick of the heat, tired of the game, and therefore vulnerable. And there were the little children; he could see them—their tiny mouths screaming—and the wave of remorse crested and then crashed, crushing him. He placed his long beautiful hands over his face and began to weep so bitterly that it seemed to Shigemasa that his heart must burst asunder. He cried for each and every man, woman, and child that he had maimed that day. Hendrik couldn't stop himself; the emotions were too overwhelming.

It must be this unnatural heat, thought Shigemasa. *First Okisato, and now Hendrik.* The sight of such strong, intelligent men in the greatest imaginable agony of spirit could not fail to elicit a sympathetic response or provoke violent revulsion. In spite of his Zen mastery, Shigemasa could not hold back a few hot tears, which welled up, unbidden in his clear, lucid eyes.

Shigemasa looked at Hendrik's clock, which read 18:30. It was time to return to either the palace or some teahouse named the Fragrant Blossom, but Hendrik showed no sign of stopping. If anything, his anguish seemed to be deepening.

Shigemasa decided that the best thing to do was withdraw quietly. In a way, Hendrik had answered all of his questions, and if he waited, he would only shame the Dutchman further by his presence. He slipped quietly out of the room and closed the door on the most open expression of cosmic grief that he had ever witnessed.

Kotetsu's abasement was insignificant compared to Hendrik's. Hendrik had removed the seals on a long-locked agony of spirit that might have daunted Buddha, if only for an instant. Even during the most brutal interrogations, Shigemasa had never seen a human being so utterly broken. To witness such despair was almost indecent, seeing what another mortal man was never meant to see.

Once outside Hendrik's door, Shigemasa turned toward it, raised his hand in benediction, turned once more, and walked out into the long rays of the setting sun.

Chapter 23

GAMBITS

Lord Ishido and Nagahisa were comfortably ensconced in the Orange Blossom room. All rooms at the teahouse bore the names of fragrant blossoms—pear, lemon, cherry—and the largest was the Orange Blossom. As a tribute to the white and fragrant flower, most of the furnishings were white from the dazzling cot to the white celadon vases filled with long white tasseled grasses. It was the most difficult room to keep clean, but on this evening it was immaculate.

Hana had agreed to remain for a short period of time to ensure that Koetsu would receive the support she needed while Hiroko searched for a suitable replacement. With the money Mariko had paid her, Hiroko could afford even a first-class geisha until Koetsu gained full status as a second-class, but given the size of the town and its distance from Kyoto and Edo, there was little need for such extravagance. It was a rare occasion when guests like Lord Ishido visited Lord Arima's province, so rare that Hiroko was trying to remember if such an exalted client had ever taken refreshment at her house.

Needless to say Hana, Koetsu, Keiko, and Hiroko were all somewhat taken aback when Ishido and Nagahisa arrived at their door. Geisha training was as formalized and rigorous as samurai training, and Hana greeted them as she would have any other guest, although her graceful bow was perhaps deeper than usual. Keiko hastened to inform the mistress that two obviously high-ranking samurai had come. Hiroko peered around a corner and could see the Tokugawa *mon* on Lord Ishido's kimono, the splendor of his *daisho*, and immediately concluded that the shogun had come, but she was puzzled by the absence of an entourage. The Tokugawa was accompanied only by a large samurai, whose kimono bore a *mon* she did not recognize. Hiroko could see that the retainer, as she thought he was, wore a *daisho* of unusual quality and that his bearing was entirely unsuited to that of someone subservient, though he seemed to defer slightly to the Tokugawa, permitting him to precede him into the Orange Blossom room. Clearly both were men of considerable wealth and of a status not commonly encountered.

While Hana made them comfortable, Hiroko spoke to Koetsu, Keiko, and Omi. Omi was not much to look at, frail and short as if a stiff breeze would blow him over, but his knowledge of unarmed combat was extensive, and the most enraged, drunken samurai—even nearly three times his size—stood little chance against him. Hiroko had hired him for a trifling sum following his release from a Kyoto prison for crippling a wealthy merchant who had confused a geisha of the first class with a prostitute after drinking his sixth flask at Kyoto's premier teahouse. Omi lived in a rudely built thatched hut behind the teahouse, ate sparingly, performed minor carpentry when needed, and ran the occasional errand. Despite her foul disposition and perpetual ill humor, Omi looked upon Hiroko as his savior.

"Now understand," barked Hiroko, "These guests are to be treated as if they were both shoguns—no, emperors. If they offer any of you anything in the way of a present I want to know instantly. If you hold out, I will know it, and you will be beaten. If the sake is too hot or too cold and I hear of it, you will get the sack. If you spill anything, if there is a lock of hair out of place, you will be beaten." She went on enumerating and explaining all the various hypothetical circumstances that would lead to beating and dismissal.

She had already made a similar speech to Hana, who had informed her that she was no longer subject to her rule.

Hiroko had apologized, and then said, "Of course, you're correct, but while you're under my roof you owe me obedience notwithstanding." Hana bowed in polite acknowledgement. To a second-class geisha, obedience to authority was second nature.

After thoroughly terrifying each and every one of her employees, Hiroko softened and said, "There is no need to be anxious or on your guard, I only expect you to do your best, make no mistakes, and represent the Fragrant Blossom as you would the finest teahouse in Nippon."

With these instructions, Koetsu, Keiko, and Hana began to serve Lord Ishido and Nagahisa, while Omi stood watchfully at the door.

Hana slid open the *shoji* to the Orange Blossom room, balancing the best lacquer tray the house had to offer. Hiroko had taken it from a locked *tansu*. The black lacquer was thick and perfect, decorated with sprays of raised silver blossoms exquisitely detailed. A flask of hot sake stood on the tray on its own little stand with two cups of fine white porcelain. To scratch such a tray was unthinkable, as it would be to spill the smallest drop of hot sake on such beauty, but Hana was equal to the task, and her consummate skill in balancing everything on the tips of her manicured fingers was suitably admired by

Ishido and Nagahisa. She bowed her way out, and Nagahisa downed his cup appreciatively before pouring another.

"I'd say that was a truly fragrant blossom."

"Remember we saw her at the festival with young Hideo," Ishido agreed.

"Yes, I recall her. She seemed fragrant then, and I think she is even more so on closer inspection. Hideo is fortunate. When I see a flower of such beauty, retirement in a small town looks very appealing."

"There are many things to be said in favor of the quiet life."

Nagahisa tilted his second cup and emptied it appreciatively.

"This is as comfortable as anything I've seen in Kyoto," he said, gesturing to the room with a sweep of his hand. "And the girl is as graceful as any I have had seen." He added approvingly, "Very polite as well. Lord Arima was right about this place. I can't imagine the other house was any better."

"No," said Ishido, "It does not get much better. Good sake, tasty radish, clean *tatami*, and a lovely lady, not to mention the company of my oldest friend. It is as good as it gets."

Despite the heat, which was palpable in the room, both men enjoyed their sake, which was the very best barrel the house had to offer, opened for the first time at Hiroko's order. She had been saving it for her retirement, but she decided to make the best possible impression on her important guests. Nagahisa called for two more flasks, which were brought in by Koetsu. Of more delicate proportions than Hana, she was in almost every respect more to Ishido's liking. Her presentation was flawless and a credit to Hana's instruction.

"That's my idea of a blossom," Ishido said, "too young to pluck, but I'll bet she will flower into a real beauty. I like delicacy in a girl's figure."

"She's lovely, I agree, but too fragile for the likes of me."

Nagahisa patted his expansive belly contentedly. Then his face tightened.

"Ishido *san*, my old friend, I've been meaning to ask you several things."

"By all means, but only if you will not take offense in the event I can't answer them."

"I agree not to be offended," said Nagahisa. He continued, "Let me get to the point. I know it was not chance that brought you to the festival today. The assassin proved that. Lord Arima insulted me; not in so many words, but I found his looks offensive. If it were not outlawed, I would have challenged him."

The brilliant evening sun seemed to set the oiled rice paper on fire with its rays. The hours were passing quickly, and soon darkness would fall.

"As you have already surmised, I am here on shogunate business. I would appreciate your company later on when I go to Lord Arima's palace, although it may well be dangerous."

Nagahisa laughed.

"No more dangerous than dodging assassin's gunfire at a festival. Arima doesn't like me, and the feeling is mutual. Count me in. One more thing, who and what is that strange policeman I saw at the festival?"

Ishido drained the last cup in his flask and sighed.

"You mean who is Shigemasa? I could take all night telling you stories, and you still wouldn't really begin to know who he is. I hardly know myself. This much I can tell you. He first came to the palace as a boy, when Ieyasu was still regent. One could almost say he grew up with Hidetada and Iemitsu. Sometime, somewhere, he learned to speak several gaijin languages. He is a devout Zen Buddhist and a master of the sword and of any number of less honorable military arts. He has no real official position, but as you may see from the insignia he wears, his access to the shogun is greater—perhaps far greater—than mine is. Let me put things that are incredibly complicated very simply. If Shigemasa walked into this room and asked me to leave for Edo this evening, I would immediately make the necessary preparations."

During this explanation Koetsu had come and gone with the fourth and fifth flasks.

Ishido concluded, "That's all I can really tell you without speculating or giving you a few specific details that I can't reveal, and believe me, you wouldn't want to know anyway."

"I'm sorry, Ishido *san,* but I have one more question," Nagahisa tipped his cup again.

Ishido smiled.

"I'm glad to see that some things don't change with time."

"Yes," said Nagahisa, "I am still curious about certain things. Are you going to invite Lord Arima onward? If you are, I would ask to take your place."

"I would be happy to allow you to do the honors, but unfortunately, it is not so simple. Besides, even at this hour, things are by no means certain. Many things are converging tonight, things that were set in motion years ago."

"Buddhism teaches us that things were set in motion eternities ago, and events here in this world of illusion are of no real importance, except in that they are positive or negative."

"Very true after the third flask," Ishido said, "and equally true after finishing the sixth, but I fear we should stop with the third, considering that, this night of all nights, we must have our wits about us."

Nagahisa laughed.

"We could share the fourth."

Keiko brought in the seventh and final flask. Both men were astonished by her graceful presentation, which was extraordinary in one so young. Hana had made certain that both Keiko's hair and kimono were arranged perfectly. She had been at some pains to hide the redness caused by Keiko's weeping after she had learned that Hana would soon be leaving. As far as the little girl was concerned, Hana was the only mother she could remember, and now she was going away. Koetsu did her best to reassure her, and to be sure, Koetsu was as kind a young woman as any girl could wish for in an older sister, but she was simply too much of an equal, unlike Hana, who was twice her age and a geisha of the second class. After all, even the dreaded Hiroko showed Hana a measure of deference.

Outside the Fragrant Blossom, Omi cursed the heat. He had seen more than the usual number of summers and Augusts, but he could not remember any month with such heat. As free of extra flesh as he was, he found himself constantly wiping his forehead. His bladder was weakened by age, and although especially vigilant given the importance of the guests, he still had to make several trips to the small hut near the river. He wanted to keep a piss jar nearby but Hiroko had told him it was not genteel.

As if it matters in the heated darkness, he thought.

There were a number of gay paper lamps, decorated with jet-black calligraphy, declaring the presence of the Fragrant Blossom in the still air from atop tall wood posts. These gave the entrance a particularly inviting appearance, although they required almost constant attention to keep them lit and from burning up. Fortunately, the night was without the slightest breath of wind.

As he returned from his fourth trip to urinate, he saw a number of samurai in a column walk up to the entrance of the teahouse, divide into two and surround the building. Each samurai was wearing a black kimono with the Arima *mon* on the back.

Good, thought Omi as he saw them standing within arms' reach of each other, *Now I don't have to worry about the safety of our guests.* He had heard of the assassin at the festival, as had everyone in the town, but he lacked any details and knew only that a man had tried to kill Lord Arima, failed, and then committed suicide. It was much better that Lord Arima protect the important clients than he, alone in the lantern-lit darkness.

An unarmed man alone stood little chance against Omi, but a man with a matchlock gun was another matter entirely.

I can't fight a man with a gun, Omi said to himself. *To even attempt to do so is suicide.*

This is the beginning of the end, Captain Yamashita said to himself as he detailed his men around the teahouse. He believed Shigemasa would see to it that he was retained in some capacity by the shogun or another *daimyo* and, Buddha willing, at his present rank. He did not think that he was in any way a traitor to his liege lord. Quite the contrary, by serving the shogun's interests over Arima's, Yamashita thought he was a patriot.

Clearly, gaijin were a threat not only to Bushido but to Nippon and even to Buddhism. The thought of being forced to worship a foreign God horrified him. Gaijin influence was a cancer that if permitted to grow would devour the Japanese way of life and with it his wife, his daughter, and young son.

The welfare of the nation and the emperor was more important than that of one province and Lord Arima. By serving the shogun, he was saving Lord Arima from himself. The lord was committing treason by ordering the arrest of the Kaishakunin.

Why Lord Arima had insisted on the arrest of Nagahisa *san* was a mystery to him. A famous martial artist, Nagahisa was not involved in politics; rather, he stood apart from them. His detention would arouse outrage among the very people Lord Arima wished to win over to his cause. Yamashita had not figured out exactly what course of action his liege lord was taking. Actually, he liked the lord and even respected him as a stern but fair master.

Everything had changed when the Lady Arima had died, which was shortly after the lord's son and heir was disowned and banished. Yamashita had been only a corporal then. He had expected the lord to remarry immediately and have more

met accomplished liars who looked him straight in the eye while telling him something utterly false, but there was still something slightly amiss with Captain Yamashita. At least he didn't bother him with cooking pots. When he had watched his captain walk out of the study, he was unsure what the precise outcome of his plan would be, which was a highly unusual state of affairs for him.

There was no sign or communication from Hendrik, or the Dutchman, as Lord Arima called him. Mariko had vanished for the time being, which was irritating only because he had asked her to meet him at the palace. She was a willful girl, but he regarded most if not all of her insolence as his own doing. For the hundredth time, he questioned the wisdom and policy of his demand that she break off all relations with Hideo.

"If I had Nobunaga's grandson leading my army, I would have a better than even chance without Dutch cannon and Dutch infantrymen. If he were married to my Mariko, then he would truly have a cause worth fighting for since his son would inherit the province. Iemitsu never had the slightest intention of allowing his youngest son to marry her. It was my cursed pride that held her out for a more advantageous match and prevented her from marrying young Oda."

He thought of his wife. Surely she would have blessed the marriage; she would have known that Mariko loved the boy, and the fact that he was Oda's grandson by a minor concubine would only have added another element of romance to the connection. That he was a bastard grandson would never have caused her a moment's hesitation or concern.

He had taken the Spaniard's guns, but he had killed the intermediary by using him in the first test at the festival. Hideo had performed magnificently, his cut almost flawless, and the Kirishitan had died bravely, a true samurai death, and now he was in paradise, or whatever the Kirishitans called it.

It makes no difference, Arima thought, *Kirishitan or Buddhist, the man will be reborn. There it is again, the one unchanging, unalterable law that until a man achieves nirvana, all men must be reborn.* Earlier in his rule, Arima would have killed Shinbei without hesitation, because the calligrapher knew things which would have been a problem had they became known.

Karma, he said to himself. *Now I am concerned about it.*

As a younger man, Arima had been very concerned about his karma. He had actually told his father at one point in his education that if he were forced to have men murdered to further a policy, he would prefer to be sent to a monastery and leave the world of illusion altogether.

The previous lord had agreed to his request, and he had found himself in a place of rigorous rules and physical mortification. The abbot of his temple was extremely strict. Arima had to rise before dawn, thoroughly cleanse himself in a freezing cold river, and then spend the remainder of the day in total silence, which was broken only by chants. All other human speech was forbidden on pain of the lash. This regimen was not at all to his liking. He had broken the rule enjoining silence, was soundly beaten for doing so, and had broken other monastery regulations as well. He had longed for the comforts of the palace, the luxuriant baths, the obedient servants, and the military training. Even the endless etiquette lessons had seemed appealing. After serving in the temple for nearly a year, he was recalled. He did not return to the temple. His father made no comments about his absence, and the time spent in the temple was never discussed. His training to be a *daimyo* continued as though uninterrupted.

When his own son, Daisuke renounced his position and became a monk, Lord Arima fully expected him to have the same reaction to temple life that he had, but Daisuke did not. Arima's spies reported that Daisuke was thriving at the temple. The monastic life suited his son, and this had incensed the failed monk. Lord Arima eventually refused to hear news of Daisuke, and the mention of his name was enough to make him lose his temper, even with Mariko.

Lord Arima had carefully considered the consequences of arresting Ishido and Nagahisa before giving Yamashita his orders. There was the problem of Ishido's retinue. He really should have arrested Ishido's samurai first, but they would have resisted and most, if not all, would fight to the death. There were the Spanish guns, but only a few men, like Mizukami, were skilled in their use. Armed with enough of the new weapons, Mizukami was a one-man army, but firing on targets was one matter, firing on samurai who were essentially guests in his province was quite another. Sending Mizukami with a sufficient number of samurai who were armed with firearms would certainly rout Ishido's men, and with the dawn, he would see the long-awaited beginning of a general insurrection.

The endless drought and terrible heat meant that many peasants were starving. The dried-out rice paddies that had provided sustenance to their families for generations were rendered worse than useless. By marshalling these peasants with *kakure* Kirishitans, masterless samurai, and other disaffected elements, his personal army could easily turn the province into a fortress much larger than Shimabara Castle. Other *daimyos*, angered by Iemitsu's insistence on their families being held hostage in Tokyo, might rise up, but Ieyasu had built the House of Tokugawa on a firm foundation of alliances, and Hidetada had accumulated an enormous treasury filled with gold and silver. The present shogun's stinginess was an almost endless source of amusing tales and jokes, but the money he possessed was an established fact. If Arima's province did rise against the shogun, that vast wealth would be unleashed against him and ultimately prove harder to defeat than the mightiest army.

An alliance with the Dutch, who had proved their worth at Shimabara, would have effectively neutralized Iemitsu's cash hoard. Nothing succeeded like military success. Then again, Shiro Amakusa's armies had scored a number of victories early in the war. Compared to China, Nippon was a small nation, but compared to Arima's province, it was very large and had many provinces from Hokkaido to Kyushu. Each had its own petty king, for that was what a *daimyo* actually was, pursuing his own agenda. It had taken centuries of conflict to unite Nippon, but it was not until Ieyasu's victory at Sekigahara that the country could truly be called united.

If only Daisuke were Mariko, and Mariko, Daisuke. Lord Arima considered this wish for the thousandth time. *Karma*, he thought. For a moment, he was bitterly disappointed by Hendrik, so much so that he could taste the acid in his stomach and feel it corroding the tissues in his throat. Then he swallowed it down.

My dream is ending, but all man's plans, even Iemitsu's, are just that, and in a year, a thousand years, it really makes no difference. They will vanish like so much smoke in the strong winds of time.

No, he said to himself, *There will be no rebellion. It is unimportant. It always was unimportant.*

Lord Arima refilled his pipe with the Dutchman's Latakia tobacco. He blew a perfect circle, which hung in the incense-filled air. He set down the pipe and toyed with one of the Spanish pistols, cocking the hammer and snapping it against the battery. He watched the bright sparks showering as iron pyrite scraped against steel. Mizukami preferred the fool's gold, as he called it, to flint, saying it gave a hotter and greater spark. The disadvantage was that iron pyrite was softer and more prone to crumble or disintegrate under battle conditions.

My guns, my beautiful, terrible guns, he thought. *They will never speak in battle.* Perhaps it was all for the best. Matchlock guns were clumsy and all but useless clubs in the rain. A samurai could smell the burning wick from a considerable distance.

He carefully set down the Spanish gun and contemplated it. He did not want to be the samurai who destroyed a thousand years of Bushido. Bushido wasn't that old, but that didn't matter at the moment, it seemed like there had never been a time in Nippon without Bushido. Amaterasu herself might as well have brought Bushido together with the sword, the mirror, and the jewel. Could the House of Arima—samurai from time immemorial—be the force that ended the way of the sword forever? Lord Arima took the Spanish gun and locked it in the iron-studded *tansu* from which he had taken the Muramasa *tanto* earlier.

The sword is the soul of the samurai. I will not be the one to destroy the soul or the sword. He made up his mind. *The name of Arima will suffer no dishonor at my hands.*

For a brief moment, he considered sending Mizukami after Yamashita to countermand his orders and have the captain and his men return to the barracks.

That fat, insolent bastard, Nagahisa, he thought. Something about him rankled Lord Arima like a foul odor he couldn't identify. *And that Ishido, Iemitsu's dog.* The very sight of that dandified lackey dressed in the Tokugawa *mon* and puffed up with importance because he is the shogun's personal valet, makes me want to vomit. *They will soon see what a real samurai is.*

Though Captain Yamashita was required by oath, Bushido, and his own integrity as a man to follow Lord Arima's orders as he crossed the threshold of the Fragrant Blossom, he knew he was making a mistake that would have fatal consequences for him and all of his men. Lord Arima had suggested that he take as many men as he saw fit, and now he felt that, confronted with arrest by many samurai, Ishido and Nagahisa would not only refuse to submit but undoubtedly feel dishonored by any action other than fighting to the death. He knew this as surely as he had ever known anything in his life, as surely as the sun rose each daybreak. Before he was fully inside the teahouse entrance, the captain turned on his heel and walked back out into the steamy night, past the smiling Omi, who thought that the captain must have forgotten something. Yamashita approached Lieutenant Zenshiro.

"Lieutenant," he said.

Zenshiro bowed. "Yamashita *san.*"

"You may dismiss your men and return to the barracks."

Zenshiro bowed and immediately walked to the sergeant, repeating the orders. After a brief interval, the only remaining samurai was Captain Yamashita. He felt a compulsion to say something, anything, to Omi, who was mystified.

First all of Arima's men had been sent to protect the teahouse from assassins, but they had all left.

Well, Omi said to himself, *samurai are queer people. Touchy, very touchy, about their so-called honor.*

"It's still so hot," Yamashita finally said.

Omi thought this was only too obvious—almost as obvious as the captain's nervousness. His right hand clasped and unclasped on the pommel of his sword.

"Yes, Captain," Omi said. He felt no fear. "It is hot." A tingling sensation at the base of his penis warned him that he had to urinate for a fifth time. To Yamashita, who continued fidgeting with his *katana*, he said, "You will excuse me, but I must piss."

Even in the flickering lantern light Yamashita saw the almost tragic expression on Omi's face; he forgot his own plight and smiled at the old man. Omi smiled back and, assuming he was excused, turned and walked to the little hut. If Yamashita had not been there, Omi would have pissed against the nearest tree, and to hell with the mother of all crocodiles. He owed her a great debt and his services, but enough was enough, and he disliked leaving his post.

When Omi left to urinate, Yamashita was gathering his thoughts, searching for the perfect introduction, when a very young, barefoot boy ran up. He was sweaty and dirty and as blown as a horse after a long race. Through the boy's ragged clothes, Yamashita could count every rib as his chest heaved in and out, like a bellows being worked furiously. The boy's eyes were brown but utterly lacking in fear.

pletely exhausted Hoki's physical resources. His mind and body were working on what little auxiliary energy remained. These reserves were tapped out. Nevertheless Hoki plucked up his courage.

Overcoming his shyness and embarrassment at his unattractive clothes and body odor, he said, in as manly a voice as he could muster, "I have a message for the lady Hana."

This simple statement took all his remaining strength. The two vinegar rice balls and the water from horse troughs could sustain him no longer after the grueling run. Hoki simultaneously burst into tears and collapsed in a dirty heap onto Hiroko's spotless *tatami.*

The last thing Hoki remembered was asking Keiko for the lady Hana, but of course, he did not know Keiko's name. When he awoke, he thought he was back in the village and it had all been a beautiful dream. However, as he opened his eyes, the face of a surpassingly beautiful woman looked down at him with concern in her lovely, caring eyes. He lay on a soft futon, and he was cleaner than he had ever been in his life as far back as he could remember. Even his chipped and cracked fingernails were clean and manicured as well as possible, given that they were filed to the quick. He rubbed his feet against each other sole to sole, and they felt smooth; the horny yellow calluses no longer caught against themselves. He was afraid to get up, afraid that the lovely dream might end.

Then the unique fragrance of freshly steamed rice and miso soup made its way into his consciousness. Having eaten nothing but two rice balls since he had left the village, Hoki was famished. He sat up and touched the soft silk of his kimono. Never had he worn so luxuriant a garment. He thought, *This is what a cloud must feel like.* He couldn't count the times he had lain on his back and looked up at clouds. Watching them, so white and pure, ever changing shape and just floating, was his favorite pastime.

Hoki opened his mouth to speak, but Hana laid a soft, perfumed index finger gently against his cracked lips.

"Wait," she said with the most beautiful voice he'd ever heard. "Eat first, then talk. You must be starving."

Hoki nodded, and Hana handed him the lovely, covered, lacquer rice bowl.

Ishido and Nagahisa were finishing a frugal but delicious repast of perfectly cooked, charcoal-grilled fish. They had been wrapped in leaves, after being rubbed with ginger, soy sauce, and other spices, and they were truly almost as delicious as those Nagahisa enjoyed in Edo.

Koetsu and Keiko took special care to make certain everything reflected favorably on the Fragrant Blossom. Although both their hearts were broken by the news that Hana would be leaving, her departure did present opportunity. While Koetsu could not possibly step into Hana's *tabi* as a geisha of the second class without further training, Hiroko would be reluctant to bear the extraordinary expense of buying the contract of an experienced geisha. She would be likely to seek the services of a geisha nearing retirement, but then she could not use and abuse a woman of great experience. She could complete Koetsu's apprenticeship herself and buy the contract of another young girl at Koetsu's level and simply do without a genuine second-class girl for a year. There would be talk in the town, of course, but the surpassing excellence of Hiroku's sake, and the freshness of her fish together with the well-known cleanliness of her house would prevail even without Hana.

The *shoji* screen drew back, sliding noiselessly on its polished wood rails. Nagahisa looked up as the light in the Orange Blossom room changed. He was expecting to see Koetsu or the diminutive, delicate Keiko with yet another flask of delectable sake. Ishido refused the seventh flask, pleading that he was still on duty but Nagahisa's tasks were over. Anything remaining of his preparations to return to Tokyo would be Musashi's responsibility.

Nagahisa was disagreeably surprised to see a tall, narrow-faced samurai of high rank wearing a kimono with the Arima *mon* and a *jingasa* bearing the same crest. The samurai hesitated on the threshold, and the handle of his *katana* knocked against the *shoji* door, causing Lord Ishido to look up from his final fish and carefully lay down his chopsticks.

"It appears we have an uninvited guest," said Ishido in a voice easily overheard by the samurai. Ishido looked directly at Captain Yamashita and addressed him. "Would you care to join us in a flask of this most excellent sake?"

Yamashita was greatly relieved that Ishido did not draw his famous Mitsutada and cut him from right shoulder to left hip. The Kaishakunin was completely at ease, as if he were in his own home.

Yamashita was so nervous his sphincter twitched, and there were gurgles in his intestines so loud he thought the two men must hear them. He felt his bowels might betray him at any moment. The heat was still blisteringly hot, but cold sweat trickled down the sides of his chest. He felt cold and would have shivered had he been alone. His mouth was dry, and he experienced the same inability to speak as he did in one of his infrequent nightmares when he tried desperately, without success, to warn his wife or daughter of some impending doom—an earthquake, fire, or flood.

He knew that whatever he said would define the remainder of his life; not only his, but more significantly, his son's. He might have only a few moments left to live before he was cut down. Everything he had rehearsed so carefully was erased. Yamashita was worried that if he opened his mouth, his voice would squeak feebly, like a rabbit in a gin. Yamashita coughed.

Ishido and Nagahisa looked at him, wondering when the man would answer. Their looks made the captain's discomfiture worse. He coughed again.

Damn it, Yamashita said to himself, *this is awful. Any-*

thing is better than nothing. His bowels underwent a wrenching spasm, which was reflected in his pale, sweating face.

"My lords," he said, "If you will excuse me for a moment, I will return in a short time."

With that, the captain bowed so low, his head nearly touched the *tatami*. He turned, slid the screen shut, and hastened through the teahouse to the small hut behind. He nearly bowled Omi over in his haste, which grew after he had reached the entrance and ran out into the steaming night.

Captain Yamashita slammed into the hut, lifted his kimono, ripped down his *hakama,* and loudly and completely voided himself. He sat briefly, anxious to return in the shortest possible time.

My life is over anyway, he thought, *I will simply tell them the truth.*

He washed himself with warm water, hitched up his loincloth, straightened his kimono, and walked back to the teahouse, feeling greatly relieved.

Nagahisa rolled his eyes at Lord Ishido.

"What was that all about?"

Ishido raised his fine black eyebrows to the ceiling.

"I don't have the faintest idea, but if I had to guess, I'd say he has orders from Lord Arima."

"I'd say he looked like a man about to soil himself," Nagahisa said. "I've seen it many times before a student has to cut his first body. The pale face, the sweat, inability to moisten the dry mouth—hell, I've felt that way myself."

"Well, I have a feeling we'll know soon enough."

Koetsu brought in two more flasks and set down the tray before bowing herself out of the room, never once turning her back on her guests.

Nagahisa watched her.

"I must say, I've rarely seen such grace in a first-class house in Kyoto. When that girl grows up, she will be sensational, and the little one is exceptional as well."

Ishido decided he would indulge in a fourth flask.

"Why did she bring two?" he said.

Nagahisa grinned.

"Since when did the great Lord High Executioner become such an old woman about sake?"

Ishido poured and drank two cups in quick succession by way of reply.

"I knew you would drink another flask if I ordered it," said Nagahisa.

"It is good sake," said Ishido.

The *shoji* slid back, and Captain Yamashita stood in the entryway, sweating less; his face showed exposure to the sun rather than the pasty, unnatural color of his earlier appearance.

He coughed once again and said in a clear voice that was certainly louder than necessary, "My lords, I have a confession to make. I was sent here by Lord Arima to arrest you."

Chapter 25

Rebellion

Attended once more by the overweight but irrepressible and skilled Genji, Hideo and Kobiyashi thoroughly refreshed themselves at the bathhouse. Hideo had paid for a hot stone massage for himself and Kobiyashi. This treat had been followed by an ice-cold bath, or at least as cold a bath as the river was in the tremendous heat. Hideo and Kobiyashi walked back to the barracks to change clothes before proceeding to the Fragrant Blossom. They decided to stop for a while in the temple to meditate and understand that even the momentous events of the day were an illusion with little effect on the truly important parts of their lives.

"There is no point in freshening our bodies without doing the same to our spirits," Kobiyashi said as they entered the temple.

"I couldn't agree more," said Hideo, who was pleased that his materialistic friend would say such a thing. Hideo loved that the Christ had actually said that prayer should be said in secret because God knows all one's secrets. It was a very good thing, as a public Kirishitan prayer would result in death.

As Kobiyashi softly chanted the Lotus Sutra over and over, Hideo inaudibly uttered an Our Father.

He was almost certain that his trespasses did not include killing Shinbei. Hana would have known by then. The barracks knew nearly everything sooner or later, though often the information was either only partially correct or otherwise altered. Still, after so many hours, if Shinbei had been killed by the test, someone would know. Hideo fervently and gratefully thanked God that that particular cup had passed from his lips. He asked God to either let him forget Mariko or, through some miracle, allow him to marry her—one thing or the other must occur for him to find some peace. He prayed for all the *kakure* Kirishitans, that they would be protected against the shogunate, who sought their destruction and that the church in Nippon would be revived.

As they finished their respective prayers, Hideo walked to the gilded image of Buddha and bowed low, prostrating himself before it. He was not the least worried about the commandment against having other gods before God; after all, he reasoned, Buddha was but a man—a very special man to be sure—not a god, much less God. God would no more be jealous of a statue than of a scroll painting. It was a question of whether or not he worshipped the wood statue as a god or a representation of God that mattered. Hideo did not worship a wooden image as a god; his god was unseen, unknowable, all-powerful, and eternal. The closest thing he had to an image of God was the tiny, painted square of copper given to him by his mother, and although he reverenced the image of Christ and kissed it, he did not worship it.

Hideo heard the crunching of sandals on the pebbles and stood up. Kobiyashi finished his chant and turned. Mizukami stood in the entrance to the temple. He was red-faced, sweating, and nearly out of breath. Hideo and Kobiyashi walked to him as fast as was respectful to the temple.

"Hideo, Kobiyashi, "Mizukami said, "you must come with me to the palace. There has been a disaster. I'll tell you on the way. Hurry!"

Mizukami's tale was shocking.

Having spent all of their pay at the festival on food and sake, nearly all of Lord Arima's retainers had returned to the barracks to escape the heat. The barracks were nearly as hot as the festival grounds, and as night fell, it was like being inside an enormous oven. Many were drunk from too many flasks of sake, and there were wild rumors about Lord Arima having replaced the corpse with Shinbei, that Shinbei had been alive when Hideo had made the cut. Others said that Lord Arima was a traitor, who would bring the gaijin and their cannon into the province. Still others said that Lord Ishido was there to invite Lord Arima onward, and they would all be masterless before the night was over. Even the officers were frightened by this last rumor; no samurai wanted to be a *ronin*. They had families, and without a lord's bounty, they would be forced into outlawry, an uncertain existence at best and unthinkable at the worst.

Lieutenant Zenshiro had attempted to calm the fears of his men, but he was cut off by Private Ando, who had urged the samurai to march on the palace, arm themselves from Lord Arima's arsenal, and then attack Lord Ishido's men.

Hideo was breathless at this sudden and unexpected turn of events.

"You know Ando and Onishi are professional malcontents, "Mizukami said. "First, Onishi seized the speaking tube, shouting, 'Buddha, help us all! We will be *ronin* by morning!' Then Ando grabbed the trumpet, saying in a loud voice, 'Lord Arima has betrayed us. We are outcasts, pariahs. We're worse than gaijin. If we don't rise up, the gaijin priests will burn our sacred temples.'"

This had gotten the attention of every man in the barracks. Lieutenant Zenshiro had made a valiant attempt to make the men see reason.

"If I am to be a *ronin*," he said, "I shall hire myself out to the highest bidder. I will not weep, wail, and lament like a toothless old grandfather."

Ando had silently sneaked up behind Zenshiro, and as the lieutenant had paused for breath, he had drawn his *katana* and cut him down from behind. Onishi had then shouted through the trumpet, "If we are *ronin*, we have no officers. All are equal. What has Lord Arima ever really done for us? I want money, not some festival designed to steal my pay. No wonder he wanted us to attend. Every *ryo* we spent on food and drink went into his pocket. He stole our money."

"Where were Hankei and the rest of the officers?" Kobiyashi asked, breaking into the story. Mizukami choked.

"I regret to say that after Zenshiro was cut down, the others were quiet. You have to understand that the men were drunk. The heat made them more stupid than they usually are, and even you must admit that, offensive as each is, Ando and Onishi can be quite persuasive."

"What about Captain Yamashita?" said Kobiyashi, "Surely, he could convince the men that this is madness."

"It gets worse," said Mizukami. "Captain Yamashita had taken some men to the Fragrant Blossom. No one except the captain knows why. Then without any explanation, the captain sent all the men back to the barracks. For all I know, he is drinking sake at the teahouse as I speak. The men are quite mad. One moment, they are raving about gaijin priests burning Buddhist temples, and the next Ando is shouting through a trumpet, 'Shimabara! Shimabara!' at the top of his lungs."

"If they attack Ishido's men, there will be war," Hideo said, "But surely Lord Ishido's men are more than a match for some drunken samurai."

"True," said Mizukami, "But if the samurai are armed

with Spanish muskets and cartridge belts, it is a different story. And if those guns are given to every peasant who has been forced off his land by the drought, unable to feed his hungry family."

"Then we will indeed have another Shimabara," said Hideo.

"Or if the rumors about Lord Arima and the gaijin are true, it would be far worse," said Mizukami.

"You really think our lord is a traitor?" Kobiyashi asked.

"I don't presume to know the lord's thoughts," said Mizukami. "I do know that if the men break into the arsenal, nothing less than the Tokugawa army can defeat them."

"But they have no leaders," said Hideo.

"If you think about it, either Ando or Onishi would make a good leader for a rebellion," said the armorer.

As the three men neared the barracks, they saw that it was deserted. Hideo and Kobiyashi insisted on stopping to get their bows and the long *utsubos* that held the battlepoint arrows. Mizukami paused to cover Lieutenant Zenshiro's body with a silk cloth; the long gash across his back began at the right shoulder and ended at the base of his spine. The barracks were silent. They could hear the buzzing of innumerable flies clustered in and on the edges of Zenshiro's wound and the pool of blood soaking into the hard-packed earth floor. Strapping the *utsubos* to their backs, Hideo and Kobiyashi left the barracks with their long *yumi* in their hands. Mizukami urged them to greater haste, and as they ran to the palace, they saw a large body of samurai at the gates.

After robbing and despoiling Lieutenant Zenshiro's body and taking his swords, several samurai had left the rebels and gone into town to sell the swords and buy more sake. The corporals and sergeants had gone in search of Captain Yamashita, leaving Ando and Onishi with the rest of the samurai.

After she left Hana at the Fragrant Blossom, Mariko stopped at a temple to give thanks to Kannon, the goddess of

to the main temple alone at night to meditate amid the candles, torches, and jasmine incense. She knew life on earth was a transient illusion, like a bubble on the river; it would disappear into Prana only to reappear in some other incarnation. Her mastery of the *aikuchi* was proof against bandits and *ronin,* so she loved the anonymity of the evening.

Yes, she thought. *At last, I have a sister.*

She recalled the last time she had seen Hendrik and the fierce embrace he had given her. It had been so tight it had hurt her nipples, and she had cried out. It was as if he had been trying to absorb her body into his. He had apologized, and she had looked into his foreign eyes, seeking an explanation for his violence. For the first time, she had seen a deep sorrow, and the huge gaijin had seemed to be on the verge of tears.

"Hendrik *san*," she had said, brushing his cheek with her hand, "Why so sad?"

To her astonishment and shame, he had begun to shake with racking sobs, a dry, hacking sound that lasted for only a few moments until he had choked it down, and the emotion had passed like a summer thunderstorm, leaving clarity in its wake.

Mariko had never thought of Hendrik as vulnerable; he had seemed so in control when he had shown her the moon through his telescope. The one time they had made love, he had played on her body like a first-class geisha on a *samisen*, touching her in places that Hideo never had. He had brought her to consummation so quickly, it was remarkable. He had touched her almost as erotically as she touched herself. He had to have sensitivity to be so knowledgeable in what gave a woman pleasure. He had told her of the girl he had left in Java and of his plantation.

Maybe, she thought, *Maybe he was just sick with longing for his home.*

She could see that life aboard ship was difficult, but he was a man and used to hardship. His sadness had deeper roots, something he had done in the past had suddenly surfaced unexpectedly.

Mariko knew the feeling. She had not been as close to her mother as she wanted to be. She had always felt that Lady Arima should have made a stand against her father and for Daisuke. The lord may have relented. Yes, she had been ill at the time, but if she had faced down the lord, Mariko would have a brother, and the family would have an heir. She knew that by blaming her mother she was being unfair, but life wasn't fair; it consisted of a series of all-too-brief joys followed by lengthy periods of sadness. Why should she be fair when life was not?

If life were fair, she said to herself, *Daisuke would be here, and I could marry Hideo with father's blessing.* She had seen Hideo at the festival, and much as she had thought that she was over him, her heart had still beat faster as she had looked at him, tall, strong, and bronzed by the torrid sun; she had deliberately looked away. Aside from his considerable physical attributes, Hideo was innately decent, which was his most attractive quality. Hendrik was decent as well, but with the gaijin, she could never be certain of his motives. With Hideo, she knew that, given a choice, he would always try to do the right thing. Mariko knew Hideo could be led but not dominated, and although he surely loved her, he would not follow her into anything negative.

When Lord Arima had told him that he could no longer be alone with Mariko, it had broken his heart, but he had respected the lord's wishes. Mariko had sought a clandestine meeting, but Hideo had demurred. At first, she had been furious with him for doing so. She had even called him a coward to his face one morning outside the barracks, but as she had said it, she had seen from the pain in his noble features that his refusal was wholly out of a respect for her father, based on honor and Bushido. He could not fail to honor his liege lord, and her father was his lord. Of course, her grandfather had been a vassal of his grandfather, but Hideo never used his lineage for personal advantage, which was another praiseworthy characteristic.

As she drew near to the main entrance of the palace, she saw a crowd of samurai in the light of the ever-burning torches. They were in small groups, and they appeared to be undisciplined. She looked for Captain Yamashita or Lieutenant Zenshiro but saw neither officer. A short, squat samurai stood on the steps; he was unattractive, with protruding front teeth and small, beady pig's eyes. She could hear him shouting instructions, something about the arsenal. She broke into a run. The samurai gave her a clear path, and she stopped near the porcine private.

"What is the meaning of this?" she asked in a clear voice that was demanding but respectful.

The private said nothing, looking at her with angry, red eyes. He motioned to a large, muscular samurai with his gloved right hand. The man stepped up and seized her around the waist. Mariko drew her dagger and stabbed the man through his right eye, releasing a spray of blood. The blade penetrated the brain, and although Mariko felt his grip loosen, he had her tightly enough to pull her off her feet, and they fell down the steps. His heavy body was on top of her, and she had struck her head on the edge of the bottom stone step, weighted down by the chest of the dead man. She felt the impact on the back of her skull and then nothing as she lost consciousness.

Ando was confused. After he had cut Zenshiro down, he had planned to march into the palace, demand the key to the arsenal, and then distribute the guns and ammunition. He would give Lord Arima a choice: he could either appoint him and Onishi as generals in his army of rebellion or spend the duration of the war in one of his dungeon cells. There were few men in the barracks who were ignorant of Lord Arima's attitude toward the Tokugawa, and this was the principal reason that Ando had counted on Lord Arima blessing their treason. The last thing he wanted was a problem with the lord, and here was his dearly beloved daughter, lying unconscious under Onishi's lifeless body. Then he had an idea. If he took Arima's only child hostage, Lord Arima would be forced to accede to his terms. Lady Mariko could remain in the dungeon under constant guard while he and Lord Arima waged war against the shogunate. Then Ando had another idea. He could take Mariko and the lord hostage and hand them over to the shogunate as traitors. Surely Iemitsu would richly reward the brave samurai who offered him Lord Arima's palace and his province without bloodshed, on a silver tray so to speak.

He looked at his friend's one-eyed body and ordered that Mariko be bound and gagged. She seemed nearly as lifeless as Onishi. Several men asked Ando for instructions, but he waved them off, saying that he needed time to think.

Ando knew that the palace guards would follow him and not rally to Lord Arima. As soon as the samurai had approached the palace, the guards at the gate had joined them. The rumors of Shinbei's death and the presence of the Kaishakunin at the festival had confirmed their belief that the fall of the House of Arima was imminent. If they were destined to be *ronin* in any event, it would be far better for them to loot the palace before dispersing through the countryside. Zenshiro was dead, so there was no turning back for all the Arima retainers, except the officers and the actual palace guards.

Ando was no fool; on the contrary, he was anything but. In spite of his appearance, he would have been an officer except for his unwillingness to submit to any authority except for Lord Arima's. On one occasion, for which he was whipped, he had told Captain Yamashita if he wanted the night soil jar in the dungeon emptied, he could drink it dry himself for all he cared. Yamashita's hand drew back to strike, and then thinking better of it, he ordered Ando to be seized and flogged. Ando was the adopted son of a modestly wealthy merchant in Osaka who had had business dealings with the previous Lord Arima and had prevailed upon the present Lord to take the unruly boy into service in hopes of settling him down. Ando was extremely intelligent and had done so well in school that his father would have sent him to the Buddhists for further instruction, but Ando had beaten his mathematics teacher senseless when the frail old man had berated him for bringing a particularly lurid pillow book to class and sharing it with the other students.

If the rumors that Lord Ishido had come to dispossess Lord Arima were true, then the lord had nothing to lose by heading his rebellion. Ando respected Lord Arima, the more so after reports of the incredible two-hundred-*oban* wager on the contest. He weighed the respective advantages of allying himself with lord against the shogun. Rebels were usually punished by boiling them in oil or simply beheading them, but leading an insurrection against an enemy of the shogunate was not treason in the ordinary sense and would be dealt with more harshly. However, if he simply turned the castle over to Lord Ishido, there would be no treasure; he would receive polite thanks and be dismissed from service. No *daimyo* would have anything to do with a samurai who had betrayed his liege lord. Ando would be forced to become a *ronin* or, worse, return in shame to his father's shop. Iemitsu would never dream of rewarding a traitor unless he was of high rank. Prejudice against treason by samurai of low rank was one factor; Iemitsu's legendary status as a miser was the other.

No, Ando thought, *All things considered, Iemitsu would not reward me richly. More likely, the shogun would torture me, sending my bones, along with those of Lord Arima, to every* daimyo *as a warning to traitors. Nobunaga would have accepted Arima as a gift. No, best make a deal with Arima. He has everything to gain and nothing to lose except his life, which he has lost anyway.*

Ando issued orders to take the unconscious Mariko to the dungeons and guard her closely if they valued their lives. His orders were instantly obeyed, and Mariko, still unconscious, was unceremoniously carried into the castle. Two of Ando's most trusted allies were left to guard the door, and the others quickly took over the palace, locking servants in their quarters. Servants were accustomed to obeying anyone wearing two swords, so the castle was secured with little commotion. Those armed samurai who had remained in the palace during the festival either joined with Ando or were cut down and their bodies piled in an antechamber. The pile was not very high; it consisted of only three corpses.

Shigemasa watched the events on the palace steps from a safe distance. He had come from the empty barracks, where he had examined the nearly naked body of Zenshiro and concluded that a rebellion was taking place. He had watched as Mariko had stabbed Onishi and had seen her being carried into the castle.

His orders were clear at this point. He was to contain any insurrection by whatever means necessary and confine it to the palace. If the means required that he sacrifice his own life, so be it. Iemitsu had been crystal clear on the meaning of "any means."

"There will be no second Shimabara," the shogun had said. "There are many Kirishitans hidden in Arima's province. Nippon cannot afford widespread unrest. The shogunate will not endure another Kirishitan uprising."

Shigemasa had reassured him that Lord Arima was no Kirishitan.

"You forget that Lord Arima hates me far more than any Kirishitan. If he had to become Kirishitan to overthrow me, he would do it in the time it takes one of their filthy unwashed priests to sprinkle him with their sacred water. Don't you ever think otherwise, Shigemasa."

The streets were all but deserted, but Shigemasa knew this would change quickly once word of the rebellion spread. All through the province, he had witnessed the devastation wrought by the heat and drought, the dry streams and rice paddies, the muttering farmers, and here and there a wooden cross standing for a day in the iron hard ground, erected by an anonymous Kirishitan to remind others of a faith that counseled martyrdom in service of their God. Shigemasa had nothing against Kirishitanity; its articles of faith were in harmony with both Bushido and Buddhism. Obedience, service to one's fellow man, and self-discipline were practices common to all three paths.

He understood Iemitsu's concerns, but he did not share them. Shigemasa had dedicated his body to the service of the shogun, but not his heart or his spirit. They were given in service to the Eightfold Path. Iemitsu was well aware of this and valued Shigemasa's service highly because he could be certain of his intentions.

Shigemasa carefully assessed the fertility of the province as a seedbed for civil strife and judged it sufficiently moist in some ways but somewhat dry and unfit in others. As autocratic as any other *daimyo* in many ways, Lord Arima financed and supported several temples, which offered medical care to the poor. He had authorized his chief steward to distribute a small yet, under the present circumstances, adequate ration of rice from the palace stores to various village headmen to feed peasants in danger of starvation. These measures were of benefit to Lord Arima in that they reduced the possibility of unrest; most *daimyos* in his place would have done nothing to alleviate their suffering people, preferring to crush any restive villages with military force.

He thought that if a truly charismatic leader made himself known, then the province would rise against the government, perhaps even against Lord Arima, though such a man would most certainly be no Shiro Amakusa. Young Oda, for instance, might be such a leader, and Iemitsu had wasted no time in making this point. He told Shigemasa that Hideo's mother was still alive. As utterly ruthless and calculating as Ieyasu was, in his own singular way, he respected Nobunaga's memory. He was extremely reluctant to destroy Settsuko and her infant son and add their deaths to his heavy burden of karma, but to have an openly Kirishitan grandson of the dictator, supported by a fervently Kirishitan mother was a danger to the Tokugawa dynasty. On his deathbed, Hidetada had made Iemitsu and Shigemasa swear to protect Settsuko and Hideo but keep them separated, making certain that Hideo be sent to a Buddhist monastery.

Shigemasa had been pleased to see that the rogue samurai did not number either Hideo or Kobiyashi among them. He knew that Ishido and Nagahisa were visiting the teahouse. He was debating whether to go to them, rouse Ishido's retinue, and storm the palace together. The two guards at the gate seemed alert and sober, but not overly formidable.

The only variable that gave Shigemasa the slightest pause was the unknown but doubtless substantial quantity of modern Spanish guns and powder that lay in Arima's arsenal. Even then, the samurai might be training cannon to rake the gate with a withering crossfire. Without question, there were more than enough soldiers who had fired cannon on occasion to make this a distinct possibility. Once this was done, it would take a formidable army equipped with siege equipment to reduce the castle. Even with the small number of samurai Shigemasa had watched enter the palace, he could have defended the structure for many months. Lord Arima surely kept enough rice in his vaults to feed an army, and springs provided fresh water.

The news of insurrection would spread rapidly, and Shigemasa knew that there were other disaffected *daimyo* nursing real or imagined grudges. They would join forces with the rebels against the shogunate, once more plunging the nation into an interminable dark age of civil war. Everything Ieyasu had worked toward for half a century would be undone by a small band of traitors in this godforsaken province. If Lord Arima joined the samurai, this nightmare would come to pass.

Lord Ishido's retainers were the only hope of averting catastrophe, assuming that Lord Arima threw his lot in with his men, and they had Mariko as a weapon against him. The Lord had no son, no wife, and the samurai held the life of his only daughter in their hands. Ishido's samurai were certainly superior to Arima's samurai, but given a gun, the clumsiest peasant could slay the greatest samurai from a distance, and Arima had amassed the greatest arsenal of modern guns in Nippon.

Shigemasa pushed the *tsuba* of his Yasutsugu *wakizashi* out with his thumb. This was an unconscious action, and when he became aware of it, he pushed it back into its *saya*.

He could easily kill the two guards standing warily in the torchlight, but this would alert others within the walls, and he was unfamiliar with the rooms and passageways. He could easily get lost and would be shot on sight. Earlier that night, he had removed his Tokugawa *mon* as a precaution. He admitted to himself that he had encouraged some of the more outrageous rumors about Ishido coming to order Lord Arima to commit *seppuku*.

Iemitsu had not told him the content of his instructions to the Kaishakunin. Iemitsu had only said what he wanted and what he didn't want. He wanted Arima's province. There was no heir, and that, as far as the shogun was concerned, was that. The point that there would be no repetition of Shimabara in the process of taking the province was made so strongly that Shigemasa thought his shogun might have apoplexy.

The quiet was deceptive, and Shigemasa realized for the first time that he might be witnessing the beginning of the very thing that Iemitsu feared most. Without a Shiro Amakusa, it could not be another Shimabara. *No,* thought Shigemasa. *With Lord Arima, who was an extremely capable administrator with considerable financial and other resources, it would be far worse.* And then there were the guns.

"The cursed gaijin guns," Shigemasa spat viciously.

"Sire, we must disrupt the shipment even if we create an international incident. I say burn the Spanish ship to the waterline, anything we have to do to destroy these guns," he had counseled Iemitsu, who had refused.

"If Lord Arima wants to buy modern weapons from the Franciscan gaijin"—as the shogun referred to the Spanish—"I will be only too pleased to take them from him when the time is suitable."

Iemitsu wanted no trouble from the Spanish, their cannon, or their soldiers, and he had consulted with Hendrik, who had told him that the Spaniards were overextended in the Philippines and would be highly unlikely to invade Nippon, despite the Japanese lack of modern weapons. The Dutchman had said that a hundred cannon of old design would counter ten of the new, and Iemitsu had many hundreds of such ordnance and thousands of men to man them.

The shogun had permitted Hendrik to trade with Lord Arima and even tantalized him with a possible alliance between the Dutch Navy, the East India Company, and his own forces. Arima was being courted by the Spanish, who were more interested in eliminating the exclusive trade franchise granted to the Dutch East India Company by Ieyasu than interested in launching an invasion of Nippon. In his right, Hendrik had really only been carrying out Iemitsu's desire to entangle Arima in a conspiracy of treason as a pretext for the shogun to seize his province.

The shogun was unaware that, as a result of his last meeting with the Dutchman, Hendrik was considering supporting Lord Arima in earnest. Iemitsu had clearly changed in the years following Shimabara, and Hendrik was no longer certain whether the shogunate would continue to be a reliable trading partner. And there was Mariko. Iemitsu's love of convolution was quite possibly exceeded by Lord Arima's, so Shigemasa was left alone to find the course out of the maze the two rulers had created that would conclude with peaceful solution to a situation that was already a war, if only an incipient conflict.

Part of him very much wanted to race to Ishido and gather

his retinue, but another part told Shigemasa that the worst thing he could do was leave the palace grounds. The voice of his internal Zen Buddhist dialog told him that none of what was happening was of lasting significance, although positive karma was preferable to negative. If he dispatched the two samurai and went in alone, the element of surprise would be very much in his favor. If a sharpshooter were watching, he would be shot to no purpose. Never in his career as Iemitsu's personal emissary and agent had he been faced with a more difficult set of choices.

By awaiting further developments, he was making the choice he liked least, that of doing nothing, which went against his nature. Meditation was action, being was action, but waiting for action was the absence of anything.

Better to go in now, he thought, *If I fail, the worst that happens is I die and Ishido inherits the problem.*

This made him smile. He knew that Ishido badly wanted to retire, and the idea that the mission, which was to be his last, would also be the worst amused him. *This had to be worse for him than being stabbed through the leg by a cowardly nobleman.* The one incident had had a logical and inevitable conclusion. This nascent insurrection had an almost infinite number of possible outcomes over months if not years.

Too early to enjoy your retirement, Ishido san, he said to himself. He sauntered up to the palace, just an anonymous samurai out for a walk on the hottest night of the year. Shigemasa's pace was leisurely, his attitude as natural as if he had walked up to Lord Arima's gate every night of his life. He resisted the temptation to put on his Tokugawa *mon,* although this was surely official shogunate business.

As he approached, one of the samurai challenged him. Shigemasa was already within two paces of the samurai. He had expected them to be fidgeting and nervous, but both were calm as if they guarded the entrance every night, which, in reality, they often did.

"I bring an urgent message for Lord Arima," Shigemasa said.

"An urgent message from whom?" asked the closest samurai.

"The message is from a gaijin. I can tell you nothing more." This answer had its desired effect.

"Please wait," said the samurai. "I think Ando should hear of this at once,"he told his companion.

Shigemasa had intended to cut down both guards the moment he reached the gate and would have done so, but the fact that one of the samurai sent for someone in higher authority in response to his answer made him reconsider.

This meant there would be more samurai to contend with. However, he was confident that he could fight six or seven of Arima's men without much difficulty.

Chapter 26

Shigemasa's Ploy

Shigemasa waited, knowing that he was wasting precious time. If he could cut the head off the poisonous snake of treason, the rebellion would wither and die, and he could return to Edo. Lord Arima's fate was still unresolved; it would be either determined shortly or left in Ishido's capable hands. The guard came back quickly but unaccompanied by anyone, much less the rebel leader as Shigemasa had hoped.

"You may give the message to me," said the man.

"My instructions are to speak only to Lord Arima," Shigemasa said, his voice filled with fervent conviction.

The samurai's face darkened.

"Lord Arima said to give me the message."

Shigemasa was undaunted by his threatening aspect, and the samurai lost his temper.

"Insolent bastard, give me the message, or I'll split you from neck to navel." The last word was almost unintelligible.

Shigemasa merely looked at the man with no more emotion than if he had been commenting on a particularly bright passing firefly. Both guards stared at Shigemasa as though he were mad.

"Are you deaf?" the guard who had threatened him asked. "Give me the message."

"I can only deliver the message directly to the lord," Shigemasa said, mildly.

The one guard turned to the other for support, but he wanted nothing to do with Shigemasa, so he turned away and looked at a firefly that was actively searching for a mate in the heated darkness.

The angry guard, whose name was Yukio, had often pulled guard duty at the palace gate. He was quite tall and well built, with a sword scar that began in the middle of his forehead and disappeared into his receding hairline. Normally, strange samurai seeking admittance to the palace were intimidated by his appearance. Clearly, Shigemasa was not put off in the least; he was as comfortable as a man in a teahouse smoking a pipe. Private, now General Ando had told Yukio to detain the man after finding out the message. Yukio was experienced in such matters; Ando had not detailed him to guard duty without good reason. After issuing the threat, he hesitated only because it failed to make any impression at all on the man. Shigemasa might as well have been the Buddha.

Yukio looked at the man's *daisho*. Both the *katana* and *wakizashi* were mounted for use. At the same time, the braided silk wrap and fine iron fittings were of the highest quality. The torchlight bounced off the solid gold *menuki,* and Yukio then saw the Tokugawa *mon* under the black silk—two in the *wakizashi* and three in the *katana*. No samurai other than one well connected to the shogunate could legally wear such adornments. Shigemasa saw Yukio's face as he looked at his swords, guessing the thoughts and conclusions in the tall samurai's mind.

Shigemasa took the initiative, speaking as if he never heard Yukio's threat. "I see you are admiring my swords."

Yukio was flustered, not knowing what to do. Such a thing had never happened to him. He had always been a faithful samurai serving Lord Arima. He would never have joined the rebels, except for the fact that he was convinced that Lord Ishido was there to dispossess his lord; he did not want to be a *ronin*. Yukio saw Ando as his only hope. Now he was faced with committing further treason—this time against the shogun. To draw his sword or interfere with, much less arrest, a shogunate official was the highest treason.

He looked at Murakami, the other guard, who usually had duty in the dungeon. He was short and taciturn. He rarely spoke, and when he did, it was usually about food. Yukio knew that Murakami had been a sergeant but had lost his rank for being drunk on duty. Murakami's drinking had coincided with his wife's untimely death, but no one in the barracks had been aware of that. Ando trusted him because he was short, powerful, and knew how to control a much larger man using only his hands. Yukio could see that Murakami was leaving the strange visitor entirely to him.

"What's your name?" barked Yukio. He was growing more uncomfortable with Shigemasa with each passing moment. Yukio sought relief from his discomfiture in anger, which reflected in his voice. To Yukio's utter amazement, Shigemasa gave him a smile as peaceful as the smile on the Great Buddha at Kamakura. His reply was as enigmatic as any Yukio had ever heard from Lord Arima, who was the most opaque person Yukio had ever spoken to.

"That is something you will never know."

The laziness in Shigemasa's tone frightened Yukio almost as much as the Tokugawa *mon* on his swords. Trapped between Ando, his own role in the uprising, and Shigemasa, Yukio knew that he had to take action. He also strongly felt there was no course open to him that would not result in his death.

Yukio did not fear death, only disgrace. It was fear of being *ronin* that had brought him to the present pass. He could see only one way out of the problem.

Yukio drew his *katana*, edge upward, in a single fluid motion, striking Murakami in the throat. The short samurai made a gurgling sound and then released a hiss of indrawn breath as the blade sliced his windpipe in two. Rich, red blood spurted from the severed carotid artery; Shigemasa deftly sidestepped the jet. Murakami's short trunk caused the body to remain on the top step rather than fall as Onishi's had. Shigemasa's face showed as much emotion as a stone image. Yukio resheathed his sword as quickly as he had drawn it. He fell to his knees, raising both hands together in a gesture of submission and supplication.

Unaware of the momentous events taking place outside the thick freestone walls of his castle, Lord Arima was also too preoccupied with his own personal affairs to notice anything amiss with the staff in his palace. He had left the strictest orders not to be disturbed for any reason whatsoever. He was unconcerned about Captain Yamashita and the success or failure of his mission to arrest Ishido and Nagahisa. Now that Hendrik and the Dutch had refused to join with him, there would be no insurrection. He sighed in fond recollection of the revolt that would never be.

"Young Oda and I would have led a fine insurrection. He would have married Mariko and been my heir. Hendrik and I would have overthrown the Tokugawa. How I would have loved to have Iemitsu in my dungeon, looking just like Shinbei. To see the look on his face would be worth my province." He would have to settle for Lord Ishido and Nagahisa and perhaps not even that. Not that any of it mattered. Lord Arima had examined all possible outcomes and decided that he would partake of the greatest luxury any man, particularly a samurai, could possibly have. He had the privilege of choosing the time and manner of his own death.

Anticipating the possibility, he had bathed in hot water heavy with exotic herbs and scented oils. His attendants had made certain that his hair was immaculate and tied loosely behind his head so it streamed down his back. He had then dismissed everyone and retired to his study. After Yamashita had left he had dismissed his personal guard. Taking off a light kimono—his study, like every room in the castle, was baking hot—he carefully wrapped a length of the finest white silk around his abdomen in the prescribed manner. He picked up his Muramasa *tanto* and wrapped the wooden handle in fine white rice paper to ensure his grip would be secure regardless of the blood.

The look on Iemitsu's face when he sees the fully signed Muramasa will be almost as good as the look that would have been on his face in his dungeon cell, thought Arima. *That I had the effrontery, the unmitigated gall, to commit seppuku with an outlawed Muramasa blade—I would give my right arm to see it.* In his mind, the image of Iemitsu, his serious face nearly black with a rage he could never completely master, was almost comical.

Tokugawa buffoon, he said to himself, *He thinks he controls everything in Nippon with his spies. When he gets the Muramasa…* Arima shook his head and smiled. *It's simply too good.* He truly looked forward to release from this spoke on the wheel of his life.

Lord Arima knew enough of the Kirishitan faith to respect it as suitable for a samurai and consistent with Bushido, but this did not lessen his faith in Buddhism. Both faiths could exist together. It was the gaijin like the Spanish who made such peace impossible. He was glad he had taken their guns and not their alliance. The Dutch he could have lived with; the Spanish, never. Of course, he never let them know that until he had the guns safely in his armory. Then he had sent Shinbei away; the boy was no longer important except as a blind to arrange the death of the Spanish go-between.

Arima hoped that the Kirishitans were right about a physical heaven. He badly wanted to be with his wife again. He had spared Shinbei as insurance, and as he examined the day's events, he was surprised to see how much his actions were affected by concern for positive karma, to demonstrate a reverence for life even though the physical world was an illusion. He had even deliberately avoided a clash between Ishido's men and his own. As he contemplated his own death, he felt an impulse to recall Yamashita.

Yes, he still hated Iemitsu, and because of that, he detested his hired attack dog, Ishido. Something about Nagahisa simply got under his skin. The tester was too self-satisfied, and it irritated him like the whine of a mosquito. They had their own karma; why should he interfere? He wished that Mariko could be there to witness his transcendence.

Bother the girl, he thought, *And I was going to send her to Hendrik to secure his allegiance.* He was not overly concerned. Mariko was frequently absent, often annoyingly so. One thing he could be sure of, she was more than a match for any man except for an Ishido. She was every inch an Arima.

"A pipe would go down well," he said audibly, and he filled the pipe with Latakia. Lighting it with a tiny coal, he drew the smoke deep into his lungs and blew out a perfectly circular, thick smoke ring. Daisuke always wore a look of disdain whenever he entered the study and saw his father smoking, as he believed Lord Arima should lead by example in this as he did in nearly every other way.

Then again, thought Arima, *Daisuke looked upon everything I did with disdain. He had the steel discipline for Bushido, as any Zen master does. He disdained Bushido. Damn him anyway. Then again, it is karma, all karma, and as long as he is at peace with himself, it really doesn't matter. Still, I would like him to see and witness how a true samurai chooses to die.*

The *shoji* to the study, which was much heavier than any other *shoji* in the palace, slid open and slammed into the doorframe. Startled out of his musings, Lord Arima was enraged.

gunate needed. There were innumerable layers of officialdom Ishido's field appointment would have to negotiate before the rank was official, but he was confident that, assuming he survived the night, Iemitsu would ratify everything upon his return to Edo. In the meantime, Ishido had nothing that he could give the new general as a badge of rank; then he had an inspiration. He handed his *jingasa*, which bore the Tokugawa *mon* in raised gold lacquer to the speechless man.

"General, you may put it on and wear it proudly for all to see. Now let us go first to the barracks and then to the palace. I believe it is now the time." He looked at Nagahisa, who was swallowing yet another bite of grilled fish. "Are you coming with us?"

Nagahisa stood and patted his belly with satisfaction.

"I most certainly am. Besides, you might need my sword."

"We might very well need your sword, my friend," Ishido said in a grim voice. Ishido settled their reckoning with Hana in gold, and the three men set off for the barracks.

There were no other guests in the teahouse. Everything was quiet, as if the heat had cast a spell over the entire town. Hoki had recovered from his faint with the help of fish soup and some cool water. He had told Hana what Shinbei had said and was now listening to Keiko play her *samisen*. The music and the beautiful little girl held him spellbound. Hana went to Hiroko's office with Ishido's gold and asked the mistress if she could have leave for the rest of the night. She braced herself, expecting a fight with the old woman. But to her surprise, Hiroko used her rare and unusual gracious tone of voice.

"By all means, my daughter."

When she told Koetsu about the conversation, Koetsu said, "I think the mistress has lost her mind. She actually gave me her best barrel of sake to serve to Lord Ishido. And she was polite to me. Lady Mariko must have given her a lot of money. Either that or Lord Ishido must have asked her to marry him."

Hana just laughed. She could afford to laugh all night, knowing that her Shinbei was alive. Hoki had given her good directions to Shinbei's village, and changing into traveling clothes, Hana kissed Koetsu, Keiko, and Hoki before walking out the door. Just before leaving, she told Hoki that the Fragrant Blossom was in need of an errand boy. Smitten with the luxurious teahouse and Keiko, Hoki thought the Fragrant Blossom was the finest and most beautiful place on earth. He would be the best boy any mistress could want.

Mizukami, Hideo, and Kobiyashi waited uneasily as they watched the samurai enter the palace. Fortunately, they had arrived too late to see Mariko stab Onishi and be carried into the castle senseless; Hideo would certainly have whistled as many arrows into the rebels as he carried in his quiver. They did see Shigemasa creep like a ninja along one wall of the palace and mount the steps to speak with the guards.

"That's Yukio," said Kobiyashi.

"I see Shigemasa," said Hideo. "I saw him along the wall."

"Now he's talking to Yukio," said Mizukami.

"How well do you know the palace?" Kobiyashi asked Mizukami.

"If anything happens to Mariko," said Hideo, "I swear, I shall have all their heads."

Hideo asked for forgiveness in a small prayer uttered under his breath. Christ had told his disciples not to swear "by the earth, for it is his footstool." He pleaded his love of Mariko, knowing that Christ and God were love. Hideo also made the distinction between killing and murder. He knew he would never murder another human being, but killing was another matter, and if killing would save Mariko's life, then he would kill and pray for forgiveness, knowing that Christ and God would understand because they could see into his heart, and he was fairly sure he had a pure heart.

Mizukami was in favor of immediate action.

"We must prevent them from breaking into the arsenal and seizing the guns. If they get the guns, we will be powerless against them."

Much to Hideo's surprise, the mercurial Kobiyashi counseled caution.

"We must allow Shigemasa to do whatever he is doing. Listen, you both know my motto, 'attack, attack, attack,' and you know that I'm impatient by nature, but I was with Shigemasa this afternoon at the festival, as you were, Hideo. I believe he knows much more than he lets on." Knowing what little he knew of Shigemasa, Hideo was inclined to agree. Only Mizukami, who had never met Shigemasa, disagreed.

"I'm telling you to look at the reality," he said. "They murdered Zenshiro. There is no denying that. They have entered Lord Arima's palace. More than one of the traitors knows of the Spanish guns, and with them, each man is a match for ten and, in the rain, a thousand."

"As if it's going to rain," Kobiyashi scoffed. "I can't remember the last time it rained. The very earth itself is dried up."

Mizukami was not deterred.

"Hideo, surely you can shoot both guards from here. Do it now." Hideo unstrapped his *utsubo* and drew out three of the best arrows. He fitted the best of the three into his bowstring. He drew the bow to its furthest extension, carefully sighting at Yukio's armored chest.

"Wait!" said Kobiyashi. "Can't you see he's wearing a matchlock-proof breastplate?"

Hideo relaxed his draw. There was no purpose in shooting against plate armor. His arrows would only shatter, fail to penetrate, and be wasted. Hideo would not risk a headshot at this distance. Although the figures were well outlined in the torchlight, they were not standing still; they were clearly engaged in conversation. Yukio was particularly animated, and it seemed to Hideo that the men's heads were bobbing up and down. No, it was too dangerous.

"Listen if anything happens to Shigemasa," Kobiyashi said, "we can shoot at will, and then with the guards down, I say we rush the gate."

Both Hideo and Mizukami agreed, but Mizukami was reluctant to give up on the idea of shooting the guards and then rushing the gate while Shigemasa was with them. Again, he said that to delay any longer would ensure that the entire renegade Arima retinue would be armed with devastating weapons, the likes of which Hideo and Kobiyashi could not imagine.

"Are they really so fearsome?" asked Kobiyashi. He was passionately interested in weapons, and as much as he loathed guns, he could not help but be interested from a scholarly perspective.

"I can tell you that, properly loaded with the new powder, I have shot through as many as four iron breastplates at one time from twenty-five paces."

Hideo sucked air through his teeth with the hissing sound he often made when he was amazed.

"So many? It's hard to imagine."

"Yes, as I have said a thousand times, barbarian guns will mean the death of Bushido, the end of honor, and the elimination of the need for samurai."

"I also hate guns, as you know, but as long as there is a Nippon, there will be a need for truth, honor, loyalty, and samurai. As long as the sun rises, the glory of Bushido will burn brightly as well."

Hideo, who had heard Kobiyashi's opinion on this subject more times than he cared to remember, was looking at the three men on the steps. He was stunned to see the samurai he thought was Yukio cut down the other guard. At first, in the uncertain light, he thought it might have been Shigemasa, but knowing as little as he did about him, the possibility of Yukio besting Shigemasa was extremely remote. The short guard fell and lay still on the wide, stone step. Yukio knelt before Shigemasa.

Hideo took only a moment to decide.

"Quickly now! Run to the gate!"

Shigemasa reached down and raised Yukio, taking hold of his right arm. As he did so, he saw three samurai bearing the Arima *mon* and armed with *yumi* coming toward him at a dead run. His intuition registered the fact that, if they were rebels, they could easily have killed him with an arrow at any time. He concluded that they were either loyalists—but loyal to whom—or Arima retainers who were unaware of the rebellion in the barracks and the occupation of the palace by disaffected samurai.

The actual situation was fluid and complicated with divided loyalties and almost opaque motives. Shigemasa was certain that Ishido had specific instructions from Iemitsu concerning Lord Arima. How the instructions would be affected by the rebellion would depend on a number of factors, including the most significant: whether the samurai were acting on orders from their lord. As badly as Shigemasa wanted to question Yukio, the sight of well-armed samurai racing toward him made it impossible.

When General Yamashita saw Zenshiro's naked corpse, black with buzzing flies, which had been feasting on his blood and the vitreous fluid in his sightless eyes for more than an hour, he was overcome with remorse. Ishido and Nagahisa had seen all too many violent deaths, but in the long period of peace since Shimabara, Yamashita had not. His grief was quickly replaced by a great and dangerous anger. He had heard rumors circulating among the samurai about the lord being a tool of the gaijin and that all Arima's samurai might soon be forced to be *ronin*, but he had dismissed it as the usual barracks talk.

Yamashita drove off the flies with his kimono belt and, taking off his own silken garment, gently recovered Zenshiro's body. Wearing only his undergarments and a loincloth, he stood and looked in Lord Ishido's eyes, but it was Ishido who spoke first.

"That was nobly done, General," he said, "Clearly, I have not made a mistake in appointing you. He was a friend?"

"No lord, not a friend. A decent, loyal samurai, who followed the path of Bushido, a most reliable officer named Zenshiro."

Ishido nodded.

"So what do we have here?" he asked. "Give me your best guess."

Yamashita drew a deep breath.

"The whole barracks has revolted. If you will excuse me, lord, before your arrival, there were rumors of a gaijin invasion. Some even said that Lord Arima was seeking gaijin help to overthrow the shogun. Soldiers are worse gossips than wrinkled old grandmothers, but the lord made no attempt to counter the talk. I spoke to him about it many times, but he said there was nothing to be concerned about, he knew his men, and I should see the horses were given sufficient water considering the heat. I know he has his spies in the barracks and throughout the province in every village and town, so who was I to question him?

"I had my eye, as did Lieutenant Zenshiro, on two men in particular: Ando and Onishi. Of the two, Ando is brighter. He looks like a pig, but he is quick with both hand and blade, and he can read and write better than I can. If the men have a leader, it is one of those two."

"That's all well and good," Ishido said, "but the question is what if any part of this is Lord Arima's doing? Are we about to be invaded by Dutch or Spanish gaijin?"

"I know nothing of gaijin, and as for the lord, I cannot believe he would permit this murder. He is a proud man, and even if he is involved in some way, he does not know of this. I'd stake my life on it."

"You mentioned two men," said Ishido. "What of young Oda Hideo."

Yamashita shook his head.

"No, young Oda would not be involved. Once more I'd stake my life on it."

"But he could be used as a figurehead without his being aware," Ishido paused before continuing, "especially by a *daimyo* as experienced and crafty as Lord Arima."

At this point, Nagahisa felt compelled to say, "Ishido *san*, in my opinion, young Oda can't be easily made use of without his will. I can say from personal experience that anyone who could make that tremendous cut while thinking that it might be a friend concealed beneath the bandages is a man to be reckoned with. Hideo would be no mascot at the head of Lord Arima's army but a true leader, a general." He bowed slightly to Yamashita. He continued, "Mark my words well, my lords, Oda Hideo is surely his grandfather's grandson."

Chapter 27

The Dictator's Grandson

Hideo was the first of the three to reach the top step. The first words out of his mouth were not to Shigemasa but to Yukio.

"Where's Mariko?" he said in between breaths.

Yukio looked at Shigemasa, uncertain whether his action and supplication were enough to vindicate him. Shigemasa said nothing. He was assessing the situation and considering his options. Now he had four men, including himself, or five, including Yukio. Regardless, he now had a small force of skilled samurai to overcome a much larger one in a castle entirely unknown to him.

He nodded to Yukio, who blurted out, "Onishi seized the lady, but she killed him. Then Ando had her carried to the dungeon. "Something happened when they fell. I couldn't see too much. I think there was some blood on her head. It might have been Onishi's."

him with one of his own guns. The scroll was a masterwork by Mitsutada Tokiwa, and it seemed to fill the length and width of the wall as he continued to contemplate it. Even his carefully choreographed impending suicide became irrelevant in light of Tokiwa's transcendent art.

I have spent my life foolishly, he thought. *The illusions of this world are just that. To make them important is the greatest possible folly.*

Ando felt an almost overpowering impulse to kill his liege lord, but without Lord Arima, his revolt was doomed to be short-lived and ruthlessly crushed. He looked at Tokiwa's scroll and saw nothing but a roughly sketched letter he could not decipher. Ando thought it might represent enlightenment, but he was no lover of art and didn't really care. He only knew that Arima was paying attention to it and not to him.

His anger needed some outlet, so he leapt across the room and seized the scroll with his left hand, tearing it from the wall. He hung the cocked pistol from his sash's long, steel belt hook. Keeping a wary eye on Lord Arima, he ripped the scroll in two down the middle of the character. The sound in the soundless room was deafening, or so it seemed to Ando.

Lord Arima's eyes had nearly closed, but the harsh tearing noise woke him from his breathing and his contemplation. Ando flung the pieces of the scroll at Lord Arima's *tabi*-clad feet, and the lord looked at Ando, who leveled his gun once more. Ando's anger evaporated, appeased by the destruction of the scroll and was replaced by curiousity. He had assumed that Arima would react violently, especially as he seemed to value the piece of paper so highly, even more than his own life. Instead, Lord Arima remained as impassive as a wood statue. He looked at Ando with great compassion. It was a look that said, *Poor man, you understand so very little. All our actions mean so very little, or* at least that's how Ando interpreted it.

Ando really was at a crossroads. He was physically and mentally spent with the effort of controlling his fellow samurai through the force of his own personality. Onishi's death had been an entirely unexpected and a bitter blow, because it deprived him of the field commander he needed. Ando was the hand, and Onishi the sword. Ando was skilled in *budo* and could defeat most of the retainers in single combat with a *boken.* His horsemanship was indifferent and his archery poor. He was a good marksman with a matchlock, and now he had command of a small army. Like every samurai, Ando had a deep and abiding fear of being masterless, of being forced to become a *ronin.* He regretted killing Zenshiro, but the lieutenant had mocked him, calling him a monkey no one would listen to much less follow.

Ando had little tolerance for mockery, having endured all too much of it from childhood, but the look on Lord Arima's face was the furthest thing imaginable from scorn. It was the look of compassion on almost every image of the Buddha. Except for the merchant who had adopted him, Ando had been shown very little compassion and understanding in his life. When given the chance, he had worked very hard to succeed and was forced to fight and prove himself again and again. He had eventually earned the respect of his fellow samurai. His rather unattractive personal appearance precluded him from being one of Lord Arima's private bodyguards, but Ando prized his status, and had only gratitude for the kindly merchant who had made it possible.

He was a samurai with a chip on his broad shoulders, and woe betide the man, like Zenshiro, who knocked it off. As he continued to look his liege lord in the eyes, Ando's head began to swim. Part of him—and this part grew with the passing of each moment—wanted to hand over his gun, fall to his knees, and beg for mercy and forgiveness. Without Onishi, his plans for the rebellion were dashed, so what was the point of continuing to kill and burn? The only people who would suffer were the poor and downtrodden—the very people he wanted to set free. If only Lord Arima had continued to treat him with scorn and stinging contempt, it would have at least made some sense.

If he had a home to go to like the officers, Ando would have walked out of the palace and gone there. He was bone-weary and heartily sick of the whole enterprise. He was an educated man, not some brutish boor.

He was about to surrender in the face of his liege lord's reaction to the cowardly and senseless desecration of Tokiwa's beautiful scroll, when one of the rebel samurai entered, leading a bloody and disheveled Mariko. Her hands were bound behind her, and her mouth was gagged. He released her, and she ran to her father, heedless of the two samurai.

"Go guard the arsenal," said Ando in a crisp voice. The samurai bowed and left without a word as Ando faced his liege lord and his daughter. Lord Arima looked at his daughter; tears ran down his cheeks. Completely ignoring Ando, he took her face between his powerful hands and smiled sadly. Reaching behind her head, he untied the gag, which was a ragged piece of silk torn from her kimono. After untying it, he stepped back half a pace.

"Mariko, are you hurt?"

Mariko hocked and spat viciously at Ando.

"You filthy insect. You will die for this."

Having vented some of her rage, she looked at her father, who stood silently with an expression of infinite sadness. In that look, all the remorse for every regret in his life—his treatment of Daisuke, his cruelty to his wife, and his situation—was distilled. Her father's soundless grief calmed her.

"I am unhurt," she said. "I killed one of them and fell on the steps, but I don't really remember. The fall must have knocked me out."

She felt her head, and there was a large lump, thick with dried blood, much like Shinbei's egg. She had come to in the very cell she had visited in the morning.

It seems I must suffer every indignity my father inflicted on

Shinbei, Mariko thought to herself. *Now this pig will kill us, but Shinbei isn't dead. Even his arrest was only a pretense. He's probably with Hana. If only Hideo were here.*

Lord Arima held out his arms, inviting her into an embrace. This was something her father hadn't done since she and Daisuke had been small children. She hesitated for a time, fearing that she might be mistaking him, but her head throbbed and she felt miserable and badly in need of comfort, so she took a step and fell into his arms. He held her in a tight embrace, something he hadn't done since Daisuke's exile, and though Mariko was a samurai to the very core of her being, she broke down in a series of wrenching, racking sobs. Ando's rebellion had smashed the high wall separating her from her father, and if the loss of her worldly position, all her wealth, and her power was the price she had to pay for her father's love, then she would gladly pay it twice over.

Arima felt her sinewy, muscular body in his arms, and memories of Mariko as a little girl, when his wife was alive and well and Daisuke was his son, flooded his mind.

What have I really accomplished in my life? I lost the love of my only son early on. No, that wasn't it at all. I, myself, withdrew my love for Daisuke and incinerated it in the flame of my anger and insufferable pride. I have made my precious little girl into the samurai my son refused to be. It was all a great mistake. Now he could see it clearly.

Just as Lord Arima opened his mouth to make the traitor an offer, he noticed that Ando was looking stupidly at an arrow point that protruded from just below his left breastbone. The nerveless fingers of his right hand splayed out, and the pistol slipped to the polished cedar floor. The sound of its fall was lost in the explosion as the weapon discharged.

Ando stood swaying for a long moment, as if contemplating the arrow that had suddenly grown out of his chest, and then he fell forward heavily on his face, pushing the point back in so that the shaft stuck far out of his back and the bright fletching of the dyed feathers stood out gaily in the lamplight.

Hideo and Kobiyashi stood for a moment at the entrance to the study, staring at their liege lord and Mariko. Hideo still held his bow in his left hand. Then he disentangled his *utsubo* and threw both it and the bow carelessly onto the cedar floor. Heedless of Lord Arima, he raced to Mariko. As Hideo reached father and daughter, Lord Arima looked at him so intently it seemed to the younger man that the *daimyo* was plumbing the very depths of his heart to determine whether he was worthy of Mariko.

Part of Hideo wanted nothing more than to wrest Mariko from the paternal embrace, and another knew that this moment of calm was an illusion. The castle was still in rebel hands, Ando or no Ando, and Ishido and Shigemasa would have need of his sword.

Hideo looked to Lord Ishido, who gestured for Hideo to follow him. There were the gaijin guns to secure. Mariko was safe for the time being, albeit in her father's arms and not his. That was enough for Hideo, and ignoring his bow, he drew his katana and followed Ishido, Shigemasa, Kobyashi, and the others out of the study.

The sword is the soul of the samurai.

Glossary of Terms

(in alphabetical order)

Aikuchi:	*tanto* without a *tsuba;* favored by samurai women
Ashigaru:	peasant soldier
Baca:	Japanese for fool or idiot
Daimyo:	hereditary Japanese noblemen, similar to an English baron, earl, or duke
Daisho:	*katana* and *wakizashi* mounted en suite and worn together by samurai; *daisho* were restricted to samurai, as were *katana* and *tachi*
Edo:	Tokyo
Eta:	despised class of Japanese; equivalent to Indian untouchable
Efu no Dachi:	type of *tachi* without a *tsuba*
Fuchi:	small, metal fitting on the *tsuka* where the *tsuka* fits against the *seppa* and *tsuba*; usually decorated and made en suite with the *kashira*; *fuchi* and *kashira* were two of the ornaments permitted as part of samurai dress
Gaijin:	foreigner, foreign
Gi Butsu:	fake
Gi Mei:	false signature
Go:	Japanese for five
Habaki:	metal collar that slides over the tang of a sword to assure a tight fit in the *saya* and with the *tsuba* and *tsuka;* usually of copper, but often covered with gold or silver sheet; occasionally decorated

No Dachi:	*tachi* of extreme length, over three *shaku*
Oban:	large Japanese gold coin weighing ten ounces
O Tanto:	unusually long and heavy *tanto*
O Wakizashi:	unusually long and heavy *wakizashi*
Sageo:	fine silk, flat cord used to secure *sayas* of *daisho* and other swords to a samurai's sash
Sama:	Japanese honorific denoting great deference; literally "great lord"
Same:	skin of a ray found in the Sea of Japan; coarse pebbly surface perfect for wrapping around the *tsukas* of a samurai sword before the *menuki* and *tsuka maki* were applied; highly prized, and individual pieces were often given as gifts
San:	Japanese honorific for sir, but more polite; both masculine and feminine
San:	Japanese for three
Saya:	scabbard of a Japanese sword; usually made of lacquered wood, such as *honoki* or Japanese cypress; often decorated with family crests in gold on black lacquer
Sekigane:	tiny, often gilt, metal fittings in a *kurikata* to prevent the *sageo* cord from fraying
Seppa:	oval spacers, like washers, made of copper and often overlaid with sheet gold or silver; used to fit and tighten the blade to the *tsuka*
Seppuku:	ritual suicide
Shaku:	Japanese unit of measure for slightly less than a foot; two *shaku* equals sixty centimeters
Shibui:	particular aesthetic of simple, subtle, and unobtrusive beauty

Shogun:	literally "generalissimo"; temporal ruler of Japan
Sun:	Japanese unit of measure for approximately one inch
Suriage:	practice of shortening a sword from the tang up; often removes the signature
Tachi:	sword generally two *shaku* or more in length of cutting edge; if signed, signed on the left side if carried edge up; generally carried slung from two loops on the *saya,* edge down; *tachi* were mandatory wear for samurai at the emperor's court in Kyoto; also worn on horseback
Tane-gashime:	Japanese matchlock musket
Tanto:	sword with a length of cutting edge generally less than one *shaku; s*ometimes worn as the short sword in a *daisho*; almost never carried as a *tachi*; *katanamei* if signed
Tsuba:	hand guard on a Japanese samurai sword; often round in shape and made of iron or copper and often elaborately decorated with gold and silver designs of great artistry; sometimes signed by artists; *tsubas* could be made by swordsmiths
Tsuka:	handle of a Japanese sword
Tsuka Maki:	flat, silk cord used to wrap *tsuka* and provide a comfortable grip
Umebari:	variant *kozuka* with double-edged, flat blade; usually of one piece used to pierce the abdomen of horses bloated from eating wet clover or other grasses
Utsubo:	large Japanese quiver; often beautifully lacquered and decorated; carried slung over the back

Wak-izashi:	sword of greater than one *shaku* and fewer than two *shaku* in length of cutting edge; occasionally worn *tachi* style, but most frequently as the *shoto* in a *daisho;* usually signed *katanamei* if signed.
Yari:	Japanese spears; made exactly the same way as samurai swords; primary weapons that foot soldiers carried against cavalry; many were superb works of art
Ya No Ne:	Japanese arrowheads; forged in the same manner as the samurai sword and often made by significant artists; water-tempered, forged, and folded
Yumi:	Japanese asymmetrical bow; usually more than eight *shaku* in length

Cast of Characters

(inalphabetical order)

Ando:	A rebel samurai in the service of Lord Arima
Mariko Arima:	Lord Arima's daughter
Daisuke Arima:	Lord Arima's son
Captain Yamashita:	A samurai in service to Lord Arima
Corporal Hankei:	A samurai in service to Lord Arima
Tokugawa Iemitsu:	Reigning shogun of Japan
Furuya:	A peasant at the festival
Genji:	A bathhouse attendant
Goki:	Lady Mariko's attendant
Hana:	A geisha of the second class at the Fragrant Blossom
Hasui Oda:	Hideo's grandmother
Hatsumasa:	A healer and witch in Shinbei's village
Hendrik Visser:	A Dutchman and high official in the Dutch East India Company
Tokugawa Hidetada:	Second Tokugawa shogun, Iemitsu's father
Toyoomi Hideyori:	Son of the Taiko Hodeyoshi Toyotomi (deceased)
Hiroko:	Owner of the Fragrant Blossom teahouse

Hoki:	A small boy in Shinbei's village, Asamu's assistant
Heisho Honami:	A member of the Honami family of sword appraisers
Tokugawa Ieyasu:	First Tokugawa shogun, Iemitsu's grandfather
Jozo:	Hana's uncle
Keiko:	Apprentice geisha at the Fragrant Blossom
Kobiyashi:	Hideo's inseparable companion
Koetsu:	Apprentice geisha at the Fragrant Blossom
Lieutenant Zenshiro:	A samurai in service to Lord Arima
Lord Arima:	Lord or *daimyo* of Kyushu Province, Hideo's liege lord
Lord Ishido:	Shogun Iemitsu's Kaishakunin
Mizukami:	Lord Arima's armorer and rangemaster
Musashi:	Assistant to Nagahisa *sensei*
Murakami:	A rebel samurai
Nagahisa Sensei:	A Hamano School sword tester
Hideo Oda:	Grandson of Nobunaga Oda, who was dictator of Japan
Okisato:	The most famous armorer in Japan

Omi:	An elderly samurai who guards the Fragrant Blossom
Onishi:	A rebel samurai
Asamu Shinbei:	Shinbei's mother
Shinbei Oyama:	A samurai in service to Lord Arima, Hana's lover
Takeo Oyama:	Shinbei's father (deceased)
Oda Nobunaga:	Dictator of Japan (deceased)
Reiko:	Kobiyashi's mother
Sato:	A samurai in service to Lord Arima
Oda Settsuko:	Hideo's mother
Shigemasa:	Shogun Iemitsu's most influential advisor
Shintaro Oda:	Hideo's father
Shiro:	Lord Arima's calligrapher
Amakusa Shiro:	The leader of the Shimabara Rebellion
Slijkerman:	A Dutch East India Company ship's boy
Toshi:	Kobiyashi's father (deceased)
Tsunahiro:	An elderly samurai in service to Lord Arima
Yamazaki:	A Kirishitan samurai in service to Lord Arima
Yoritomo:	A samurai in service to Shogun Iemitsu
Yukio:	A rebel samurai